DREAM, ANNIE, DREAM

Waka T. Brown

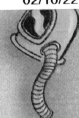

Quill Tree Books
An Imprint of HarperCollinsPublishers

Quill Tree Books is an imprint of HarperCollins Publishers.

Dream, Annie, Dream
ISBN 978-0-06-301716-0

Typography by David Curtis
21 22 23 24 25   SB   10 9 8 7 6 5 4 3 2 1

First Edition

For all the dreamers

ACT I
ANNIE

CHAPTER 1

You can be anything you want to be.

My sixth-grade teacher's parting words to the graduating class of Iron Hills Elementary rang in my ears, even over the deafening roar of the rocket motors.

I could be anything I want to be, and this fine summer morning, I was an astronaut.

"Blue skies. Winds are steady. In T-minus ten seconds we have blastoff. Ten, nine, eight, seven . . ."

"Chibi!" a voice called out from ground control. "Chibi!"

Since my name isn't Chibi, I ignored it.

". . . six . . ."

"Chibi!" Ground control was annoyingly loud and insistent this morning.

"Five . . . oh, forget it. Rocket launch aborted," I mumbled to myself. My mom calling for our cat totally did not work with my make-believe trip to the moon. It was hard enough, at twelve, pretending *anything*, and my mom's interruptions didn't help.

To be fair, it's not completely her fault. After all, I *am* kind of too old for these games, but Jessie, I mean *Jessica*, and her mom are late picking me up and this sycamore tree is the best place for me to watch for their car. And this is where Jessie and I used to pretend, when we were little kids, that we were pilots, or astronauts, or princesses stuck in our towers. So I guess I just slipped back into it out of habit.

Even though it wasn't 9:00 a.m. yet, it felt like the sun's rays were arms pushing down on me as heat waves rose from the ground, threatening to press me into a sweat sandwich. My hair was already sticking to my neck and the rash on the backs of my legs was starting to itch. We don't have AC—well, we do, but we don't use it unless we absolutely have to—so the inside of my house isn't any better. At least in this tree there's shade *and* a breeze.

I had brought my tattered copy of *Alice's Adventures in Wonderland* up with me and had been planning on reading it while I waited for Jess . . . ica. Although I knew the story by heart, I still giggled at its sheer silliness—her expanding and shrinking! Flamingos used as croquet mallets! But, before I knew what happened, my imagination was off and running in another direction, and I soon found myself inside an abandoned yet still fully functional spaceship. I flipped a page to see if it could offer any hints as to how to resume count-down mode.

"Chibi!"

My mom's voice pulled me from my launch *again*.

"Okaasan, Chibi koko ni iru yo!" I yelled back as I glanced down at my gray-and-white tuxedo cat sharpening her claws on the trunk of the tree. "Chibi's right here!"

I snapped off one of the fuzzy broad sycamore leaves from a branch and shoved it between the pages where I had stopped reading. I stuffed the book inside the back of my jean shorts and clambered down.

Honk!

Not a moment too soon, either, because my ride had just pulled in!

I scooped Chibi up mid-scratch and gently set her down inside our rickety screen door.

"Ah, arigatou! Jessie-chan no okaasan ni yoroshiku ne!" my mom hollered out after me.

"Yeah, okay. Bye!" I jumped down the front steps toward my friend's car.

Jessie opened the car door for me, and I slid inside, my sweaty legs squeaking against the beige leather seats. I sighed as a blast of cool air hit my face.

Being in the Kellys' fancy car—a Chrysler Fifth Avenue is

what it was called—was what I imagined a limousine was like, or . . . Apollo's chariot! I read a lot of mythology last year, and sure, the Kellys' Fifth Avenue wasn't pulled by fiery horses, but being inside it felt like I was floating in the sky.

My mom waved from the front porch and Mrs. Kelly waved back as we drove away. For the next five weeks, Monday through Friday, this would be our routine. Theater camp instead of school (thank goodness), and a posh ride instead of the school bus.

Which reminded me. "My mom says hi . . . and thanks."

"Well, you tell her 'Hi . . . and you're welcome!' right back, okay?" Mrs. Kelly chuckled as she steered us around the corner.

I liked how Jessie's mom never seemed to mind how our carpool arrangement was kind of one-sided and *not* in her favor. With my dad at work today, my mom didn't have a car to drive us in. And the one we had was nowhere near as nice as this one that glided over streets like a boat in still waters, the potholes barely registering on the wheels. I sank into the sofa-like "Corinthian leather" seats (I didn't really know what that meant, except that Jessie made sure to point them out when her family bought the car).

Did I just say "Jessie"? I meant *Jessica.*

"Hi, *Jessica!*" I finally greeted my best friend. She was no longer "Jessie," as she had been since the day we met in kindergarten. That's when we became best friends because she liked

4

dinosaurs and so did I! Now that we were finished with elementary school, she decided she would be *Jessica* from now on.

My friend's blue eyes twinkled, and her freckles seemed to sparkle on her cheeks when I called her by her new name (or was that because she was wearing *blush*?!). It had only been a few weeks since the last day of school, but she already seemed older. Her sandy blond hair was pulled back in a neat French braid and her bangs were curled, teased, and shellacked in place with a healthy dose of Aqua Net hairspray.

I wished my hair would do that, only it wouldn't. If I curled it—*even* when I used hairspray—within hours it would resume its natural state: a stick-straight black waterfall that tumbled just below my shoulders. Except for when I had it up in a ponytail, which was almost always in the summer to keep it from glomming onto my neck with sweat.

With her new hairstyle, my friend was *much* more like a "Jessica" now than a "Jessie."

"Hi, *Annie*."

Annie. It felt weird to hear Jessica say my new name, too.

I used to be Aoi Inoue, but if there's one thing I've learned, it's that it's easier for people to pronounce "Arnold Schwarzenegger" than it is to pronounce a short name like mine.

I could count the number of people who could pronounce my name correctly on one hand even though it's really easy. Three syllables—Ah. Oh. Ee. A-o-i. See? Piece of cake.

But for my six years of elementary school, "Ooey!" "A-OK!" and "Owie!" were the names I answered to. But not anymore.

And my last name, Inoue? That was a disaster, too.

"I know you?" they asked. "In owie?"

My dad discovered, though, that if we pronounced it "Enoway," it sounded vaguely Irish, which people seemed more comfortable with than "Ee-no-oo-eh."

So, on this first day of summer theater camp, 1987, I declared that I was Annie Enoway. Together with my new old friend Jessica Kelly, I was shedding my elementary school past and was on my way to becoming anything that I wanted to be.

CHAPTER 2

I *am a sunny-side-up egg.*

A skillet, cast iron, heated up over the blue flames of a gas stove. Two eggs, cracked with one hand, plopped into smoking bacon fat.

I sizzled and twitched as my clear gooey insides whitened and gelled. I flung my arms into the air like the grease that spat and hissed out from the pan. My sunshine-yellow yolks, runny at first, hardened as I finished cooking.

"Two eggs, sunny-side up!" Jessica yelled.

"Yes!" I leapt up from the stage floor, as black as the skillet I was frying in. Jessica stood up to take my place.

"No fair!" pouted Ben Prescott, the puny green-eyed boy who had been in theater camp with us for the past several years. Although he looked taller, and maybe not as puny as he used to be, he was clearly still a baby, whining over the fact that

Jessica and I had always ruled, and still ruled, at these improv games.

Not that it was a competition or anything.

But as Jessica took the stage, our theater camp director, Ms. Tracy, clapped her hands.

"Very nice, Annie! Very realistic egg frying. Now, before we continue, I have an announcement to make."

Jessica sat back down next to me and we focused all our attention on Ms. Tracy. Tall, pale, dark-haired, and dressed entirely in black, Ms. Tracy looked like she was born and raised in the theater. She *oozed* drama.

Silence fell over us as we waited for the news. Jessica's mom had mentioned something exciting might be coming up and we both had our guesses. We didn't dare jinx it, though, by hoping for it too much.

"As you all know, the Topeka Repertory Theater puts on a summer production every year. While in the past it had only been for adults and actors sixteen and older, this year we're putting on the play *Annie*, so . . ." Ms. Tracy paused here for maximum suspense. Entirely appropriate since this *was* theater camp.

Jessica and I held our breath.

". . . we're opening auditions up for actors older than ten."

Squeeeee!! Unlike the older, more established Topeka Civic Theatre, Topeka Repertory had only been around for a few

8

years. But it quickly established a name for itself when it wowed everyone with its flashy and professional production of *Oklahoma!* last summer. You'd think that Kansans wouldn't be all that excited to see a musical about the even-less-exciting state immediately to our south, but after that show, every actor in town wanted to be part of Topeka Repertory.

Jessica grabbed my hands. We couldn't stop ourselves from squealing and wriggling and stomping our feet. *Annie* the movie had come out a few years ago, and the rags-to-riches story about the spunky little redheaded orphan was our absolute *favorite*. Between the two of us, we'd seen it at least twenty times. We knew all the songs by heart. We sang them at recess, at home, and even in the sycamore tree because dreaming and imagining we were Broadway stars was easier up there, for some reason.

In true Ms. Tracy fashion, she inhaled deeply and drew herself up tall, raising her hand in a flowing swoop over her head. When she lowered her arm gracefully, like a ballerina would, we all quieted down as we exhaled along with her.

"Now, TRT plays are *real* productions. You must prepare for your audition and even then, you might not get the part you wanted. You might not even get a part at all."

At this point, her eyes seemed to rest on me. But only for a split second. So fast that I might have imagined it. In fact, I'm sure I did.

Ms. Tracy gathered a stack of papers from a nearby stool and began passing them out. "Auditions are next week. There's more information on this sheet, but make sure to complete it and have it ready by . . ."

As Ms. Tracy rambled on and Jessica read through the handout next to me, a rumpled and frazzled lady who had just huffed and puffed her way into the theater caught my attention. She was probably the same age as my mom and Mrs. Kelly, but there was nothing motherly about her. Her mousy brown hair was a partially grown out, chin-length perm, and her oversized faded camo-green G.I. Joe T-shirt was half tucked in, half out. She wiped the sweat off her forehead with her sleeve before she interrupted.

"Hey, sorry I'm late. Town's changed since I was here last. Not the heat, though, Jesus Christ, it's still hotter than hell here—"

"Mrs. Glick!" Ms. Tracy turned with a flourish and held out her arm toward the guest like she was the Queen of England. "Everyone, it is my honor to mention the most exciting part of TRT's summer production. We have a bona fide Hollywood director on board! Please, let us all welcome—"

"Sam! It's Sam," the director mumbled gruffly, her voice low and gravelly like one of the back roads that led out past the cow pastures on the outskirts of Topeka. "Mrs. Glick was my mother, not to mention the fact that I'm not married, thank

God. What a train wreck *that* woulda been!" Perhaps realizing she was veering off topic, Sam cleared her throat and continued. "Yeah, so. It's been a while since I've done theater, and like Tracy here said, I was out in LA for a while. But now I'm back and, uh . . . Guess I'll see some of you next week? Cool."

And with that, Sam not-Mrs.-Glick shuffled out of the theater.

Wow! Quick and to the point and didn't talk to us like we were a bunch of babies. I could tell she was the Real Hollywood Deal.

I looked down at my audition form.

You can be anything you want to be.

Those words rang in my head again.

The truth is, I want to be so many things, but at this moment, more than anything else . . .

I want to be Annie.

Little Orphan Annie.

CHAPTER 3

"Tadaima!" I announced my arrival home as soon as I bounded up our front porch steps and into my home sweet hotter-than-Hades. But not even the late-June Kansas heat could quell my excitement about playing Annie in this year's community theater production.

My little brother, Tak, careened down the stairs, his black hair sticking up like little demon horns. He would have toppled headfirst if I hadn't been there to stop his forward momentum.

"Oof!"

But instead of "Sorry" he hollered "Cowabunga!!!" and leapt as far as his five-year-old legs would catapult him. Luckily, the sofa was there to catch him as he face-planted into its faded floral cushions.

My mom sighed from the kitchen. "He's been like this all day," she told me in Japanese, too tired to even practice her

English. "How was theater camp?"

"It was great!" I sat down at the table and answered my mom in English, too excited to use my Japanese. "I'm going to be Annie!"

My mom frowned. She was *not* on board with my name change, but after hearing my real one butchered at the elementary school graduation ceremony, she relented. Pretty sure the way the principal pronounced my name ended up meaning something like "evil demon" or "bug guts" in Japanese (not that I know how to say either).

"Can't I call you 'Aoi' at home at least?" My mom began chopping an onion into slices so thin you could almost see through them.

"Nope! In fact, you should call me Annie even more. To help me get in character."

"'Character'? Dou iu imi?" My mom paused.

I sighed. I didn't know how to explain "character" in Japanese. "You know, like Little Orphan Annie? The movie we saw all together a few years ago?"

We saw few enough movies together as a family that my mom remembered.

"You mean the curly redheaded girl who gets adopted by the rich bald man?"

"Yep!" I pulled the folded paper from my shorts pocket. I smoothed it out, moved the junk mail and three days' worth of newspapers that cluttered the kitchen table, and set it down on the small patch where I'd made some space. "Can you sign this?"

Tak bounced into the kitchen. "You don't look anything like that Annie girl."

I rolled my eyes. "There are things called wigs, butt-head."

"You're the butt-head," Tak retorted as he turned around and slapped his bottom at me.

My mom was actually reading the form rather than just signing it like she usually does.

The screen door rattled. "I'm home!"

"Daddy!" Tak stopped slapping his butt to run full speed toward the front door.

Our dad let go of the handles on his square black leather work satchel just in time to swoop Tak into his arms and use the little demon's forward momentum to swing him high in the air.

"Can we play basketball?" Tak pleaded.

"Ooh, can we?" I chimed in. I knew we should have let Dad change out of his shirt and tie first, but . . .

"I need Aoi to help with dinner." My mom appeared in the entryway of the kitchen, her dark silhouette blocking the sun behind her like a fun-squashing villain.

"No fair! *I* want to help with dinner!" Just as quickly as Tak had greeted Dad, he ran back into the kitchen. "Aoi *always* gets to help with dinner."

"Okay, Annie, I guess you're with me!" My dad loosened his tie and stepped outside again. I scooted close behind him, both of us trying not to notice my mom's accusing glare. I know we should have felt bad about leaving the little goblin inside with her, but Tak wasn't exactly great at moving out of the way for cars or not having meltdowns when he missed his shots (which was almost always).

I grabbed the basketball from the corner of the front porch and then rushed across the street with my dad. Our neighbors had a hoop and didn't mind when anyone used it.

Dribble, dribble, dribble. I laid up a basket to my right. *Swish.*

My dad passed it back to me and this time I went to my left. *Clonk.*

He rebounded it and now it was his turn. While I waited, I jumped up and down, as high as I could, with my eye on the rim. I wanted to make my legs as strong as they could get. They would have to be if I was going to play in the NBA!

Then he dribbled circles around me, like he was *asking* for me to steal it from him. Even though he was forty years old, he was still pretty spry. He certainly didn't *look* like he was that old, especially compared with Jessica's dad, who had already lost most of his dark brown hair. Professor Kelly was so self-conscious about it that he carefully combed the strands that he had left over the top of his head.

"It looks like a bar code," my mom observed. When I burst into giggles at this description, she tried to keep a straight face, but couldn't. She warned me never to tell anyone she had said that.

I never did, even though I wanted to. Especially when the wind blew and made Professor Kelly's hair fly up and dance in the breeze. When this happened, it reminded me less of a bar code and more of a tattered flag indicating, "Never surrender!"

Dad, on the other hand, had a full head of black hair and barely any gray. He'd even grown a mustache in an attempt to make himself look older.

"I can't have the students thinking I'm just the teaching assistant," he explained to my mother when she complained about it. "It'll make them respect me more."

I was getting a little tired of waiting for my turn as my dad managed five shots off me.

"What did you do today, Daddy?" I asked just as he released from the "free-throw line," which was a black tar smudge in the middle of the street.

Ka-thunk!

"Brick!" I yelled.

"Brick?" Dad rebounded his own ball. "What's that?"

"It's a really ugly shot," I explained. My dad's English wasn't bad, and he knew a lot about basketball, but he wasn't always up-to-date with American slang.

He laughed. He knew I only asked about his day to distract him. And it worked.

"Well, I learned a new math riddle today." He passed me the ball.

I groaned. My dad's a math professor, so naturally, he's obsessed with numbers. I, on the other hand, inherited none of those math-loving genes.

"So, let's say I gave you a hundred dollars—"

"You're giving me a hundred dollars?" I interrupted.

"And with it, you bought a hundred animals. Your choices were a goldfish, a turtle, and a cat—" my dad continued, unfazed.

"Why would I buy a cat? We already have Chibi." I laughed.

"If the turtle cost three dollars, the goldfish cost fifty cents, and the cat cost ten dollars, how many of each type of animal did you buy?"

"Well . . ." I pretended to seriously consider his riddle. Dad looked so excited that he might have actually piqued my interest that I *almost* felt sorry for him.

"Four times five is twelve, and four times six is thirteen, and four times—" I had no clue where to even begin with his riddle, so I recited *Alice in Wonderland*'s multiplication tables instead. You know, to remind my dad how much I personally hated math.

"Oh, Annie." My dad sighed.

But I could tell he wasn't upset with me because he just smiled and shook his head.

Instead of a layup this time, I got right up under the basket and launched myself as close to the rim as my legs would take me. I let go of the ball.

"Almost, Annie!" My dad clapped. He knew how much I wanted to dunk that ball! After several months of practicing, I was pretty sure it was only a matter of a few inches now.

My dad's the one who told me about Muggsy Bogues, the shortest basketball player in the NBA, and got me fired up about basketball in the first place. At 5'3", *he* could dunk, so why not me? I mean, I'm not 5'3" yet, but I think I might get there eventually. After all, my dad's 5'7" and my mom's 5'1", so averaged out, that's *at least* 5'3".

My mom gets mad at my dad for encouraging me and my "silly ideas," as she's been known to call them. But they're not silly. They're *dreams*, and my dad's a dreamer, just like me.

When he graduated from college in Japan, he could have just gotten a job at some company and worked there for the rest of his life. But he was addicted to Hollywood movies and the glossy, exciting "you can be anything you want to be" way of life they introduced him to. That's what made him dream of coming to the US.

He told me that for a long time, America didn't allow in many immigrants who looked like him. Well, they had before, like when they used the Chinese to help with things like building railroads. But then in the late 1800s . . . they stopped. Apparently, there were a lot of people who thought the Chinese were taking their jobs, so the US government no longer let them come over anymore. But then, Japanese people, Koreans, and even South Asians came to work in the US. (So I guess there *were* enough jobs?) But people complained once more and made it harder for people to immigrate *again*. Then there were a couple of wars and even though the US still had laws to shut non-Americans out, people around the world really believed the US was a land of freedom and democracy. And I guess finally, that's when some American leaders started to think, *Maybe our immigration laws should reflect that!* At least this is what my dad said. I think. I have to admit, my mind wanders a little when he gets on these tangents. When US immigration laws eased up around the same time my dad was trying to figure out what to do with his life, he took it as a sign he should come here for graduate school.

He didn't have much money, so he created some matrix that determined which schools in the US were cheapest but paid the most for their graduate teaching assistants, and then he took cost-of-living expenses into account and *ta-da*! He ended up getting his PhD in math at KU (aka the University of Kansas), which led to a teaching position at the small college where he's at now.

I'm sure he misses Japan some, but my dad seems really happy with his life here. After dinner most nights, he likes to take in the dramatic red and fiery oranges of the Kansan sunset and say, "Look at this sky! Look at our yard! We could never have this in Japan."

Then we all sit and stare at our yard, which is way smaller than Jessica's but way bigger than anything we could afford in Japan. My mom usually doesn't say anything, though.

Speaking of my mom . . .

"Gohan dekimashita yo!" she called out to let us know that dinner was ready.

My dad passed me the ball and I went in for one last (attempted) dunk.

"Aoi!" my mom yelled sharply, causing me to miss. I grabbed the ball and bounded back into the house.

CHAPTER 4

Inside on the dinner table was a large platter of battered and golden-fried little fishies, slivered onions, and red bell peppers tossed in an oil-and-vinegar dressing with parsley and garlic. At each of our place settings was a bowl of steamed rice, as well as chopsticks. Except at Tak's spot—he always used a fork and spoon because his chopstick skills totally sucked.

"Itadakimasu." This is how we began dinner in our house. Jessica asked if it was similar to saying grace and I said yes, but it isn't really. It's just what Japanese people say before they eat their meals—there's nothing religious or anything like that. But I found that saying "Yeah, it's our version of grace" seemed to satisfy people like Jessica and kept me from having to answer too many questions about how we were different.

I don't love this particular meal that my mom makes, but Tak seemed really proud of his contribution today.

"I chopped the vegetables," he announced as he crunched into the fish. "With a *knife*."

Sure enough, my mom's expertly sliced onions and red peppers were mixed in with big uneven chunks that looked like they were hacked at with an ax.

"Wow, thank you for helping with dinner!" As my dad praised Tak, he looked up at my mom sheepishly. We all knew that supervising my little brother with a sharp blade probably wasn't as much fun as shooting baskets across the street.

"See? That's another thing that's really nice about America. Tak can help with dinner and Annie can play basketball outside." My dad liked to talk about how great it was here, almost like he was trying to convince someone. "In Japan, I bet Annie would have to be in the kitchen and Tak and I . . . I bet there wouldn't even be a hoop out in front of our house like . . . Oh, what's this?"

From under the pile of mail my mom always set off to the side of our forever-cluttered table, my *Annie* audition form caught his eye. As he pulled it out, my mom spoke up. "Aoi, I think we need to talk about—"

I knew that tone my mom's voice took.

"I'm going to audition for *Annie*, Dad!" I cut in. I realized it was rude to interrupt, but I had to plead my side before my mom could make her case against it. Because it definitely sounded like she was against it.

22

"*Annie*? Like the movie?"

"Yep! Could you sign it? It's just the permission form."

"Aoi . . ." my mother tried again.

"I'm finally old enough to audition for actual shows, Daddy! The kind TRT puts on. You know, the new community theater?"

"Ah, *ii na*, sounds good to me!" Dad took a pen out of his pocket and signed.

I practically yanked it out of his hand and dashed upstairs before my mom could take it from me. After stashing it inside my copy of *Alice's Adventures in Wonderland*, I was about to head back downstairs when I heard Mom's words floating up toward me.

"Why do you encourage her like that?"

"Like what?"

"She doesn't look a thing like Annie. We all know she's not going to get the part."

I froze in place. Why would my mom say that? *No one* looked like Annie. But we all *could* with a wig, some makeup, and *acting*. Last summer, at our little end-of-camp show, Mom said I did a good job. I was really proud then because she's not the type to slather on the praise. But maybe she *wasn't* that impressed. How else could you explain why my own mother didn't think I even had a chance?

"It's like when she said she was going to be a princess like

Diana, and you actually said that was a great idea."

Ugh! I couldn't believe my mom had to bring that up. I was six then! And highly impressionable. That was some wedding. Even Mom couldn't take her eyes off the TV and Princess Diana's poofy dress and long silk wedding train that went on for ages. I dreamed about finding my own Prince Charming someday.

"What?" my dad responded to my mom. "Technically she *could* still be a princess."

I stomped down the stairs, eager to put an end to them taking apart my dreams. Even the silly ones.

Their conversation stopped.

When I entered the kitchen, I pulled my chair out hard so that it scraped obnoxiously across our linoleum floor. I wanted them to know I'd heard.

Tak wanted to make sure, too. "Mom thinks you won't get the part."

I scowled as I skewered a fish and stuffed it in my mouth. I chewed so I didn't have to talk.

"But what do we know about theater?" My dad responded to my thundercloud expression with his own ray-of-sunshine optimism. "*I* know you can do anything you set your mind to."

That's right, I thought as I avoided making eye contact with my mom. *I can.*

CHAPTER 5

For the following week, Jessica and I worked on our audition materials during camp—where Ms. Tracy taught us how to command the stage from the moment we walked on and announced our names—and also after, usually at Jessica's house.

The Kelly house was older, like ours, and only five blocks from where I lived. Even though it was so close, Jessica's home felt like a wonderland compared to my place. Starting at about three blocks away from the Kellys', the houses and lawns grew much larger, like what might have happened if my house had taken multivitamins and drunk lots of milk growing up.

Jessica's dad works at the local university like mine. *Unlike* my dad, he's the university president. Jessica's grandparents actually owned the house her family lives in now, so when they moved to a retirement home, they basically gave the house to Jessica's parents.

If my parents had stayed in Japan, I guess we could have had a similar arrangement, too. Dad would have taken care of Obaachan (that's "Grandma" in Japanese) and we would have all lived with her. Since he decided to immigrate to the US, though, he sends money back to his younger brother, who ended up taking care of their mother instead.

"We don't have much to spare," I overheard my mother telling her sister in Japanese over the phone one day. "But he feels guilty for leaving them to follow his dream."

When you walked into Jessica's house, soft, cool air enveloped you as you stepped inside. Even when we used the AC at our place, it was only a window unit that rattled and hummed. And it never got our place as refreshingly chilly as Jessica's place.

Plush ivory-colored carpet covered almost all the floors in her house. When I stepped on it, I felt like I was walking on a cloud. Even though the Kellys wore shoes in their house most of the time, the carpet seemed resistant to dirt and stayed the same light ivory, day in, day out.

It was on this soft, triple-cream carpet in Jessica's room that we hung out on the Wednesday before auditions (only five more days to go!).

Jessica jumped onto the cotton-candy-pink comforter that

covered her canopy bed, and closed its sheer lavender-colored drapes embroidered with butterflies around her. She waited for me to introduce her.

"Next. Jessica Kel—"

Before I could finish, she burst through the fabric and leapt onto the floor.

"Hi! My name is Jessica Kelly," she shouted dramatically. "And I'm going to be singing 'Tomorrow' for you."

"Ms. Tracy said to make sure not to yell."

"I'm *not* yelling. I'm *projecting.*"

"Okay," I responded, not convinced.

Jessica then proceeded to belt Annie's signature song at the top of her lungs. As she got toward the end, when the notes went higher and higher, her voice cracked. She paused and tried again.

"You don't have to go up that high, you know. She did in the movie, but—"

"I'm just a little hoarse today, that's all."

At that moment, Mrs. Kelly arrived at Jessica's bedroom door. She held two tall glasses of Coke with ice.

"Working hard, girls?"

She handed Jessica her glass and then the other one to me. I took a sip. My mom only let me have pop about once a week, so Tak and I would take tall glasses and fill them with ice so it seemed like we had more than we actually did.

"Thanks, Mom."

"It's Diet Coke, so you can have as much as you like, okay?"

Diet Coke? That explained the funny aftertaste. My mom refused to buy anything "diet" because she said it was mazui, or "yucky," and that she didn't trust the chemicals in it.

Jessica's mom—like mine—didn't work outside the home. Otherwise, they were like night and day. Mrs. Kelly letting her daughter have sugar-free drinks wasn't the only way in which they were different. My mom is *really* pretty, but you might not notice at first glance because she's not *fancy*-pretty. She doesn't use much makeup—just some lipstick if she's going out—and she wears her hair the same way every day, pulled back into a bun. At home, she always has an apron and slippers on.

Not Mrs. Kelly, though. She's *definitely* the fancy-pretty type. Every time I see her, she's all done up. Foundation, eye shadow, mascara, lipstick, and blush swooshed across her face to "accent her cheekbones" was how Jessica explained it. I don't understand how she keeps it all from melting off her face during the summer. And her hair is shorter than my mom's, but it's always curled and styled. In fact, she spent hours at the salon to get it "frosted" recently. When Jessica told me how much it cost, I could hardly believe it. We *never* spent that much on anything.

Today, Mrs. Kelly was wearing turquoise-blue pumps to match her turquoise-blue blouse. From her ears hung large, golden hoop earrings, and her nails were long and painted a glittering pink. I asked my mom once if I could grow my nails out like that, and she told me not to be ridiculous. That I'd never be able to get any work done that way.

I took another sip of Diet Coke. Even though Jessica's mom said we could have as much as we wanted, I was pretty sure I'd be okay with this one glass.

Mrs. Kelly tucked a flyaway strand of hair behind Jessica's ear.

"Well, you sound *fantastic*, princess. I can tell that new director is just going to think you're something *special*."

As I watched Mrs. Kelly gaze at Jessica like she was the sun, moon, and Wonder Woman all rolled into one, I wished for a split moment that my mom would talk to me like Jessica's mom did to her. "Fantastic," "princess," and "special"? Those weren't the words my mom would have used. More like, "Are you sure that's the song you want to try out with? It's too high for you, you're straining."

Then she would have finished with, "And you should make sure you fix your hair before you go onstage."

"It's so nice of you to help Jessica with her audition!" Mrs. Kelly patted me on my back and looked down on me warmly.

"Um, I'm helping *her*, too, Mom!" Jessica snorted in objection to having her good deed overlooked.

"Oh?" Her mom looked surprised. "For what part?"

I thought it was funny that it wasn't obvious. There was only *one* part any girl wanted. Jessica answered before I could. "For Annie, *DUH*, Mom!"

I almost choked on an ice cube.

But Mrs. Kelly only looked confused for a moment, not mad. Then she shone a big smile at me—it was so wide I could see her molars. "What song are you going to audition with, dear?"

"Umm . . . 'Maybe,' I think."

"Well, you should definitely sing. Not 'maybe'!"

"She's gonna sing the *song* 'Maybe,' Mom. Geez!" Jessica sighed with exasperation.

"Oh!" Mrs. Kelly let out a laugh that clinked and twinkled like the ice cubes in our glasses. "You know, I was thinking of auditioning for one of the adult parts, too! How about I join you and we could all take turns? Annie could go first—"

"Uh . . ." I looked at Jessica. *Save me!* I tried to tell her with my eyes.

"God, Mom, get outta here! We're working!"

Sometimes I couldn't believe Jessica got away with how she talked to her mom. If *I* talked to my mom that way . . .

"Fine . . . Fine!" Mrs. Kelly laughed again, like it was no big deal that her daughter just mouthed off to her big-time.

When she left and closed the door behind her, I let out the breath I had been holding. "Thanks."

Jessica raised an eyebrow at me. "How're you gonna sing onstage in front of a huge crowd if you can't sing in front of my mom?"

I hopped on the bed and peeked through the canopy drapes. "I *can*, I just . . ."

Jessica giggled. "I know, I don't like to sing in front of her, either."

I peekaboo'd through the light purple canopy drapes a few more times until we were both laughing so hard we could barely breathe. Jessica was the first to calm down. Or try to at least.

"Come on, we . . . don't have that much more time. Let's hear it."

I took a deep breath and centered myself, like Ms. Tracy taught us at camp. I hopped off the bed, stood up tall, and looked straight ahead.

"Hi! My name is Annie, and I'm going to sing 'Maybe' for you today."

Jessica burst into applause. "Nice *projecting*!"

I tried not to smile as I took another deep breath and started singing softly. What would it feel like to be an orphan? To have no home, no parents? To be waiting for my mom and dad day after day and have them never show up? I channeled all those feelings into my words.

When I finished, Jessica didn't applaud. She just sat there.

"What? Was it *that* bad?"

"No. No! It was great, Annie! It really was."

I blushed. Jessica and I usually joked around a lot. It was almost weird for her to be so sincere.

But then it hit me. In this room we could both be Annie, but not after the auditions. Even though this should have been obvious from the start, I realized that only one of us would get the part.

And maybe it would be Jessica . . . which would be okay because she's my best friend.

But maybe it would be me.

Maybe.

CHAPTER 6

The adults who were trying out for parts like Daddy War-bucks and the evil Miss Hannigan auditioned over the weekend. For us kids, though, ours were on Monday evening at the concert hall of the university where my dad works. Since he didn't need the car then, my mom insisted on driving. "We can't take advantage of the Kellys' generosity," Mom insisted. Even though we offered to take Jessica, too, they said no thanks. I'm not surprised—I knew her mom wouldn't miss Jessica's audition for the world.

Not mine, though. She was going to help our church prepare for its annual "International Food Bazaar" event while I did mine.

"Are you sure that's what you should wear?" My mother looked back at me through the rearview mirror.

Ms. Tracy had told us that it was okay to dress casual for

auditions. That we should be comfortable but not sloppy. And *definitely* not like we were trying too hard.

I looked down at my pastel plaid romper, matching pink socks, and clean(ish) Converses we'd bought from a garage sale a month ago.

"Yeah," I answered. "It's fine!" Although I wasn't 100 percent sure now that it was.

I was *totally* okay with the fact that my mom wouldn't be at my audition.

Jessica and my other friends' parents attended all their school events and recitals and performances, but mine didn't. They came to some, but a lot of times, Mom said she would have to stay home with Tak, who wasn't really old enough to sit still during them without fidgeting or whining, "How much longer now?" But I could tell she actually *wanted* to stay home. While other parents chatted and socialized, my mom often hung out by herself off to the side, holding Tak's hand as tightly as he held on to hers.

When my dad came to my events, he usually ended up falling asleep. One time during the informational parent meeting for my sixth-grade basketball team, he nodded off. He tried really hard not to, but that only made it worse. First his head dropped down and then quickly jerked up. And try though he did to keep his eyelids open, they fluttered shut, and not only did he doze off again, he snored so loudly he scared himself awake. The next time he fell asleep, he swayed to the right and almost ended up in Mr. Holmes's lap. Then his whole body bobbed to the left and he almost fell out of his chair.

To make matters worse, all my teammates were there, too, so they couldn't help giggling with each snort and sleep tremor.

I know my dad's only tired because he works *really* hard, but after that I didn't mind all that much when my parents said they couldn't come to my events.

"Nanji ni pick up su re ba ii?" My mom mixed in English sometimes with her Japanese to make sure Tak and I understood what she said.

"Umm . . . nine o'clock?" That was *way* later than my audition should last, but I wanted to make sure she wouldn't be there when I sang.

"Okay! Ja ganbatte ne." She drove off after wishing me luck.

I ran into the university concert hall, where Ms. Tracy stood at the entrance. I handed my form to her and she read through it quickly.

"Annie? It says here that you're only interested in the part of Annie. Is that right?"

It *was*, but now I felt embarrassed that I had only checked that one box.

Ms. Tracy handed her clipboard and pen back to me before I could even respond.

"I thought I checked off more," I fumbled as I tried to hide my reddening cheeks from her. I checked the boxes next to the other orphans' names, too, then handed the sheet back to her.

As she reviewed my form again, I took in the stage from the back of the auditorium where we were standing. Rows and rows of padded maroon seats, dipping down in the middle and flattening out, all facing a girl in the spotlight who I had never seen before.

"That's Jennifer Miller," Ms. Tracy whispered. "She's fourteen, but I think she looks like she could be eleven, don't you?"

I gulped. Jessica and I would be competing against *high school* students? I knew Topeka Repertory Theater was big-time, but I didn't know it would be *this* big-time.

I felt *really* embarrassed now about checking only the "Annie" box on the form. After watching what was unfolding before me, I knew I'd be lucky if I even got a part, let alone the lead role.

Jennifer delivered her rendition of "You're Never Fully Dressed Without a Smile." It was an upbeat number and even though we weren't asked to, Jennifer performed her song with some snappy dance moves that made it clear she would be fine with any choreography thrown at her, if she were cast.

Jennifer finished with a pose, fluttering jazz hands, and a huge smile plastered across her face. Her almost-platinum hair bounced over her shoulders. Her teeth were dazzling white, like those toothpaste commercials where stars burst forth from the actor's smile.

Ms. Tracy clapped. "Okay, Annie. Head on backstage and I'll make sure Sam gets this. Break a leg!"

As I made my way down the aisle, I passed Sam, the director, and another woman with cat-eyed glasses sitting next to her. I hadn't noticed them when I first walked in, sitting about ten rows from the stage and the gaping orchestra pit in front of it.

"Okay . . ." Sam paused to double-check the name on the form. ". . . Jennifer. We'll be in touch."

Wow. No smile, no applause, no "That was really great!"

Before I lost my nerve entirely and threw myself into the orchestra pit out of despair, I scurried toward a black door on the side of the stage.

Once I was safely out of sight, I peered around, hoping to see Jessica. Where was she? She said her audition was tonight, but she didn't mention exactly what time. She said she'd check, but then she forgot to tell me after camp.

"Hey! Annie!"

Instead of Jessica, I found Ben. And I was actually *really* relieved to see a familiar face, even if it was his.

"Hey, Ben," I greeted him as I made my way over.

We didn't say anything more as we watched a little girl in dark brown pigtails skip onto the stage, probably just making the age cutoff since she looked like she was barely ten. She sang a really cute and peppy version of "Maybe."

Unfortunately, "Maybe" is a pretty sad and depressing song. This kid's bouncing and smiley version of it was kind of . . . confusing? Like I wasn't sure if she was trying to be ironic?

Whew, mine's better.

I'm kind of ashamed this thought crossed my mind, but it did.

On the other side of the stage, the little girl's mother watched her intensely. She grinned from ear to ear as she mouthed the words to the song along with her little girl.

Well, I guess we know who taught her how to perform it all happy like *that.*

"What are you singing?" Ben whisper-asked.

"Same." I pointed to the girl who had just finished and skipped off the stage. "Ugh, I'm so nervous." I wiped the sweat from my palms.

Ben gave me a thumbs-up. "Oh, you're gonna *demolish* her."

A laugh almost burst out of me, but I covered my mouth before it could.

"Ben! That's not nice."

"Into little pieces. She's gonna hear you sing, and she'll know it's *over.*"

Ben was being so over the top about crushing that cute little girl's spirits that my nerves went away. A little.

"Annie?" a voice called out from the seats. "Annie . . . ? Ino . . . Inoo . . ."

"That's you!" I felt all the blood rush from my body as Ben gave me a shove.

And then . . . I was onstage. *Onstage.* The biggest stage Topeka had to offer. The lights that shone on it blinded me for a second, and my legs were deciding what to do. Crumple? Or stride?

"Annie Enoway!" I stated my name and strode out onto the stage with all the confidence that I did not feel *one bit.*

"Hi, I'm Annie Enoway," I repeated with a smile. "And I'm going to be singing 'Maybe,' too."

One nice thing about the lights was that it was hard to see anyone out there in the seats. *Huh.* I hadn't figured it would be like that.

I took a deep breath like Ms. Tracy taught us to. I looked over to my right, where the piano player had his hands poised over the black and white keys. He reminded me of a grandpa who always had candies in his pocket to give to his grandkids. His hair was white, but his eyes were a bright sky blue. He winked when I made eye contact. Then he gave me a little nod.

As the opening notes to the song played, I closed my eyes for a moment, remembering all the sadness I conjured up at Jessica's house when we were practicing.

I looked out over the director's head as I began to sing. "Maybe" was about Annie dreaming about who her parents were, and I knew all about dreaming. Maybe I didn't really know what it was like to be an orphan. But once last year, my dad didn't pick me up from basketball practice on time. And I waited and waited as it got darker and darker and other parents picked up their children. I didn't cry then, but I burst into tears when he finally arrived over an hour late. Turns out his department meeting had run long, but I thought he had gotten into an accident and died.

I mustered up all the sadness from that time and put it into my singing. My voice cracked on the last *"May . . . be . . ."* not because I was straining but because I was actually *sad*. In fact, I sang the last word so softly that I was pretty sure only the accompanist and I could hear it. He was with me the whole time, though, adjusting his tempo to mine and the piano volume to my voice. I was pretty amazed that he could do it just like that, too. Without knowing me or ever rehearsing with me prior to this. Like I said before—Topeka Repertory Theater was *big-time*.

When I finished, I paused for three seconds before I looked up. Ms. Tracy clapped for me in the back of the theater. The director didn't, but I already knew not to expect her to. She hadn't clapped for anyone else.

But she did say this:

"Nice."

I glanced over to the side of the stage, where Ben gave me a huge double thumbs-up. I guess he noticed Sam's compliment, too.

"All right . . ." Sam examined my audition form. "Annie? Ha! Well, whaddaya know. Name fits at least. We'll let you know soon."

"Thank you!" I squeaked as I practically floated off the stage.

Nice. She said my audition was nice! I know that doesn't sound like much. Not like "Amazing!" or "Fantastic!" or "Great job!" but *it was.* Coming from that grouchy director, "Nice" meant *a lot.*

I checked my watch: 8:10. *Oof.* Looked like it would be almost an hour before my mom came to pick me up.

Ben was next. He sang "It's a Hard-Knock Life," which I thought was really funny since all the orphans who sing that song in the play are supposed to be girls. But why not? There weren't that many parts for boys Ben's age anyway. How hard could it be to add a little boy orphan in the mix? Plus, the way he hammed up his audition had me and a lot of other people backstage giggling. I peeked out toward Sam and I'm *pretty* sure I saw a smile on her face, too.

When Ben finished, I gave him a big double thumbs-up just like he did for me.

"Thanks," the director said right after he ended. "We'll let you know in a few days."

Thanks. Ben and I were pretty sure that meant *awesome* in Sam-speak.

Turns out that the woman sitting next to Sam was Midge Prescott, Ben's aunt. She was helping with the auditions, which meant he had to stay late, too. Even though I thought he was just a whiny boy before this summer, he now seemed, well . . . I dunno. Different. We hung out backstage together and watched the next five auditions, all girls, all singing Annie's big signature song, "Tomorrow." Natalie Moreno was the fifth girl to sing it, and she did so in a matter-of-fact, almost *scientific* manner. She was twelve like me, but towered over all of us. She was even taller than Ms. Tracy. That, combined with how Sam sighed, long and loud, after Natalie finished her song, did not bode well. Plus, Sam's only comment was "Okay," and not like *ooookay!* but like *ok*. Then she searched her many pockets like she desperately needed to find something. When she finally fished out a box of Good & Plenty, she seemed disappointed but poured a bunch of the pink and white candies into her hand before popping them into her mouth.

Ben and I knew where she was coming from. Sam had been here a lot longer than me, and I was already tired of the song, too.

"Where's Jessica?" Ben asked.

I shrugged. "I was about to ask you the same thing." I looked around. I thought for sure she would have gone on by now.

"Last, but not least," Ben's aunt announced. "For tonight's final audition, we have . . . Jessica Kelly?"

From the other side of the stage, Ben and I watched as Little Orphan Annie stepped out into the spotlight.

Like, *the* Little Orphan Annie. Jessica looked *exactly* like you would imagine Annie to look. Frizzy strawberry-red curls had replaced her sandy-blond French braid and poofy bangs. Instead of her stylish acid-wash jean shorts and pastel polo shirt that she often wore, she was dressed in a drab, oversized dress and a ratty gray cardigan.

My jaw dropped.

From the audience, Sam muttered, "Oh, for cryin' out loud."

I guess she was as blown away as I was.

Even though Ms. Tracy had insisted we should just wear regular clothes to our auditions, I remembered how my mom questioned what I was wearing.

No matter how much I didn't want to admit it, after seeing how transformed, how very *Annie* Jessica looked, the thought *Mom was right* shoved its way into my brain.

"Hi, my name is Jessica Kelly and I'm going to be singing 'Tomorrow' for you."

Out of the side of my eye, I noticed Sam emptying the last of her Good & Plenty candies directly into her mouth.

Jessica took a deep breath and began.

I really wanted Jessica to do well . . . but a small voice inside me started to question her motives. Why hadn't she told me she was going to go all out? Was *that* why she hadn't told me what time she was auditioning?

But then I felt awful. What kind of friend thinks that way? I told that little mean voice inside me to "shut your face!"

Great job, Jessica! I channeled all my best thoughts to my best friend. *You're totally awesome!*

I peeked out into the audience and saw Ms. Tracy and Mrs. Kelly sending all their positive energy toward Jessica as well. Her mom was practically *glowing* with pride.

As she neared the end of the song, the part where the music swelled and the melody rose, I tensed.

Jessica did, too.

Right as her voice cracked, Mrs. Kelly's smile froze on her face.

Jessica kept going, though.

But something changed after that note. I could tell Jessica no longer believed she was Little Orphan Annie. I wondered if the people watching also felt that way.

I felt doubly, triply bad for the little green monster of jealousy that reared its ugly head earlier, even if it was only for a moment. It wasn't *her* fault she could morph into Annie like that. I never asked Jessica what she was going to wear to the audition, either, so should I care that she didn't tell me? Friends support each other, no matter what.

There was a moment of silence after Jessica's last note. I peeked out. Sam had a finger in her mouth in an effort to free a molar from the grips of a glob of Good & Plenty. It was hard to tell *what* she thought of Jessica's audition.

"All right, that's a wrap then, right?" Sam gathered her purse and handed the stack of audition forms to Ben's aunt. She sounded relieved to be done. No "Nice!" or even a "Thanks!" for Jessica. My heart sank for my friend.

"Results will be out . . . as soon as we talk everything over. Shouldn't be more than a few days. Or more. Later, everyone!" Sam waved once—to no one in particular—and headed out the door.

When I turned back to the stage, Jessica was already gone.

CHAPTER 7

"Ms. Tracy, have you talked to the director? Did she say anything about us?"

"How 'bout you, Ms. Tracy? What did you think of our auditions?"

"Ms. Tracy, will we know *before* or *after* the weekend?"

"If you already know, would you tell us? If we promised not to tell anyone else?"

After a few minutes of this, Ms. Tracy pretty much immediately banned all of us who auditioned last night from talking about anything and everything relating to *Annie* while we were at camp.

During our first lunch break, Jessica explained that her mom *made* her get all dressed up like Annie and said that the hair dye they used would wash out eventually. That's why they were so late, because her mom was freaking out so much. As she said this, she played with her still-slightly-orange hair and rolled her eyes, like she couldn't care less.

I knew my friend, though.

"You were great," I insisted. "You looked just like her!"

Her eyes lit up for a second. "You think so?"

I nodded. I wasn't lying, because she really did *look* great.

"You were awesome, Annie," Jessica told me, in between bites of her yogurt. "You totally were."

"Thanks," I responded, really wanting to believe my friend. I hadn't realized that she was even there when I sang my song.

"Girls, I hope you're not obsessing over the audition." Ms. Tracy overheard our conversation as she walked by. She clapped her hands then, and signaled the end of lunch to everyone else at camp. "Chop chop, everyone! I hope you're ready for some *improv*!"

I didn't know *how* I was gonna be able to wait to know whether I was cast as Annie or not. The couple of days after the audition dragged on forever, and each minute felt like it lasted an hour.

Turned out that my mom had thought of the perfect thing to take my mind off theater.

"Aoi, you have a doctor's appointment on Thursday morning."

I groaned. "*Morning?* But I have camp th—"

"Your rash isn't getting better. I want to have it looked at—"

"It's fine!" I retorted as I also resisted the urge to scratch the backs of my legs at the same time.

My mom raised her eyebrow at me. I knew not to argue. "Fine."

I hated going to the doctor. My earliest memory of going was when I was five and my mom had taken me in for my yearly checkup. Even though that was years ago, I still remember how my heart pounded when the nurse came in with that tray of needles. *Shots? No one said anything about shots!* Without thinking, I *bolted* through the partially open door and ran as fast as I could until I careened down the hall and a doctor and two nurses cornered me. My mom dragged me back into the exam room, where they held me down, readied the needle, and gave me a big ol' shot in the butt.

I hated the office corridors, with their fake lighting that we had to walk down until we got to the door for pediatrics. I hated the waiting room with old magazines whose pages were torn out. Not that they were the least bit interesting—they were pretty much all about gardening or what gifts you could crochet for your friends at Christmas (even when we went to the office in June).

But the morning of my appointment, we turned right onto SW Huntoon Street instead of the usual left.

"Mom, the hospital's thataway."

"We're not going to the hospital." My mom pulled a notepad

with directions scribbled on it out of her purse. "Your old doctor retired, so I thought we'd go to this one. I heard good things about her."

The new office was in a building that looked more like a house than a medical facility. I wasn't sure if that was a good or bad thing. We got there early because my mom was hypersensitive about being on time, which actually meant getting there fifteen minutes before the appointment. But since my mom was also worried about getting lost on her way there, we were thirty minutes early. Not that it mattered much because I knew we wouldn't be seen on time. We never were!

I scanned the stack of magazines. Surprise, surprise, all of them were from *this year*. In fact, they were from the past couple of months. Of course, there wasn't a single copy of *Seventeen*. Only *TIME*, *Newsweek*, and *People*, which was a tiny step up from the old gardening and craft magazines that my former doctor's office had. I pulled out my copy of *Alice's Adventures in Wonderland* anyway and began to read.

"Again?" My mom side-eyed me as she smoothed back her hair and checked her lipstick in her compact mirror. "What is it about that book?"

"I like it," I grumbled. Now it was my turn to side-eye my mom. Why she felt the doctor's office was worth dressing up for was a mystery to me! Granted, she didn't get out *that* much, especially without smudgy Tak, whose hands attracted dirt no matter where we went.

"Aoi?" A nurse poked her head into the waiting room. Whoa, that was quick. I had expected that we'd be waiting for at least an extra fifteen minutes. *And* she said my name right. I instinctively looked over at my mom to see if she'd noticed too. She didn't smile, but she didn't look annoyed either, so I could tell she was already pleased with this new office. My mom stood up first and let me go in ahead of her, almost like she was trying to make sure I went in.

When we reached the exam room, I sat on the crinkly paper (that I hated, new doctor or no) and scratched at the backs of my legs.

"Aoi, yame nasai." My mom stopped me.

"So, it looks like we're seeing you for a rash? And some coughing at night?" The nurse checked my chart.

Cough? What cough? I thought. This was the first I'd heard about any *cough*.

"Yes. Yes, she scratches here . . . and the cough. Bad at night. I hear, I can hear—"

"I don't hear it," I interrupted my mom as she searched for her words.

"Well, Dr. Wang will be in soon." The nurse scribbled down some notes before she left.

I glared at my mom. "My cough isn't bad at all."

"You don't notice it because you're sleeping."

"How bad can it be, then?" By the way my mom's eyebrows were moving into a V formation, I knew I was pushing my luck. But I couldn't believe I was having to miss camp and hanging out with Jessica—and Ben—for this!

"I can hear it from across the hall," my mom countered. "I heard this new doctor is good with allergies too."

As if on cue, a young woman in a white jacket opened the door. Her wavy, shoulder-length black hair was pulled back from her face in a neat clip. Two glittering diamond studs shone from her ears.

"Hello, Mrs. Inoue!" She greeted my mom with a warm smile and a handshake. My mom smiled back. Like *really* smiled back.

"And you must be Aoi." She shook my hand, too.

Not only did this doctor pronounce our names correctly, she spoke perfect English, and . . . she was Asian.

Like me.

Don't get me wrong, there were a few other Asians in town, but I didn't know of many other Asian *Americans* . . . I thought me and Tak were the only ones.

As Dr. Wang listened to my heart with her stethoscope, my mom asked, "Are you from China?"

Mom! I thought. Even though I was only twelve, I had already been asked this question enough to know it got old pretty fast. The "where-are-you-from"-ing that wouldn't stop even when you told them you were born in Kansas, in Topeka, in this hospital, in fact. Not until you mentioned someplace outside the US that fit into that "other" category that the person asking the question had already put you in.

No one ever asked Jessica to provide them with her ancestral history!

But Dr. Wang only smiled, and not in an annoyed way at all. "My parents are from Taiwan, actually. And judging from your name, I'm guessing you're Japanese?"

"I was born here," I blurted out.

"Same here!" Dr. Wang moved her stethoscope. "Deep breath in . . . now out."

"You were born in Topeka?" my mom asked. Normally, my mom was pretty quiet around new people. I didn't know why she was being this chatty *and nosy* all of a sudden.

"Well, no, not *here*, here. More like Houston. But my husband is from Topeka, so . . ." Dr. Wang moved her stethoscope again. "Deep breath in . . . now out."

"Lungs sound good." Dr. Wang moved on to examine the backs of my knees. "Looks like we have some eczema going on here. How long has it been like this?"

"It only happens when it's really hot." I was embarrassed with how bad I knew the rash must look. I knew I wasn't supposed to pick at it, but . . .

My checkup continued with questions about seasonal

allergies (yes, hay fever for both my mom and me), if we had pets (yes, our cat, Chibi), and food sensitivities (too much milk makes my tummy hurt). While Dr. Wang and my mom talked, I looked around at the posters and framed certificates on the walls. There was a diploma from Brown University and a diploma from the University of California, San Francisco, medical school. *Brown and San Francisco?* Board certifications in pediatrics *and* allergy and immunology. I wondered how Dr. Wang ended up out here. I swung my legs out of boredom until my mom shot a look my way.

"So, there are many people like you at medical school?" my mom asked Dr. Wang.

What? I must have missed something because at what point did the conversation veer from my health to Dr. Wang's educational background?

Dr. Wang laughed. "Yeah, sure. If you're talking about other women, yes. And if you're talking about other Asian Americans, then yes to that, too." Dr. Wang turned and winked at me.

Huh? I wondered what *that* was all about. Dr. Wang certainly wasn't like all the other old doctor dudes I'd seen before. Maybe she was trying to tell me her mom was like mine, too. She certainly wasn't acting like anything my mom said was weird or too out-of-bounds (even though it totally was).

At the end of my appointment, Dr. Wang sent us home with

some steroid cream samples for my rash and some suggestions to try at night for my cough.

On our ride home, my mom rolled the windows of our Chevy Chevette down since the air conditioner had broken a while ago. "Because it's an American car," my mom always explained. "That's why the turning radius is so bad, too."

The broken AC and lack of maneuverability were the least of our car's problems. If the Kellys' car was like Apollo's golden chariot pulled by fiery horses across the sky, our car was like a rickety rickshaw pulled by some unfortunate guy, sweating buckets while pulling his passengers over bumpy cobblestoned streets.

When I told my dad this a while ago, he got really excited and told me that "rickshaw" actually is from the Japanese word jinrikisha, which means "human-powered vehicle." Instead of feeling bad that I didn't like our car, he laughed and said if he was driving a rickshaw, then it was like the next best thing to driving an actual Japanese car.

"Why *don't* we buy a Japanese car, then?" I asked a few years ago, but didn't anymore because the question made my mom's jaw clench and eyes grow steely.

"Because when you're Japanese in America, you just can't drive a Japanese car." We used to have one—a Corolla, I think—but we traded it in. "Japanese cars use less gas, so more people buy them. That makes some Americans angry. So angry that they even attack people who look Japanese. In Michigan, there was a Chinese man who was attacked—"

"The eggs were hard to clean off of it," Dad interrupted quietly. *People threw eggs at our car?* I wondered. *Why would they do that?* I thought I remembered him shaking his head at Mom not to say anything more, but I don't know—I was only seven.

"No use dwelling on it," my dad said. And then he never talked about it again. His approach to these types of incidents seemed to work for him. Was it the same for Mom? Of that, I wasn't so sure.

But even though my mom was driving in a car that she clearly hated, and the breeze from the wind only tangled up our hair and didn't do much to cool us down, she was energetic and smiling. Which I thought was a pretty strange way to react after an appointment about my weird leg rash.

"Did you like her?" my mom asked. "I did. She was smart."

"How could you tell?" I countered. I didn't even know why I asked since Dr. Wang seemed pretty smart to me, too. These days, contradicting my mom felt like a reaction I couldn't stop even if I wanted to.

"You have to be intelligent to be a doctor," Mom answered matter-of-factly. "Doctors are smart, and they get paid well. So, they're rich, too."

"Okay, so—"

"Didn't you see those diamond earrings?" My mom didn't have much jewelry of her own, but the pieces she had were real. Even if they were small and not flashy at all, she was proud that what she had wasn't fake. She knew her stuff. "Dr. Wang's earrings . . . very high quality and at least a carat each."

I stared out the window, dreading where this conversation was going.

"Smart, respected, rich . . . I know what you're going to be." My mom patted my head as we waited for our stoplight to turn green.

I held my breath, cringing at what she would say next.

"You're going to be a *doctor*."

Clearly my mom had misunderstood what my teacher said to us at our elementary school graduation. It was "You can be anything you want to be."

Not "You can be anything *I* want you to be."

CHAPTER 8

Doctor, huh? Yeah, right! Over my dead body. I mean, Dr. Wang was cool and all, but the one thing I desperately did not want to ever be was a doctor.

For one, I hated needles. And blood.

"The nurses deal with most of that!" Mom assured me.

And day in, day out, being stuck in that exam room looking at nasty rashes like the one on the backs of my legs?

No thanks.

Once my mom saw how good I was onstage, I knew she would stop with this doctor dream of *hers*, not mine.

On Friday, Ms. Tracy had us gather around as she told us audition results had been posted out in the hall.

Jessica, Ben, and I squealed with excitement, but Ms. Tracy immediately brought her hands down, like an orchestra conductor telling the musicians they needed to be pianissimo—basically, that they needed to be quiet and simmer down. Because she had that kind of hold over us, we all obeyed without a word of complaint.

"Now, before I let you all go to see whether you've been cast"—Ms. Tracy paused dramatically here as she looked at each and every one of us—"I want you to remember what I told you earlier. Auditioning doesn't mean you're guaranteed a role. Actors audition, and there are usually years, I'm talking *YEARS*, of rejection. Of not getting the part they want. Of not getting *any* part. Sometimes it might seem like there's no rhyme or reason for why you were cast or not, but you *cannot* take it personally. So, I don't want to hear any 'but she did this' or 'I did that' or 'the director didn't like me' or 'if I had only worn my purple shoes and not my blue ones—'"

"I don't have blue *or* purple shoes," Ben sighed with exaggerated remorse.

Ms. Tracy cracked a smile, which was basically her way of giving us all permission to smile, too.

"So, with that in mind . . ." Ms. Tracy stepped aside and stretched her arm out toward the door.

We leapt up and ran toward the doors that led to the hallway. We were in such a rush that a bunch of us got stuck in the doorway for a split second, but we were able to burst through the bottleneck and into the hall.

Only which way were we supposed to go? Was the sheet

posted on our left? Our right?

Like we were in a mad scramble of an Easter egg hunt, we dashed in all directions. Then we heard Ben yell, "Here!"

The rest of us practically trampled him on our way to the sheets taped up on the dark wall of the hallway.

"Jessica's Annie!" a girl named Angie shrieked.

Only that couldn't be what I heard. Maybe she yelled, "Jessica, Annie!"

That *had* to be what she said. Otherwise that would mean Jessica was Annie.

Not me.

Ms. Tracy's words echoed in my ears:

You cannot *take it personally.*

"I'm Sandy!" yelled Ben. "Woof, woof!"

At first I had been wondering, *hoping* that I'd be cast as Annie. But as some of the camp kids scanned and scanned the list while others celebrated, my hands became clammy and cold, and I worried that maybe I wouldn't be cast at all.

I finally made my way to the sheet and plain as day, it was written:

ANNIE: Jessica Kelly

I took a deep breath and held it in as I continued down the list. Past Daddy Warbucks, past Miss Hannigan, past the orphans: Molly, Pepper (Jennifer, the high school student from auditions, got that part), Duffy, Kate, and Tessie (oh my

59

God, the cute girl with the happy rendition of "Maybe" got that part . . .).

Auditioning doesn't mean you're guaranteed a role.

I know, I thought. *I know, Ms. Tracy, but I really, really, really want a role,* any *role.*

My heart was beating so hard I was sure everyone around me could hear it. My stomach started to hurt. *Please, please have my name somewhere, anywhere, I don't care about not being the lead anymore, I just want to be a part of—*

And that's when I saw it:

JULY: Annie Inoue

July was the name of the quietest orphan. She was supposed to be named Julie, but her mom couldn't spell and so she left her at the orphanage with a note that said the baby's name was July. And . . . that was it. That was the most exciting aspect of the girl I'd be playing. But like Ms. Tracy had said, I wasn't guaranteed anything.

But . . . I got *something.* And who cared if I barely had any lines, I made it! I was in the play, my very first real theater production. I finally let out my breath. Whew!

Jessica found me and grabbed my hands.

"We're in the play!"

We jumped up and down. "You're gonna be Annie, Jessica!" I squeaked with so much excitement I almost convinced myself that this was the outcome I wanted all along.

"I can't believe it!" Jessica squealed back.

Natalie, the tall girl who auditioned right before Jessica, was sniffling. When I glanced toward her, she turned her back on us.

"Jess, maybe we should . . ."

"Yeah," Jessica agreed. We quieted down as we walked past her on our way back to Ms. Tracy.

"Congrats on getting the part, Jessica," Natalie mumbled over her shoulder in a manner that didn't sound congratulatory at all.

"Thanks," Jessica responded. "I'm really surprised."

Before she walked away, I noticed Natalie's eyes were red. I also thought I heard her say, "Yeah, me too."

CHAPTER 9

The next day, Dad brought Tak and me to the campus where he worked. It had thunderstormed the night before, so the ground was wet and raindrops still clung to the blades of grass. Even though it was a little muggy, it was nowhere near as suffocating as it usually was at the end of June.

The buildings on the outside were made of off-white stone and there was even a clock tower that chimed every hour, all of which made the university grounds feel ancient and scholarly. Once we were inside where my dad worked, though, unflattering fluorescent lights illuminated the halls, which had the same dull linoleum floors you'd see in any boring old building. My dad's office itself was cramped, cluttered, and looked like a tidal wave of papers had crashed into it.

The best part of his workplace was the kitchenette in his department. It was stocked with all sorts of goodies my mom wouldn't let us have at home. My dad prepared a cup of hot chocolate for Tak, but he made sure it wasn't very hot *or* very chocolaty. We all knew what happened when Tak had too much sugar.

"Hot." My dad blew on the cup, though, when he handed it to Tak. "Be careful." If he didn't say this, Tak would chug his drink and turn into a hyper wildebeest within minutes.

I guess you could say my dad was tricking his son, but I liked to think of it more as acting. Maybe I got that from him.

Tak accepted the cup gingerly and took a tentative sip.

"Good?" Dad asked.

Tak nodded.

"Too hot? It's too hot, isn't it?" My dad reached for Tak's cup, even though he knew it was lukewarm at best.

Tak shook his head and disappeared around a corner so he could drink his "big boy" hot chocolate in peace.

Once Tak was out of sight, Dad mixed me a cup of decaf Sanka instant coffee, two powdered creamers, and one packet of sugar. Since my mom had stayed home, he added one more for me.

"That's for making the play!" He presented me with the cup of steaming hot, extra sweet "coffee." I'd loved the smell of coffee ever since I could remember. I always begged for a taste, but my parents would never let me since they said the caffeine was bad for me. But a couple years ago, Dad discovered Sanka.

Since it was decaffeinated, he decided it would be fine for me to have a sip. When I did, I thought it was unlike anything I had ever had before. Ever since then, hot chocolate had taken a back seat to Sanka, two creams, two sugars.

"Thank you." I took the cup and blew on it a few times to cool it. "But I'm only one of the orphans. Not a big part at all."

"Hmm." My dad moved some stacks of paper around. "I think it's pretty unusual for people to get what they want right away."

I took a sip. "Yeah, but Jessica did," I grumbled.

"I guess that's true . . ." My dad looked through another folder as he continued his conversation with me. "And who knows why?"

I sipped as I thought the same thought to myself. *Why? Why Jessica and not me?* Jessica *did* look exactly like Little Orphan Annie . . . but Ben was cast as Sandy the dog, so did it really matter all that much that I didn't "look" the part? I mean, a family across town had just adopted a baby girl from Korea. Would it have been *that* hard to imagine *me* as an orphan?

Or maybe my audition didn't go as well as I thought.

"You made the play! Celebrate that. Your first play. Use it to study what goes on, learn from other actors, you know. What is it that they say here? 'You can't run before walking'? Is that how that saying goes?"

I didn't answer because I was still replaying my audition in my mind. *What went wrong?*

My dad gathered a few folders and added them to his already full black bag. "You know, KU was really hard for me at first."

"I know." My dad liked telling stories about his hard-knock graduate math student life. Kind of like how Jessica's dad always talked about having to walk to school uphill both ways in the snow when he was a kid.

"With all the classes in English, I had to go back to my dorm room and study twice, maybe three times as hard. But after a while, I didn't have to translate everything into Japanese in my head. And now look at me!"

I looked at my dad standing tall and proud in the one square of clear space in his cramped little office.

"A university professor! *And* department chair."

"Yay, Daddy!" I responded with as much enthusiasm as I could muster.

My dad was a dreamer like me, sure, but I never understood how anyone's dream could be to fiddle around with numbers and teach other people how to fiddle around with numbers. I *definitely* didn't take after him in this regard.

"You know, in Japan teachers are highly respected."

"Uh-huh." *In Japan.* I thought about all the ways my sixth-grade classmates talked back to our teacher or passed notes when she wasn't looking.

"Especially *professors*," my dad clarified, as if he could hear what I was thinking.

"You know," my dad continued with a twinkle in his eye. "Maybe *you* could become a professor too!"

I groaned. "Daddy, you *know* I don't like school."

Dad feigned shock. "How could you not like school? Come on, there must be at least something you like."

I thought about it. "Recess!" I answered with an evil grin, knowing full well that there were no recesses in college. Or middle school, for that matter.

"Another thing!" Dad demanded. "Besides recess."

"Lunch!" I responded this time without having to think at all.

"Oh!" he said like he couldn't wait to let me in on a secret. "Did you know there's a new little café on campus? They have the most delicious paninis and even frozen yogurt."

I frowned. I didn't know what a panini was, and even though I could live forever on frozen yogurt, that was *not* enough to entice me into teaching math with my dad.

"Just think of it." Dad looked out the window at the courtyard.

My eyes rolled so hard they almost fell out of my head. I had heard this particular dream of his before. More than a hundred times!

"We could have offices next to each other. Maybe even

66

research a paper together. This building could be renamed to Inoue Hall."

I sighed. Even though Dad was better at letting me have my own dreams, sometimes he let me know what some of his dreams for me were too. Not in a "do this!" "be this!" type of way, but in more like a "here's another option to consider" way. Still, the fact that he hadn't given up hope on my future university math professorship made me sad.

Thankfully, at that moment a *thud!* diverted our attention to Tak, who had been running sprints back and forth in the hallway after finishing his drink. I guess my dad's acting didn't fool Tak. After a couple of sips he had figured out that the hot chocolate—so hot that it had to be sipped slowly—was more like chuggable chocolate.

My dad and I dashed into the hallway, where Tak was on the floor, rubbing his knee.

"I tripped."

"Are you okay?" My dad picked him up.

"Yeah, it was just my knee."

Tak was definitely a handful, but he was a tough little booger, I had to give him that.

My dad tried to hoist him onto his shoulders.

"Daddy, watch out!" Tak hollered. "You almost hit my head on the ceiling!"

"Oh, sorry." Dad brought Tak back down and carried him

toward the kitchenette for another cup of consolation hot chocolate.

"If I'm gonna teach math like you, I have to make sure to keep my head good," explained Tak.

My dad's eyebrows shot up and we traded surprised glances. This was the first we'd heard of my little brother's plans. It was hard to imagine the little tornado sitting still long enough to learn anything, but . . . if he did, maybe my dad would let up on me about math for once.

My dad broke into a huge grin. "Wow, with *three* Inoue math professors, this place would *definitely* be named after us!"

Or . . . maybe not.

CHAPTER 10

Tonight was the night! Jessica and I were about to pee in our pants, we were *that excited* for our first rehearsal with the entire cast—The Initial Readthrough.

Jessica and I had already received our script books a few days ago during our lunch break at theater camp.

"Hold out both hands, ladies," Ms. Tracy had commanded.

When Jessica and I did as we were told, she handed us each our own copy of *Annie*.

"Now, you are not to mark in these with pen *ever*. All markings need to be made in pencil. And *lightly*. At the end of the play, you must erase all the marks you made and return these to us in pristine condition. If you don't, we'll be fined, which means *you'll* be fined. Do you understand?"

When Jessica asked, "Can't we just photocopy them?" Ms. Tracy was aghast.

"No! Absolutely not! Photocopies are certainly *not* authorized, either!"

Ms. Tracy was normally light and fun at camp, but when she talked about anything to do with *Annie*, she was all business.

Our hands were still held out with the heavy script books resting gently on top. We were afraid to move.

"Yes, Ms. Tracy."

"Now, the experienced actors like the adults playing Daddy Warbucks and Miss Hannigan will probably come to the first rehearsal with their lines pretty much memorized—"

"*Memorized?*" Jessica squeaked. "But first rehearsal is in three days!"

Ms. Tracy took in a deep breath and exhaled slowly. Although she didn't tell us to, we did the same.

"If you had let me finish, I was going to add that this *is* community theater. And yes, while we do take our productions seriously, we also realize that children are part of this production too. And that you have a lot of lines . . . and are a beginner. Sam and I thought five weeks would be enough time."

Five *weeks*? Piece of cake. I could have my lines memorized in five days since I barely had any. But Jessica still wasn't breathing.

"That's all of July." Ms. Tracy framed the five-week time frame in a different way, as if that would help. "Don't worry, I'm sure July can help you."

Who? Then I remembered that was my character's name. I got it. Calling *me* Annie would be too confusing during this production.

"July in July!" Ms. Tracy laughed at her own joke.

Ms. Tracy was a really good teacher, but . . . she was not funny.

Jessica wasn't laughing because she was too busy flipping through the pages of the script and hyperventilating.

For a moment, Ms. Tracy looked back and forth between us. "Would you like some extra help during lunch, Jessica?"

Jessica looked up. She had stopped on a page that was particularly dense with Annie's lines.

"Oh, could I?" she pleaded. "You'd do that for me?"

Ms. Tracy looked like she might have had other plans for her hour off. But Jessica did seem like she was going to have a meltdown even before our first rehearsal. And since Ms. Tracy was our teacher . . .

"Well, a bit of a head start never hurt anyone, did it?" Ms. Tracy relented. "Come on now, open them up and let's begin."

For the next few days before the initial readthrough, she worked with both of us during our lunchbreak.

Although I didn't have many lines at all, Jessica had a *ton*. Ms. Tracy knew we were friends, though, so she included me in her noontime sessions with Jessica.

"*July*, read all the orphans' lines. Jessica, read Annie's, and

I'll read everything else. How's that sound? Good? Let's get to work."

For the first readthrough, instead of the cast meeting at the theater, we all met at Ben's aunt and uncle's house. There was a potluck beforehand. Ben told us that the kids didn't need to bring anything, but my mom insisted we bring *something* since it would be rude to show up empty-handed. I brought a salad, cringing a little that I'd be bringing something that everyone *should* eat, but wouldn't want to.

"Hosting so many people." My mom shook her head, like she was trying to imagine how that would even be possible. It wouldn't have been in our house, and it wasn't just because our place was small. . . . My mom struggled enough in smaller settings in which she only had to attend. Shouldering the responsibilities of a host, engaging in effortless small talk, *and* making sure all the guests were having a good time? I knew I couldn't ask that of her.

We didn't need to pick up Jessica since her mom would be staying (of course) for the potluck and readthrough. The Kellys were going to bring me, too, until my mom heard it was going to be at a stranger's house.

"They're not *strangers*, Mom!" I tried to explain. "It's the choreographer's house."

That didn't mean anything to her.

So, she waited in the car until Mrs. Kelly stuck her head out the front door and waved at her.

"We'll bring her home when they're done, all right?"

My mom nodded and waved. "Thank you!"

I watched her drive off, half—no, a third, no, more like a fourth of me wishing she was the type of mom who would join the other parents, at least for the potluck.

But she wasn't, so when she was out of sight, I stepped back into Midge Prescott's house, which was more like Jessica's house than mine. White walls, bright brass fixtures, oak everywhere, and big soft beige sofas that wrapped around a large TV.

I set the salad my mom had made on the table.

"Vegetables! Oh my God, that's all there was in LA." The director, Sam, appeared out of nowhere. She grabbed the salad tongs and scooped some onto her paper plate. "There's only so much Hamburger Helper and tortilla chip casserole a person can eat, know what I mean? It's like I've had flippin' cream of mushroom coursing through my veins ever since I got here."

I nodded even though we never ate those things at my house.

Mrs. Kelly, looking even fancier than usual, descended upon us. "Director Glick! I'm Cathy Kelly, Jessica's mother? Not to mention Maid Number Two."

"Oh, yeah. Hi." Sam plunged her hand into a bag of chips and stuffed some into her mouth, almost like she was doing it to avoid talking with her.

"Anyway, we're just thrilled you're back from LA to direct at our humble little theater." Mrs. Kelly extended her hand to Sam.

Sam nodded and crunched. She wiped off the sour-cream-and-onion chip dust on her jeans and looked toward the clock as she shook hands. When Mrs. Kelly went in for a two-handed shake, I may have been imagining it, but it seemed like Sam pulled hard to extract herself from it. I grabbed a chip, too, as I watched this scene unfold before my eyes. I didn't know exactly what was going on, but *something* definitely was. . . .

"I, uh, should get set up." Sam pointed toward the clock and shuffled away.

Mrs. Kelly turned her attention to me. "Is that a salad?"

"My mom made it," I responded apologetically.

"Oh, she's such a doll." Mrs. Kelly scanned the guests. "Jessica? Jessica, did you have some of Mrs. Enoway's salad? You really should."

Wow. I guess my mom was right that I should bring it.

After everyone had their fill (except for Jessica, who told me she was too nervous to eat), we retreated to the basement, where a mishmash assortment of chairs had been set out. Folding chairs, dining chairs, stools, beanbags off to the side.

Since I knew I wouldn't be reading most of the time, I grabbed one of the beanbags in the back. Jessica grabbed another. Giggles burst forth from my belly when she smushed me with it. Ben grabbed a third beanbag and began battling with Jessica right above me. My giggles turned into full-on guffaws.

"Ben!" His aunt Midge was definitely *not* laughing. Ben immediately threw his beanbag on the carpet. I knocked Jessica's off me. At the same time, they both plopped down in their bags obediently, like puppies who had gotten in trouble.

"Jessica, how 'bout you sit in one of these chairs?" Her mom patted the chair farthest away from us.

I quieted down, embarrassed that at our first rehearsal with the adults we had to be scolded like little kids. But then Ben winked at me like he knew what I was thinking, and that our horsing around would be forgotten in no time. Thank goodness for Ben! I mean, he really was the *best*.

Once the rest of the actors took their seats, Sam galumphed down the stairs with a can of Mountain Dew. She looked for a place to put it. Seeing none, she set it down on the carpet. Midge ducked in, quietly took it, and set it on a nearby table (with a coaster underneath).

"Hey, so, as you all know, I'm Sam. Really excited to be directing back here in my hometown. I know it's Topeka and everything, but I was actually pleasantly surprised with the auditions." At this point, Sam paused and looked around.

Was that it?

"You know, for the most part."

There was a moment of silence before the adults burst into laughter.

Funny, because I didn't think Sam was joking. But she joined in after a couple of seconds, so maybe she was.

"All right then, let's get started."

Midge read all the scene descriptions and actors' cues while Sam listened and took notes. The adults transformed into their characters when they read their parts, even though they weren't in costume and were just sitting around a circle in folding chairs.

The man playing Oliver Warbucks, the billionaire businessman who would eventually adopt Annie, already had his lines memorized and said everything to Jessica so convincingly I half believed he *was* a billionaire businessman in real life.

The lady who played Miss Hannigan, the evil woman who ran the orphanage, seemed really nice during dinner, but she became super nasty when she delivered her lines, also off book.

The cute little girl in pigtails who played Tessie, the youngest orphan, delivered her lines with the cutest lisp. She had her lines mostly memorized, too, although it was pretty clear her mom had something (maybe everything) to do with that because when Tessie said her lines, her mom's mouth moved along with them. It just so happened that her mom had a bit part as one of Mr. Warbucks's servants, as did Mrs. Kelly.

Jessica, who probably had the most lines out of anyone, did great, I think! She stumbled over one of the words, but her mom jumped in to help her right away, so no one noticed at all. At least Sam didn't; she kept her nose buried in her script book the entire time.

Ben didn't have any lines since he was Sandy the dog.

"We'll figure out good places to put in your barks, kid, okay?" Sam let him know.

When it was my turn, I delivered my lines from the sidelines. All memorized, but I could tell no one really cared.

At least I got a part, I reminded myself. *I should be grateful.*

CHAPTER 11

Rehearsals were two hours long, three times a week, and took place in the evenings since most of the adults worked during the day. This meant I wasn't home until nine a lot of the time. My mom grumbled, but since I had such a small part, I didn't have to go to all of them. Even though I wanted to because . . .

REHEARSALS WERE SO MUCH FUN.

First, we always started with movement exercises. Lots of jumping jacks and stretching. Then vocal exercises such as arpeggios, which were like walking up and down stairs but with our voices, or ones where we'd all sound like sirens. I was so used to doing these with other kids as part of theater camp, but seeing all the adults do it too was really funny.

But once warm-ups were over, we were all *business*.

And I know "business" doesn't sound like *fun* necessarily,

but it was pretty cool to see how *real* actors worked.

"Good, good." Sam would always start her comments this way. "But this time, could you be more . . . repressed? Your character's not the expressive type, so you should be holding it all in. Try starting out like that, and then loosen up as you go on."

Then the actor who played the stern Oliver Warbucks would nod, take a deep breath, and like a spirit possessed his body, he would deliver his lines in the way Sam directed.

And Sam wasn't exactly *mean* to Jessica, but she didn't heap on the praise like Mrs. Kelly did, either.

"Well, what do you think Annie must be feeling here now?" Sam didn't just care about our lines; she made sure we knew *why* each character said what they did.

"I mean, I think she must be . . . sad?" Jessica shot a glance over to her mom while Sam shot a glance over to Ms. Tracy.

"We'll work on it," Ms. Tracy would say, looking up from Sam's script notes that she had been erasing and rewriting in a lighter pencil. I guess Ms. Tracy wasn't joking around when she told us earlier that we shouldn't write in our script books. Sam didn't seem to care, though, which clearly stressed Ms. Tracy out. Our three lunchtime sessions with Ms. Tracy ended up being an indefinite number of extra practice sessions now that *Annie* was in full swing. In fact, it was hard for me and Jessica to keep our mind on camp theater much anymore, and

Ms. Tracy had interrupted our side conversations more than once to tell us to "focus, girls!"

Just like my dad had told me to, I listened and watched and watched and listened. I was learning so much, and frankly, I was a little *relieved* I wasn't Annie. I'm not sure I would have been ready for what Jessica was being asked to deliver!

Maybe that was why I was cast in a minor role. Maybe Sam sensed I wouldn't have been able to handle anything more. I let go of my disappointment about not getting to be Annie and decided to enjoy everything about my first *real* theater experience instead.

Like hanging out with the other kid actors. Jennifer, the high school girl who knocked my socks off during her audition, played the oldest orphan, Pepper. She often told us stories that began with, "Well, in high school, we . . ."

Since Jessica and I hadn't even started middle school yet, I was all ears. Homecoming? Dances? Friday night football games? High school sounded *awesome*. I didn't have an older sister to show me the ropes, so having Jennifer give us the low-down—well, that information was *gold*.

But maybe the best part of practice was hanging out with Sandy the dog.

I had known Ben for several years and he used to be really annoying. But what I discovered during rehearsals was that he was also *really* funny.

When it came time to work on blocking (basically figuring out where we moved and when), he ran around the stage on all fours.

"Hey! Knock it off!" Sam yelled.

But when he lifted his leg to pretend pee on an imaginary fire hydrant, Daddy Warbucks cracked up, and then Miss Hannigan, and then the boy who played the dogcatcher. In spite of herself, Sam laughed too.

"All right, all right, you're in character, I get it." She patted her leg. "Here, boy, here, boy," she called to Ben. He trotted over and she scratched him behind an ear. His right leg twitched and shook in response. "So, Sandy? When the dogcatcher appears, you do a couple loops here and then exit there, okay?"

"Woof!" he replied in dog-speak to indicate he understood.

The more I watched Ben, and the more we worked together during rehearsals, the more I wanted to spend even *extra* time with him. He made me laugh nonstop, and when I could make him smile his cute lopsided grin back at me, I felt like I had won an Academy Award.

His eyes reminded me of trees in the way that they're green, but they sparkle like leaves in a breeze when the light hits them just right. When we talked, he made me feel like there's no one else around. When he got excited, he'd run his hands through his yellow hair and then it'd stick up adorably like straw.

Before, he was always like that frog in the fairy tale, but now he'd turned into a prince. Maybe *my* prince.

On one of our recent theater camp lunch breaks, Ms. Tracy walked us all to the ice cream parlor across the street where Ben introduced me to the wonders of Baskin-Robbins' pink bubble gum flavor.

"You can pick the bits of gum out." He showed me as he assembled a pile of gum on his napkin. "So you can chew them after you finish your scoop. It's like you get two treats, not just one!"

And during rehearsals, when it was all about Little Orphan Annie searching for her long-lost parents, or Daddy Warbucks growing increasingly charmed by her, Ben sat next to me and whispered alternate dialogue in my ear while I tried not to laugh.

"Annie, I've decided you need to go back to the orphanage."

"What? Why, Daddy Warbucks?"

"Your hair drives me crazy. There's so much of it and it's so curly and red. Since I have none, I am hugely jealous."

"But Daddy Warbucks, I hate the orphanage!"

"I have dreams of shaving your head and fashioning a wig out of it."

"Oh no!"

"I know. I would look like Ronald McDonald. But I can't stop thinking about it."

"Okay, maybe the orphanage wasn't so bad."

Sometimes it's so hard not to laugh, my giggles squeak out of my eyes in the form of tears.

It's like between last summer and now, Ben drank some sort of potion like the ones Alice drank in Wonderland and it changed him from annoying to dreamy. I know it might sound weird to say I like a boy who acts like a dog. Okay, it actually *does* sound weird. Maybe *I* drank some sort of potion by mistake and it's clouding my judgment.

My feelings for Ben aren't like anything I've ever read about in books or seen in the movies. I guess some people would call it a "crush," but it's a lot more than that! Last year, a few kids "went" with each other, which meant they held hands in the hall and at recess. Most of the time, they looked really awkward when they did, and it was weird for the rest of us to witness, too. Ben and I weren't like that, either. The only romance (if you could call it that) I had to compare it with was the story of how my parents met—a story that my dad loved to tell over and over again. . . .

Basically, my mom was a flight attendant for a Japanese airline. My dad was traveling from Japan. They met. The end.

I'm sure my dad would object to my summary of their romance.

"Your mom was the most beautiful woman I had ever seen." This was how my dad always started telling their "love story" (ugh, gross). "I was traveling to the US for the first time, to Kansas City, and your mother was on the flight. I asked her if she had ever been there and she said yes, but that she hadn't spent much time outside the airport. I told her that I was going to study math at the University of Kansas and that impressed her so much."

"I don't believe I used the word 'impressed,'" my mom would interject. "I believe the word I used was mezurashii, as in 'unusual.'"

"But I told her that the next time she flew into Kansas City and had a layover that she should look me up. And she did!"

"Yes, four years later," my mom teased my dad.

"Couldn't forget about me even after four years!" Dad teased right back.

"I admit I was curious what happened to that odd man I had met. And I felt that maybe I was being close-minded about not exploring Kansas a little more. I had made a point to explore all the places I had layovers in. Seattle, San Francisco, London, Hawaii, Sydney . . . But never Kansas. I *was* surprised that he was still in school."

"Hey! PhDs take time. And I was on my way out—I had just accepted my job offer!"

"So, he met me at the airport—"

"And I drove her to a campus party in Lawrence. She was amazed at the wide roads, how fast I could drive—"

"Again, not 'amazed,' more like 'alarmed'—"

"And at the party she said Kansas was unlike any place she had ever visited. That the sprawling openness made her feel free."

Then, no matter when my dad told this story or to whom, he would hold his breath and look over to my mom for confirmation.

Only when my mom quietly responded "Yes, I did say that" would my dad exhale. I'm not sure he realized he was doing that.

"And she said she wished someday she'd live someplace other than Japan, not just visit. But she was worried about how difficult it would be to get a visa. So, I said, hey, why don't we get married?"

The first time Dad told us this story, even Tak was shocked.

"Whaaaat?? That's crazy!"

"Didn't you guys just meet?" I asked.

"No, we met four years earlier," my mother clarified in a way that seemed kind of defensive to me.

"And six months after the party where I proposed, we got married in Vegas!" My dad was always gleeful when he told this part of the story. "The wonderland of America! Neither of us had been there, and so we were able to get married *and* have a honeymoon all in the same place!"

As you can see, my parents' romance was *nothing* like what

was developing between me and Ben. At least what I *thought* might be developing. He was always hanging around me and Jessica and trying to make me laugh. That *might* mean he likes me, right? And even so, I told myself I wouldn't get married until I graduated college, which was twenty-two at the very earliest. I would have known Ben for more than a decade by then! *Way* more responsible than my parents and their whirlwind romance.

"July, come on!" Sam's holler pulled me out of my daydream. "We gotta choreograph the orphans' number. Hurry it up, would ya?"

I hustled onto the stage, hoping no one saw me patting Sandy the dog on the head.

CHAPTER 12

"Hi, Mrs. Inoue, thank you very much for having me over."

My mom just nodded and smiled as Jessica slipped her shoes off at the entrance. She always did this without ever having to be asked—it was one of the reasons my mom liked her, not to mention the fact she was one of the few people who could actually pronounce our last name correctly. Plus, Jessica was way more polite to my mom than she was to her own.

"Come on!" I ran upstairs. I knew our time to practice would be limited because of the "Tak Factor." He was out with my dad right now, but when he returned, it was always a toss-up as to whether or not he would leave us alone.

Jessica knew the drill too. As soon as we were both in my room, she shut the door behind her and shoved my desk chair up against it. The lock didn't work, and the chair would only thwart Tak for a few minutes, but every little bit helped.

I also piled my pillow and stuffed animals on the chair. They didn't provide much weight, but they might be able to absorb some noise (to discourage eavesdropping). I wished I had some of the pillows from Jessica's bed—she had tons!—but when I mentioned wanting "decorative pillows" to my mom, she stared at me like I was an alien.

"Why do you need more than one pillow? Is your neck hurting?" she asked.

"Well, no, it's to make my bed look . . . pretty."

"So, you want pillows that aren't for sleeping?"

Although language was an issue sometimes, her not understanding me in this instance was not due to that.

It was way easier to relax at Jessica's place, or at least it *had* been before the play. But now, Jessica always asked to rehearse lines at my house. I was happy to since her mom always drove us everywhere, but it also meant that I had to clean up beforehand. With everything in its place, it looked a *tiny* bit bigger. Jessica never said anything about our house, but it was hard *not* to notice how different it was from hers.

I arranged the last stuffed animal onto our barricade. They stared at us with their plastic eyes, actually looking happy to be tossed about and given a purpose for a change. Dr. Wang had recommended I not sleep with them anymore to see if that would help me with my cough at night, so they had been ignored and left idle for weeks until now.

"You're too big to sleep with stuffed animals anyway, right, Aoi?" my mother had asked me at the last appointment.

The cream that Dr. Wang prescribed for the rash on the backs of my legs worked wonders, so it was clear she knew what she was doing. Still, it made me sad to banish my plushies to the closet.

"An audience! Great idea." Jessica arranged my stuffed chicken so it faced more our way and handed me her script book.

I read everyone's lines except hers, we skipped the scenes she wasn't in, and . . . she had all her lines down, right to the very end.

"Yay, Jessica! You did it!"

Jessica threw her hands up in the air. "Yes!"

"And in four weeks, not five!"

Jessica collapsed onto my bed, almost squishing my favorite fluffernugget, Chibi, who leapt off with an annoyed "Mrow!"

My friend wrapped herself in the indigo-and-white patchwork quilt my mom had sewn me. "Well, yeah. If I didn't, Sam would have *killed* me. She *hates* me."

"No, she doesn't. She's hard on everyone."

Jessica stared up at my ceiling with the glow-in-the-dark stars still stuck to it from when my parents put them up for a birthday surprise years ago.

"She keeps on asking, 'What do you think is going on here?

What's Annie *feeling*? Do you think she might be saying *this* but meaning something else?'"

I flipped through Jessica's script book where she had marked in pencil (lightly, like Ms. Tracy had told us to) notes such as "louder here!" and "with a smile" and "stage left."

"Where?" I asked. I couldn't find any notes about character anywhere.

"The part where Annie was trying to tell Daddy Warbucks she liked him very much and she was honored that he wanted to adopt her, but . . ."

"Oh yeah!" I remembered Jessica working on that during the last rehearsal.

"You sound *waaaay* too chipper, here, Annie." Sam had stopped Jessica before she could finish her lines in the section.

"I do?" Jessica squeaked.

"Yeah, she says she's not happy about hurting Mr. Warbucks's feelings, but this desire to find her parents is what *she* wants. She's conflicted. You ever feel that way?"

"Umm . . ." Jessica fidgeted with a lock of her hair. "M-m-maybe?"

"Whaddaya mean, 'maybe'?" Sam barked. "Are you saying you *don't know* if you've ever felt an internal conflict?"

A wave of guilt washed over me. When we weren't in the scene, Ben and I goofed off together a lot. Since he wasn't there that night, it was the first time I really noticed how much Jessica was struggling. Some friend I was!

I would have listened more, but a scornful snort from behind me pulled my attention away.

It was Natalie, the tall girl who wasn't cast in the play. She was at rehearsal tonight, though, because she and a few other people were working on the set instead.

"What?" I asked.

Natalie rolled her eyes. "Nothing."

What was *her* problem? "Ms. Tracy said not to take it personally if you didn't get a part."

Natalie laughed. "Me? I'm not worried about me. But do you really think she was the best person for this role?" With the paintbrush she was holding, Natalie pointed toward Jessica.

"That's my best friend you're talking about." I bristled.

"Oh, I know." Natalie turned her back to me and dipped her brush in a bucket of brown paint. Without looking at me, she continued.

"Ms. Tracy also said absolutely don't show up to the auditions in costume. What does your buddy do? She shows up dressed *exactly* like Annie. Can't really hit those high notes, either, can she?"

During rehearsal last week, Sam rearranged the music so it better fit Jessica's range. The final musical medley was supposed to showcase a big song and dance number between Annie and Mr. Warbucks. But Sam adjusted it so the chorus joined in more than what was written in the script.

"Doesn't it make you wonder at least a little?" Natalie painted the side of what would become the president's office. "That—as Shakespeare would say—something might be rotten in the state of Denmark, if you catch my drift."

I had *no* idea what Natalie was talking about.

I watched Jessica working with the director. Jessica was still struggling with the concept of Annie feeling conflicted by Mr. Warbucks's offer. "Conflicted?" Jessica asked Sam. "About what?"

"Wanting something, but it's not what someone else wants you to want," Sam pushed.

"Give her a break." I scowled at Natalie. "She's doing her best."

"Wow." Natalie shrugged. "Whatever you say."

Remembering that conversation, I flipped to the scene that had been giving Jessica trouble.

"Do you want to work on this part?" I pointed toward the section where Jessica had just drawn a huge frowny face.

"What? Why? I have that memorized." Jessica stood up and paced around the room. She stopped in front of my fortress of stuffed animals.

"Tiffany? You still have Tiffany!" She grabbed a stuffed triceratops from the pile and the rest of the animals came tumbling down.

"Of course I do."

Jessica had given me Tiffany the Triceratops during my "archaeologist phase." After seeing *Raiders of the Lost Ark*, I dreamed of being the girl version of Indiana Jones. Running away from boulders, traveling the world, and chasing down old relics before bad guys could get them sounded like the most amazing life ever. But then Dad brought home a documentary in which a real-life archaeologist spent what seemed like months dusting off layers of dirt with a toothbrush. To find buried treasure? No, a piece of broken pottery. He seemed really excited about it, too, at which point I decided maybe I should move on from that dream.

I held my hands out and Jessica threw Tiffany at me.

I gave the dinosaur a hug. She smelled like friendship and simpler times.

"I'm . . . bad, aren't I?" Jessica stared at herself in the mirror hanging next to my door.

"What are you talking about?"

"I know Sam is hard on everyone, but I can tell the other actors are frustrated with me too."

"That's not true! You memorized your lines in four weeks, not five—"

"But I don't understand what she wants!" Jessica flopped on my bed again. "Like, how would *you* say those lines?"

I set down Tiffany next to Jessica as I thought about how Sam described Annie's emotions during this scene: *About wanting something, but it's not what someone else wants you to want....*

I knew ALL ABOUT THAT.

But . . .

What Jessica was asking me for was a line read, which was what she had asked Sam for. "Can't you just say it like you want me to say it?" she had asked, and Sam had turned her down flat.

"You want a line read? No way, kid. That's not how I direct, and that's not how I want you to learn how to act."

But would it be all right for *me* to help a friend that way?

I looked over at Jessica, her poofy bangs less bouncy than usual. I guess not even Aqua Net stood a chance against the Kansas humidity and the thoughts that were weighing her down. My friend had picked Tiffany up and was staring into her dark eyes, still shiny after all these years. Tiffany the Triceratops, that Jessica had given me because we both loved dinosaurs so much. Jessica, who was Jessie when I was still Aoi. Jessica, whose mom took me to theater camp almost every morning even when my mom couldn't return the favor.

Didn't I owe my friend at least *something*?

I picked up Jessica's script book and began giving Jessica line reads, even though Sam was against it.

Jessica repeated each line after I read, and we worked this way until we finished the script.

CHAPTER 13

After seven weeks of hard work, it was finally opening night! Mrs. Kelly drove me and Jessica to the theater early to get ready.

We didn't talk much in the car. At least Jessica and I didn't. Mrs. Kelly talked enough for the both of us.

"Well, girls, this is the big night! Your first step toward stardom! I bet years from now, people will look back on this day and say, 'I knew them when!'"

Only I knew that Mrs. Kelly was basically saying this all to Jessica, not me.

Jessica looked positively ghostlike as she stared out the car window. I punched her lightly in the shoulder and made a silly face at her. She tried to smile back at me, but it looked more like she was about to throw up.

"Annie? Your parents are coming tonight, right?"

"Yes, Mrs. Kelly. My little brother, too."

"Oooh, Tak will love it, I'm sure!"

Only Mrs. Kelly pronounced my little brother's name like "Take" and not "Talk," which is how it should be pronounced. Jessica rolled her eyes and then made a face back at me because she had corrected her mom a million times about this before. I snort-giggled, which made Jessica laugh. She tried to hold it in, but that made her squeak-fart, which of course made us both cackle so hard we almost cried.

"Girls? What's so funny? Girls?"

"Nothing, Mom. Nothing." Jessica smiled back at me for real this time.

I could tell Mrs. Kelly really wanted to be let in on the joke, but she seemed okay with not knowing . . . as long as it meant Jessica no longer looked like she wanted to barf.

Getting ready for opening night was like playing make-believe and dress-up, but *way* more intense. Like, the university stage was the big grown-up version of Jessica's canopy bed that we used as our dolls' and stuffed animals' stage when we were younger. Instead of the tiny bit of lipstick and little-girl glittery fingernail polish that we were allowed to wear back then, now we had trays of stage makeup. The lady who played Miss Hannigan helped me with mine—foundation, eyeliner, lipstick, and then a big smudge across one of my cheeks to help me transform into the ragtag orphan I was supposed to be. My face felt stiff—even though we had gone through this in dress rehearsal, I still wasn't used to how all this makeup felt. I mean, how was I supposed to be expressive with all this gunk on my face?

Mrs. Kelly was really caking it on, too. Jessica was pale to begin with, but she became even more so when her mom coated her face in foundation, which covered up all her actual freckles. So then she had to draw a bunch of fake freckles onto Jessica's face too.

"God, Mom, I'm not a clown!" Jessica pushed her mother away. With camp having ended several weeks ago and her mom at all the rehearsals, those two were practically *always* together. My friend stomped toward the door where I had been watching. I could tell she *definitely* needed a break.

"Hey, Jessica, wanna see something cool?" I whispered as she approached so her mom couldn't overhear.

"Omigod, yes!" By the desperation in her voice, I'm pretty sure I could have shown her a moldy potato and she still would have been grateful for the distraction. We ran out of the dressing room before her mom could object and I hustled backstage.

"Annie, you look adorable!" Jessica exclaimed like she just noticed me. "So . . . *orphan-y!*"

I laughed as we rounded a corner. "I'm an orphan. What did you expect?"

"I don't know." My friend made a face. "I just didn't expect you could look the part as much as you do!"

I was only half listening to Jessica as I navigated through the actors milling about the hallway. "I'm taking that to mean you had no idea that I could look so poor, raggedy, and unloved. So, thanks!" I responded. *We were almost there. . . .*

Jessica looked confused for a split second, like that *wasn't* what she meant. But then she smiled and said, "You're welcome!"

Jessica and I finally made it backstage. "Look!" I peeked out at the audience members beginning to make their way to their seats.

"What? No!" Jessica pulled me back.

"They can't see us!" I promised. "It's really cool!"

Jessica opened the curtains ever so slightly but then leapt backward like she was afraid her head would get lopped off.

"No, it's not! It's . . . it's . . ." She took in a deep breath and exhaled. And then she did it again . . . and again. I don't think she was doing it in the way Ms. Tracy meant for us to.

I had never seen Jessica like this.

"Remember our auditions?" I tried to get Jessica to look at me.

My friend groaned. "*Why* would you bring that up now? I choked!"

"No, you didn't," I reassured her. "What I remember about

it was the lights. How they shone so bright, it was actually hard to see anyone out there. Didn't you notice that?"

Jessica stopped her panicked breathing for a second to think. "Yeah, I guess, but—"

"That's actually what calmed me down. If you focus on the light and only what's happening onstage, then it'll help you not to worry about what's going on out there. Helped me, anyway."

Jessica peeked out again. "Huh. I never thought of it that way."

"Jessica? Jessica, what on earth are you *doing*?" Dressed in her maid costume, Mrs. Kelly stomped toward us.

"Break a leg!" I called out.

Jessica turned back and yelled, "You too!"

Of course, things go wrong on opening night. Both Ms. Tracy and Sam had told us they would and not to worry about it. The Topeka Repertory Theater production of *Annie* was no exception.

For instance, when Ben was running away from the dog-catcher, he got a little too into the chase and knocked over the fake fire hydrant. Everyone acted like it didn't even happen and during the set change, it disappeared anyway.

"You're supposed to *pee* on it, not destroy it," I joked around with Ben backstage. He laughed. See? I could make him laugh too.

In one of Annie's scenes with the orphanage manager, Miss Hannigan, Jessica repeated the same line twice. But the actor who played Miss Hannigan was such a pro, she was able to improvise and make the scene flow seamlessly. I doubt anyone in the audience even noticed.

In the orchestra pit, a trumpet player honked once after the song had ended, almost like a musical sneeze. The audience (and even Daddy Warbucks) cracked up a bit about that, but it was no big deal.

The scenes I was in went fine. The orphans had choreographed group song and dance routines so there was a *little* pressure not to mess up, I guess, but not a lot. It's not like any one of us was the focus of the scene.

And Jessica . . . Jessica did great! She really did. After I had read the lines for her that day in the way *I* thought they should sound, and Jessica repeated them back to me, Sam complimented her during the following rehearsal, and that was a really big deal because Sam usually found something to grumble about, especially with Jessica. She didn't even have to calm herself down with Good & Plenty like she usually did when she was frustrated. When Sam said nice things to Jessica about how much she'd improved, I beamed inside. Sure, Jessica was the star of the play, but by helping her, maybe I was a little bit of a star too. Like stardust.

Even though I didn't have a huge part, it was really amazing to see the show all come together that night. Aside from dress rehearsal last night, cast and crew had only worked in bits and pieces up until then. A few scenes here, a few members of the cast there. Songs one night, dance routines another night. Tonight, though, with the set, the lighting, the costumes, the music, the actors, and the *audience* all together . . . Well, it was like magic that we all had a part in, no matter how small.

As the play closed, the audience roared and gave us a standing ovation. Mrs. Kelly rushed out with a huge bouquet of multicolored roses for Jessica, who took a bow with the actor who played Mr. Warbucks. One by one, cast members for the roles of Miss Hannigan, Rooster, Lily, and Grace stepped to the front of the stage. After the other orphans and I took our bows and stepped back, Jessica caught my attention, and she waved me closer.

"Annie, come on!" I looked around. The orphans had just gone—my turn was over.

"Annie!" Jessica motioned to me again. Then she turned around, grabbed me from the row behind her, and pulled me into the center with her.

That's when I looked out over the audience and saw what Jessica saw. Hundreds of adoring fans, applauding, whistling, cheering. The lights illuminated the stage and the audience remained in the dark. But when I shielded my eyes and scanned the crowd, I could make out my mom, dad, and Tak applauding, too.

The orchestra was still playing, and the music rose up toward us like a sparkling cloud that I could ride on. Jessica lifted my hand high before we took another bow. I could scarcely breathe—never had I felt the happiness that I did in that one moment.

When I stood back up, Jessica squeezed my hand and then let go. I knew that was my cue to make room for more of the performers. I stepped to the side.

Ben, still in his dog costume, pranced out on all fours to renewed audience cheers. He sat (like a good boy!) next to Jessica and she scritched him behind an ear, which made one of his legs twitch back and forth. The audience laughed and continued clapping.

Finally, it was Sam's turn and as she walked past me, I thought I heard her mumbling, "... deserve a flippin' Tony for this ..."

Once Sam reached the front of the stage, Mrs. Kelly brought out a bouquet of flowers for her as well. Not as big as the bouquet she gave her daughter, but Sam didn't exactly strike me as the kind of person who liked flowers all that much anyway. Sam bowed awkwardly and waved to the audience as she took a few steps back. We followed her lead and stepped back too.

Finally, the audience applause began to die down as the heavy maroon curtains inched closed.

Even though opening night was over, that feeling I had onstage looking out beyond the lights, at the audience, hearing the music and the applause envelop us like a warm hug... I held on to that feeling as long as I could.

You can be anything that you want to be. That's what they told us at the end of elementary school. So, I'd thought I wanted to be Little Orphan Annie and that didn't happen. But I watched and listened during all the rehearsals just like my dad told me to do. I learned so much about what goes into making a show—a *real* show—that whatever that *anything* was, I knew this:

I want to be something that makes me feel like I did tonight.

ACT II
THE KING AND I

CHAPTER 14

It was hard to imagine anything could equal the excitement of the play, but within a couple of weeks, Jessica and I embarked on another great adventure together: middle school.

Even though Westridge Middle School, otherwise known as WMS, was made up of only two grades—seventh and eighth—there were more kids there than all the grades combined from our previous school.

A few different elementary schools, like the one Ben had attended, fed into WMS, so there were a lot of new faces. There were also a lot of familiar ones, but even those had changed over the summer. The girls wore their hair bigger than ever—it seemed like everyone but me had a perm now—and their shoulders were wide and padded. Maybe they needed to be to balance out all that hair! Not to mention there was so much purple eye shadow it was like being in a field of lavender. A lot of kids were also taller, the boys' voices had dropped, some of the guys were hairier. Staring out at everyone as we made our way into the gymnasium for the first-day-of-school assembly, it occurred to me that it was as if some of my classmates ate the same cake that Alice in Wonderland did, and now all of a sudden they were giant versions of themselves.

By the time we'd graduated from Iron Hills Elementary, we knew everyone in the school, and everyone knew us. In a way it was comforting, but it was also constricting—like wearing a pair of jeans two sizes too small. Jessica and I were ready to move on after all our years there. TRT really let us spread our wings, so by the end of the summer we felt larger than life. I mean, we had worked with *adults* in *Annie*, our first real community theater production! Plus, we didn't arrive home until close to eleven the night we had our three evening shows. But none of that prepared us for how *small* we felt here. Throngs of students in the unfamiliar hallways, most of whom we didn't recognize. The older students jostled and bumped past us like we weren't there. There was no "Excuse me," or even a "Watch where you're going!" No one knew about our triumphant summer. No one *cared*.

I had woken up an hour earlier than usual so I could work on my hair. There's no way my mother would let me get a perm, so I just had to use an old curling iron instead. The end-of-August heat and humidity destroyed my work in no time flat, though, so I figured a headband might help it look better. And at the time, I thought it did, but now I wasn't so sure. I adjusted it—not sure why since I didn't have a mirror with me and who knows how it looked now?—but I did it anyway. Jessica fiddled with her large red plastic earrings, too, so I knew she was feeling the same.

"Ben!" I spotted another familiar face through the crowd. "Ben!"

He turned and saw us. Even though it had only been a few weeks, I missed not being able to hang out with him during rehearsals, and backstage during the four shows we put on. When the show wrapped on a Sunday afternoon, Jessica had to go hang out with her relatives who came in from out of town to see her perform. Ben and his family pretty much immediately left for vacation. I went from almost two months of "Real-Life Ben" to two weeks of just "Fantasy Ben." So seeing him smile at me now, in the present, was hard to describe. It was like making an impossible shot from half-court (*swish!*), like in the movies when the boy turns to the girl in slow motion and gentle synthesizer music starts playing, like I was back onstage with the spotlight on me.

But then my dream froze and a chill ran through me. Ben was from the theater. He was from the summer. We hadn't ever gone to the same school. Would we joke around like we used to? Or would he walk on by?

"Hey, Jessica! Hey, Annie!" His clear, cheerful voice cut through my worries.

The three of us sat together during the assembly, but our group vibe disappeared as soon as it was over. It was time to head to our classes. Unlike last year, where we only switched for math and English, *every* class this year would be with a different teacher.

Jessica and I already knew our class schedules by heart. Our lunch was at the same time, but we were bummed that we only had one class together: physical education.

Ben pulled his schedule out and compared it with Jessica's first. "We have English and social studies together!"

"Cool!" Jessica smiled at him. He smiled back.

"How 'bout you, Annie?" Ben asked.

I retrieved my class list from my backpack and checked it against his. "Math and science!" I squeaked.

"Awesome! Want to walk together?"

My face flushed as I nodded. Since science was first period, it made sense to go with each other. Not *go* with each other in that sense, but, you know, *go* as in *walk* to class together.

Poor Jessica. It was too bad she didn't have the same schedule, so she'd have to walk by herself. But when I looked up, I saw that I didn't need to worry.

"Hey, Jessica! Need any help finding your class?" Two girls I'd never met waved my best friend over. Although I didn't recognize them, they reminded me of Jessica with their matching poofy hairstyles and brightly colored blouses with padded shoulders.

"Who are *they*?" I asked. I thought Jessica and I knew all the same people. It felt strange to realize we didn't. I reached up and adjusted my headband.

"Oh, our moms are on the PTO leadership committee together," she responded casually, like it was no big deal. "Bye! See you at lunch." She patted me on the head before she walked away.

Ben and I watched as Jessica disappeared around a corner. "Do you even know where the class is?" Ben abruptly pulled out his school map and studied it for a second before turning it right side up.

I laughed. "I think so." I was *so* relieved Ben was with me.

"Then after you, my lady!" Ben bowed and I laughed again. What a dork.

I stepped in front of him and we made our way to first period together. He hung on to my backpack as I wove through the throngs of people on our way to class.

"So, how was the first day of middle school?" my dad asked when he came home about an hour after everyone else had finished dinner. "Did you make some new friends?"

I was in my room arranging all the papers from my classes

in my new Trapper Keeper binder. After the morning assembly, the rest of the day was a bit of a blur. Between rushing to my classes, to remembering my locker combination, to finding Jessica at lunchtime among the sea of unfamiliar faces in our ocean-sized cafeteria—I hardly had a chance to breathe, let alone chat with anyone new. I could barely keep track of all my teachers' names, not to mention all the kids in each class I hadn't met yet. By fourth-period social studies, I was having a hard time concentrating. It was the last class before lunch, so I was *starving*. When the teacher described how we were going to travel around the world and back in time, my interest was piqued and I was able to ignore my stomach's growls. But when she said we'd begin with the *great* civilizations of Sumer and Mesopotamia, I remembered that pottery shard documentary that made me lose interest in being an archaeologist. Her description started off sounding like an Indiana Jones type of rip-roarin' adventure, but when she continued on about the *earth-shattering* Greek civilization, and the *awe-inspiring* Roman Empire, I sensed she was trying a bit too hard. By the time she told us we'd even learn about the *jaw-dropping* Industrial Revolution, I was pretty much convinced this class would end up more like sifting through a plot of dirt with a toothbrush. On top of all that, starting tomorrow, PE was gonna be *awkward* with having to change into our uniforms in the locker room *every day*. Thank goodness it was at the end of the day and we wouldn't have to take showers in front of everyone.

"It was okay." I finally answered my dad's question.

Dad looked sad. I felt a little bad that I didn't have more to offer him. "How was *your* day?"

"My day?" He scratched his mustache and looked off to the side, pondering. "It was okay."

I rolled my eyes and he laughed.

My dad sat down at my desk. "Do you like your new math teacher?"

I groaned. I couldn't believe my dad spent all day working in the university math department and now what did he want? More math! And he had to ask me about my math teacher, and not my bubbly young English teacher who was so excited about all the books we were going to read that it was hard not to get excited, too. Or Ms. Johnson, the giant PE teacher (honestly, I'd never seen a woman that tall before) who used to play basketball during college.

My new math teacher was Mrs. Olds and the name fit, if you ask me. Her hair was a faded grayish-brown curly cap of frizz. She wore drab gray "teacher clothes"—a vest over an off-white blouse with a prim collar buttoned all the way to the top, and even fastened with a cameo brooch to double/triple ensure that—God forbid—she show part of her neck. Her face was wrinkled, like an apple left out in the sun too long.

"Just like my name, I'm in the class of the 'old folks,' so we do things the old-fashioned way in *my* class. When I speak, you listen. You will have homework every night and you will turn it in every day. You won't get better at math unless you practice. Math is just like anything else; practice makes perfect." And then she passed around two handouts: a list of class expectations and a worksheet with a set of thirty problems, all lined up in even rows.

"May I see?" Dad asked as he spotted it on my bed by my Trapper Keeper.

I handed it to him and this time it was his turn to groan. "No wonder you don't like math! There's nothing fun about this." He spotted the class expectations sheet too. "Does this have her number? Maybe I should call her—"

"No, don't do that!" I snatched the paper away before my dad could reach it. "I mean, it's just to see what we're able to do. I don't think the rest of the year will be this way," I lied. Judging by the look of Mrs. Olds, I pretty much knew this *was* the type of work she'd hand out every day. Plus, there was something else about her. Not her frumpy old outfit, or the creaky ol' singsongy voice she used when she talked to us like babies. There was *something else* that I couldn't put my finger on . . . that I just didn't like. *At* all.

"Oh, okay." My dad frowned as he scanned my worksheet. "You can do this, right?"

I took the paper back from him and almost yawned as I looked over my problems. "Oh yeah. No problem."

"*Ja*, how about you finish those and then we shoot some baskets?"

I looked out the window at the dimming light.

"Or . . ." My dad scratched his mustache again. "We play basketball first while we can?"

I jumped up and ran down the stairs. "I shoot first!"

"Only until you miss!"

"Which will be never!" I shouted back as I ran outside ahead of him and grabbed our basketball.

Even though I said I'd shoot baskets first, I only fired off a couple before I passed the ball to my dad as soon as he reached the street. I felt sorry for him, huffing and puffing like an old man! But he seemed to shed a year with each basket he shot.

Middle school was like a storm, threatening to blow me over with all that was new. Still, I couldn't help but feel hopeful. I gave my dad an extra-long turn as I jumped up and down, higher and higher, always reaching for that rim.

CHAPTER 15

With school came back-to-school physicals, which we should have gotten done during the summer, but my parents aren't exactly on top of those things like Jessica's parents. Phone calls especially frustrated my mom. The person on the other line would often ask her to repeat herself, and each time she did it was like stretching a rubber band—you could sense the tension. She said she'd schedule my doctor's appointment, but I got tired of waiting and did it myself instead. By the time I ended up calling Dr. Wang's office, we had to wait another three weeks before they could fit me in for an appointment, even though she was new in town. I guess the word had gotten out about how good she was. I was a *little* stressed about missing school, but I needed to have this physical so I could try out for the middle school basketball team.

After checking in, my mom and I sat down in the waiting

room. Instead of the same magazines as last time, there were all new ones, including a *TIME* magazine that caught my eye. It had a photo of a bunch of Asian kids on the cover with the caption: "Those Asian-American Whiz Kids."

I'd brought along *Alice's Adventures in Wonderland* like I always did, but I didn't feel like opening it up this time. I reached out toward the glossy magazine, flipped through it, and began reading.

In the article, it talked about how Asian American kids were doing great in school and attending all these prestigious universities. It talked about how high their SAT scores were in comparison to everyone else. Plus, there was all this stuff in there about how Asian American kids were unusually awesome at math, science, and engineering. *Ugh*, I thought. *That doesn't sound anything like me.*

There weren't any other Asian American kids like me at my elementary school. This year, I noticed that there were maybe a couple? But they were in the grade above me, not mine. I only knew about them because some of the older kids called me "Grace" a few times and I was like, "Who?" The eighth graders who called me that seemed confused and mumbled, "Oh, it's just that you look like her." When I finally located this mythical "Grace Anderson," I didn't think I looked like her at all.

Then, people always asked if Daniel Yu was my older

brother. This confused me too. Like, in what world do "Inoue" and "Yu" sound like the same last name?

Even Jessica *and* Ben asked me if I knew them. I responded to both of them with a "No. Why would I?" But then they weren't able to answer that, either.

"What are you reading, Aoi?" My mother interrupted my thoughts.

"Oh, nothing." I walked over to the other side of the waiting room to bury the magazine under a pile of others, but Mom stopped me.

"Can I have it?" she asked.

It wasn't like I could tell her no. But for some reason, *I really didn't want her to read it.*

"Why?" I stalled. "It was really boring."

"Let me see it." My mom held out her hand.

"Aoi? Aoi Inoue?" The nurse popped her head into the waiting room.

I breathed a sigh of relief. "Here!" I answered like roll call for a class. I dropped the magazine into a rack where I stood and strode over. This time, I waited for my mom to go first so I could make sure she didn't grab that magazine.

"So, Aoi." Dr. Wang looked over my sports physical form. "You want to play basketball?"

I nodded.

"Okay, let's see how you're doing."

Like last time, Dr. Wang listened to my heart and my breathing, and she made me stand up and touch my toes as she examined my spine. She checked the rash on the backs of my legs.

"Well, that's looking a lot better!" Dr. Wang seemed happy for me.

"Yes, thank you," my mom gushed. "You're the first doctor who gave her something that worked."

I don't know why mom turned into The Compliment Machine around Dr. Wang, but it was really weird.

Dr. Wang smiled. "I'm glad it helped. I'm sure Aoi had something to do with it, too, right? Sometimes the younger kids have a harder time following directions. How's her cough at night?"

"It's good," I responded before my mom could.

"Well, you know, we did what you suggested, but . . ." I could tell my mom really wanted to pile on some more compliments, but something was holding her back.

"So, no more stuffed animals on the bed?"

"Nope."

"But she's still coughing?" Dr. Wang directed her question to my mom and not me.

What? My mom didn't say anything more about my cough.

"Yes . . . in the middle of the night."

"You mentioned you have a cat." Dr. Wang reviewed the notes in my chart. "Her lungs sound fine, but I'm wondering, Aoi, if maybe you're allergic."

Allergic? Allergic to Chibi? Chibi had been around for as long as I could remember. I even ate cat food with her when I was a toddler (before my mom caught me and made me stop).

"Does your cat sleep with you, Aoi?"

Since I couldn't snuggle with my stuffed animals anymore, I had been snuggling with Chibi instead. Ten years ago, I chose her from a litter of four kittens. The rest of them were all gray, but she was dressed up and ready to go—with white gloves on each paw and a fancy white diamond on her chest. When I picked her up for the first time, she snuggled into the crook of my arm, kneaded it, and purred. From that moment I knew she was the one for me and I was the one for her.

My insides twisted. I couldn't be allergic to her. I just *couldn't.*

My mom didn't seem happy about the idea, either. "Do we . . . we must give her away?"

"Oh, no!" Dr. Wang smiled reassuringly. "It doesn't sound severe. Let's just start out with no more cat in the bedroom, how about that?"

I nodded, but wasn't happy at all about this situation. Chibi's purring at night helped me fall asleep. Without my stuffed animals, and now without my fuzzy friend, I'd be awake forever.

"Thank you, Dr. Wang!" My mom smiled and nodded like "no more cat in the bedroom" was the best medical advice she'd ever heard.

That wasn't my worst doctor's appointment ever, but it was close. Sure, I came away with a completed sports physical. But now because of Dr. Wang, I couldn't sleep with my fluffy cat anymore. The only good part of the visit was that on our way out, Mom wasn't able to find the *TIME* magazine I stashed away.

CHAPTER 16

Although it didn't seem like it would be possible when middle school started, soon all the newness became routine and we fell into a rhythm. Not exactly an easy, relaxing rhythm, but a rhythm nonetheless. Elementary school recesses became a distant memory, and the worries we had about being able to open our lockers seemed so silly now.

Like elementary school, that feeling of being onstage with the spotlight dazzling my eyes and thunderous applause filling my ears started to fade, too, as the weather began to cool and the green leaves of summer turned brown and yellow. But I wasn't ready to let go yet.

Ben and I had two classes together: math and science. In the past, these had been my two least favorite subjects, but at least with Ben they were tolerable. Since science was first period, the class was subdued and quiet since we were all pretty sleepy, teacher included.

Math with Mrs. Olds was as bad as I predicted it would be, but in some ways it was so bad that it united all the students against her and her awfulness. Although I wasn't a big fan of the subject matter, her lectures about the "good ol' days" were even worse. It was a struggle not to giggle at the faces Ben made behind her back.

I guess in the "good ol' days" it was okay for teachers to blatantly favor boys over girls too. When Natalie dug through her backpack in search of a pencil, instead of just lending her one from the class set, Mrs. Olds felt the need to point her out.

"Girls," she sighed as she brought a pencil over to Natalie. "So flighty. Always losing things."

Even though I hadn't forgotten Natalie's surly attitude from this summer, I didn't think she deserved *that*.

Sometimes Mrs. Olds needed student volunteers to distribute worksheets (so many worksheets!) or take a trip to the office, or staple handouts together. She *always* chose a boy for these tasks even though each and every one of us was desperate for something to ease our boredom.

One day, she needed someone to drop off folders with all the other math teachers in the school. It was the best type of chore because it got us *out* of that math-and-good-ol'-days prison and moving around.

"Now, who would like to help your little ol' teacher out?"

Everyone raised their hands. Mrs. Olds scanned the class.

"Ben Prescott," she announced. "You seem like a capable young man."

The rest of us groaned together. Ben was one of her favorites. It was no secret to any of us, especially to Ben. Around her, he used his acting skills from this past summer to act like the "capable young man" Mrs. Olds believed him to be instead of the goofball we all knew he was.

"Yes, Mrs. Olds." Ben practically leapt out of his seat. But then he did something completely unexpected.

"Would it be all right if I chose someone to come with me?"

We gasped. Mrs. Olds *never* entertained requests like this. Once, she showed a video in class. As the tape neared the end, she abruptly shut it off even though we had a good ten minutes of class left before the bell rang. It wasn't a very interesting video—I mean, it was a *math* video—but it gave us a break from hearing her speak. We whined with disappointment.

"Mrs. Olds, can we see the ending, please?"

"Come on, Mrs. Olds! We have enough time!"

"Now, now, I just don't want your brains to turn to mush. We all know that's what happens when we watch too much TV. All your complaining makes me think you need another page of problems to solve tonight."

Her reasoning didn't even make sense! *She* was the one who showed us the video in the first place. Mrs. Olds was *that* mean.

So, we all held our breath when Ben made his request, wondering if this was what would topple him off of his teacher's-pet pedestal.

"Why, Ben, what a nice young man you are."

"Oh, thank you, Mrs. Olds! Can Annie come with me?"

I almost fell out of my chair, but I was able to keep it together as Mrs. Olds turned her faded, watery eyes toward me.

"You mean, *may* Annie come with you?" I could tell she wished she hadn't granted Ben this extra favor.

"Oh, of course. *May* Annie come with me . . . please?" Ben corrected himself for her like it made him happy to do so.

"As long as you're finished with all your work, Annie. Are you?"

Truth was, even though she had us working on math problems for the bulk of the period, I wasn't. She had assigned us four pages—two double-sided pages—but I had only done the last page where the hardest problems were. The first three pages just felt like mindless busywork that I simply couldn't bring myself to do at the moment. They weren't due until tomorrow, so I spent the rest of the time writing a note to Jessica that I was going to hand her during the next passing period.

"Yes, Mrs. Olds." I showed her the last page of completed problems.

Ben wasn't the only one who could act. Some might call what I did lying, but not me, not when it involved Mrs. Olds. Especially since she only asked *me* if I had all my work done, and not Ben.

"All right then."

As soon as Ben and I rounded the corner away from Mrs. Olds's classroom, I raised my hands in victory and he started dancing.

"Thanks for saving me," I whispered. We calmed ourselves down as we walked past the windows of the other classes still in session.

"I just needed someone to help me carry these." Ben handed me the stack of folders.

"I knew it!"

It was great to joke around with Ben again, just like this past summer. With school beginning and so many other kids around, I had started to wonder if our friendship was as important to him as it was to me.

Ben knocked on the door to Mr. West's classroom and I handed him his folder.

"Hey, how's Jessica doing?" Ben asked me as we continued on our errand. "We're seated clear across the room from each other in both our classes, so I haven't had much of a chance to talk with her recently."

Jessica? I still rode the bus with her to and from school and we always sat next to each other for our stretches at the beginning of PE class. At least once a week we still hung out after school to do our homework (or more like gossip!) together. She walked to some of her classes with girls I didn't know, but I didn't have those classes with her, so that wasn't a big deal. She was the same ol' Jessica, at least as far as I could tell. It was *Ben* who *I* hadn't hung out with much since this summer.

But then I had a brilliant idea.

"Why don't you sit with us at lunch?" While our summer connection wasn't gone, he still had been sitting with his elementary school pals in the cafeteria. But maybe . . .

Ben blushed. *Oh no*, I thought. *He knows I like him.* Plus, who was I to think he'd rather sit with a couple of girls than all his buddies from his old school? But then he answered in a way that I could only dream he'd answer.

"Really? You guys wouldn't mind?"

I almost dropped the folders I was carrying. "Mind? Why would we mind?"

Ben looked right at me with those green eyes in a way that made me feel like I was the only person in the hallway (which technically I was, but who cares?).

"You're the best, Annie!"

Now it was my turn to blush.

CHAPTER 17

"**O**f course I don't mind," Jessica answered when I asked her if it was okay that I asked Ben if he wanted to sit with us at lunch. "I like Ben. Not as much as *some people* I know, though."

Jessica nudged me with her shoulder as we sat on the gym bleachers waiting for basketball tryouts to start.

"Ha ha, very funny." I nudged Jessica back. She knew I liked Ben, but she was nice about not making too big a deal out of it.

Tryouts started at 7:00 p.m. sharp, and my dad had actually been free to drive me and Jessica there. In the car, my dad tried his hardest to make small talk with Jessica.

"You like basketball?" As a die-hard KU Jayhawks fan from the moment he stepped onto campus years ago, he was always looking for someone to talk with about the team.

"It's okay, I guess."

"I think KU has a great chance to win the championship this year," my dad tried again. "Especially with Danny Manning leading the team. What do you think?"

When Jessica responded with, "Who's Danny Manning?" he thought maybe he didn't understand her, like "Who's Danny Manning?" was some sort of new American slang that didn't mean what he thought it meant. He almost went through a red light when Jessica followed up with "And what championship?"

Danny Manning was only one of the best college basketball players in the US, and KU had been on the hunt for the NCAA basketball championship for years. Coming close, but never winning it, at least not since 1952.

Not knowing about Danny Manning did not bode well for Jessica, I thought. In fact, I was a little surprised when she'd asked for a ride to tryouts tonight.

The writing seemed to be on the wall for Jessica when our PE teacher, who was also the basketball coach, came bounding out of the locker room decked out in a red-and-blue KU Jayhawks T-shirt and shorts.

"Hey, everyone, thanks for coming out to tryouts! Parents, my name is Amanda Johnson and I'm going to be the seventh-grade girls' basketball coach this year. As many of you know, I also teach PE. . . ."

As Ms. Johnson introduced herself and described what the

season would look like—that is, *if* we were to make the team—I looked around the gym and spotted Natalie. Even though she seemed gangly and awkwardly gigantic when she tried out for "Little" Orphan Annie, something told me she'd feel more at home on the basketball court.

A shrill *tweet* signaled the beginning of tryouts. We started with lines, which I loved. I was already pretty low to the ground to begin with, so running back and forth in the gym and bending down to touch the lines on the court not only got my blood pumping, but it was fun.

Then we formed two rows and shuffled in one direction until we heard Ms. Johnson's whistle for us to stop. Then we switched directions when she whistled again, all the while passing the ball back and forth between rows. The gym echoed with the sound of our squeaking shoes and the *boom* of the ball against the floor.

Layup drills followed by free-throw shooting rounded out the first fifteen minutes of tryouts. So far, so good!

Maybe not for Jessica, though. She missed a pass because she was looking at the clock, like she was counting the minutes until this would end. During lines, she stopped to retie her shoe not only once but twice (same shoe). She finished last but didn't seem to care at all. I wondered what was going on. Maybe she wasn't feeling well?

Ms. Johnson then divided us into two teams and handed

half of us stinky red mesh jerseys to scrimmage in. Jessica, me, and Angie, Kirsten, and Paige—three girls I'd faced off against in previous years of recreation basketball—were on one team. But the rec ball days when everyone made the team ended with elementary school, and now we had to compete against each other for limited spots.

Natalie and four other players made up the other team. When Ms. Johnson tossed it up between them, Natalie tipped the ball my way by accident. I began dribbling. I'd never played with this particular combination of team members before, but being at the point guard position felt like home. Before I crossed the half-court line, I scanned the possibilities. Kirsten was by the basket. "Annie! Annie!" she called out to me. With her curly flaming-red hair, she was an easy target to spot. But Natalie was on her like a pesky mosquito out for blood, so I couldn't pass it her way. Angie motioned to me. She set a pick against my defender, so I'd have a clear path to the basket. I drove down the lane for my first layup!

SMACK! Out of nowhere, I ran into a tree—a tree called Natalie. I practically bounced off her and onto the floor.

"Nice try, Shorty!" She smirked as she snagged the ball.

The other team took off down the court with the ball. Natalie's height was an advantage, but not when she was dribbling. Since she didn't keep the ball low to the ground, I was able to run back and steal it from her pretty easily. Bringing the ball up was usually something the guard was responsible for, not someone like Natalie, who was most likely going to be a forward or center.

Everyone was just so much *taller* this year. Who knew that a few inches could make such a difference? When Alice in Wonderland took a bite of a magic mushroom, it made her neck very long, like a serpent. I know I'd look very weird if I had a long, snakelike neck, but I would have made that trade-off at this moment because I couldn't see over or around anyone!

Back and forth, we went on like this for twenty minutes, until Ms. Johnson blew her whistle and switched up the teams. It didn't make much of a difference—I hadn't made a single basket yet. I fed a few to Angie—she was so tall, too, that it seemed like all she needed to do was hold her hands up over her head and then gently toss the ball into the net. But me? I was knocked down, blocked, and shot over, again and again, usually by Natalie, who was still on the other team. I was good last year, I swear! I never stopped practicing, yet here I was, struggling to hold on to the ball, let alone score.

BAM! I was on the floor again. This time because I planted myself in front of Natalie as she bulldozed her way to the basket.

Tweet! With Ms. Johnson's whistle, we paused and looked her way. Both of us knew there was a foul, but we didn't know if it would be against Natalie for charging, or me for blocking.

"Annie, two shots!" Ms. Johnson called out.

Yes! I leapt to my feet and for the first time during the tryout, I glanced my dad's way. He grinned and clapped twice. "Way to take the charge, Annie!"

"Come on, Coach!" Natalie groused. "She *totally* flopped!"

"Two shots!" Ms. Johnson stayed firm in her call.

Swish and *CLONK!* At least I made *one* shot tonight.

Within a few more minutes of scrimmaging, it became apparent that Jessica, who was on Natalie's team now, didn't really need to be guarded. This allowed for us to double team whoever had the ball. Usually, this was Natalie. After about forty minutes of playing as hard as we could, we were all panting and trying to catch our breath.

For the most part, Natalie had been untouched during the scrimmage . . . until now. With me and Kirsten both on her, I waved my hands in front of her face.

"Get off me," she muttered.

"Get rid of the ball!" Ms. Johnson shouted.

Seeing no other choice, Natalie passed the ball—hard—to Jessica.

Almost as if it were flying through space in slow motion, I watched as the orange orb hurtled toward Jessica's unsuspecting, clock-watching face.

"Ow!" she screamed.

Ms. Johnson blew her whistle. "Good hustle, girls. We're done for today."

Jessica immediately brought her shirt up to her nose.

"Are you okay?" I ran over.

"Mind if I take a look?" Ms. Johnson gently pried Jessica's hand from her nose. "Here, hold your head back."

"Is it broken? It's broken, isn't it?" Jessica sounded hysterical.

"Nah, just a bit of a bloody nose." Ms. Johnson pulled a couple of Kleenexes from her pocket and brought them up to Jessica's face. "Hold it there and apply some pressure for a minute, okay?"

I sat in silence next to my friend until her breathing evened out and she calmed down. "Sorry that happened, Jessica."

With her head still tilted back, she side-eyed Natalie, who stood off to the left, cleaning some dirt out from under a thumbnail. "I bet she did it on purpose," she grumbled.

"Coach *did* tell her to get rid of the ball." I don't know why I jumped to Natalie's defense like that. "But she totally didn't need to throw it that hard," I added so Jessica knew that I was on *her* side, not Natalie's.

"At least this way, my mom will *never* make me play again," Jessica muttered.

My jaw dropped. "You don't want to make the team?"

"Mom just thought I should get more exercise," she admitted.

"That's the only reason I'm here."

"Oh." I *really* wanted to make the team. But with every basket shot I took, someone taller either blocked it or stole it. How did Muggsy Bogues handle it? At only 5'3" he made it to the NBA, but it was looking doubtful as to whether I'd even make my seventh-grade team. I only made one free throw tonight. *One* point. I seriously doubt that made an impression on Ms. Johnson. It felt kind of strange to sit next to someone who didn't care about something that I personally wanted very much.

"Don't worry if you don't make the team, though," Jessica whispered to me.

Ugh. I looked down at my ratty old high-tops. I guess Jessica didn't think I played well enough to make it, either. Clearly, she thought that would be a good thing for *me*, too, since *she* didn't care for basketball at all. Even though she was trying to be nice, her comment stung.

"Because I've heard there's going to be something *much* better to occupy our time." Jessica removed the tissues from her nose, which had stopped bleeding.

"Oh yeah?" I looked up. Usually there wasn't much Jessica knew that I didn't know of, and vice versa.

"For the annual WMS show, it's going to be a joint musical production with the high school," Jessica whispered. "My mom made me swear to keep it secret, so don't tell anyone, okay?"

Another theater production? And with the *high school*? My mind flashed back to that moment onstage this past summer— the lights, the applause, that *feeling*.

That feeling I'd been looking for again ever since middle school started. That feeling I hoped for with each basket shot, but was dashed when I missed.

Maybe the annual school show would be where I'd find it.

CHAPTER 18

Although I begged more than a couple of times, Jessica wouldn't share anything more about the school show to me.

"I swore I wouldn't say anything," she explained. "But I promise, the announcement will be made *soon*."

How did Mrs. Kelly come by this top-secret information? The thought *did* cross my mind. But she couldn't tell me *that*, either.

Having to wait for basketball team announcements was driving me crazy too.

Luckily, I was put out of my misery the Monday morning after Thanksgiving.

There was an all-school assembly and as we filed into the gymnasium where it was being held, I noticed Sam talking to the principal by the school stage.

Sam? What's she *doing here?*

Then I put two and two together. *The show!*

"Jessica! Annie!" Ben waved at us and made his way over. Jessica scooted over to make room for him.

Ben made a big show of settling in between the two of us. But then he scooted against me, so I scooted back against him.

Jessica rolled her eyes and flipped her hair at us. "Now, now, children."

Ben dropped his head and looked like a puppy who had been scolded. But then he turned toward me and winked.

My heart fluttered and flopped.

"Good morning, Wildcats!" the principal began. "I'm glad to see you're all still students and didn't turn into turkeys over Thanksgiving!"

The principal was always pretty corny, but usually his jokes at least made us groan. This one was met with complete silence.

"You know, because you are what you eat?"

More silence, except for the very loud sigh that Ben let out. I wanted to giggle so badly at that point, but I was starting to feel sorry for the principal. Starting to, but not completely, because he was *not* funny at all.

He cleared his throat and moved on. "As the eighth graders already know, Westridge Middle School puts on a show every March. This year will be a little different."

Jessica looked straight ahead and smiled. I sat up straight. *This was it!*

"The WMS Wildcats are teaming up with the South Topeka High School Thunderbolts to put on the largest theater production our district has ever seen. We all thought this would be a perfect way to show off the high school's new auditorium."

A buzz welled up across the gymnasium.

The principal smiled. He was probably happy that this news was going over better than his earlier attempts at humor.

"In the past, Mrs. Hall would have overseen the production."

The choir director halfheartedly waved to us from where she stood behind the principal.

"But since this will be a much bigger production involving two schools, we're enlisting some outside help. Mrs. Sam Glick worked in LA as a director, worked on *Annie* with the Topeka Repertory Theater this past summer, and has now been brought on to help us with *our* production of *The King and I.*" The principal stepped aside and applauded as Sam waved to us from her seat. She wore brown corduroys and a buttoned-down collared shirt—which was pretty darn dressed up for her—but she looked uncomfortable as a result.

After the principal explained when and where auditions

would take place (after the winter holidays in the high school auditorium), my mind wandered.

The King and I? I didn't know this musical as well as I knew *Annie*, but I *had* seen it before! It was on TV a year ago when Mom was out running errands, Dad was working, and I was supposed to be babysitting Tak. Which I *did* because we watched the show together. ("It has explosions!" I had lied. "But they're real little, so if you're not concentrating, you might miss them.") It was actually about an English woman named Anna who traveled to Siam (which is what people used to call Thailand) to teach the king's children. I didn't remember much else except that Anna and the king had a lot of misunderstandings due to cultural differences.

As the principal droned on now about grades and the importance of studying, I only thought about *The King and I*. And the more I thought about it, the more excited I became. I knew I wasn't guaranteed a part, but hopefully my experience in *Annie* over the summer would help.

"You think you'll try out?" I whispered to Ben. Memories of all the fun we had over the summer flooded back.

"Yeah!" he whispered back right away. Maybe he was thinking about our summer too?

"Are you going to audition?" Ben asked Jessica.

She laughed as if he just asked the silliest question in the world. "Of course!"

"All right, Wildcats. I know there are only three weeks until winter break, but let's keep our focus and make them good ones!" the principal finished as the bell sounded.

I might have been imagining things, but Ben looked embarrassed with the way Jessica responded to him. I couldn't be sure, though, because he got up and rushed out of the gym as soon as the assembly finished.

"See? I told you there'd be *way* more interesting stuff than basketball to look forward to."

While I walked alongside her, Jessica lifted her heel up to the side and kicked me in the butt as we made our way out of the gym. For some reason, kicking each other this way when greeting friends was a thing in middle school. I didn't love it, but I guess it's just what we do.

"Way more." I kicked Jessica's bottom in response. Or tried to anyway, but she dodged and I just kind of stumbled.

"Hey, congrats!" Natalie waved to me from across the hall.

"For what?" I was genuinely confused. With my mind stuck in Thailand for the past few minutes, I felt almost jet-lagged when Natalie pulled me from my thoughts back into the real world.

"For making the team, Shorty!" Natalie laughed.

"Ugh, who cares about basketball when you can be in *theater*?" Jessica rolled her eyes.

Without missing a beat, Natalie responded, "How's the nose, Jess?"

My friend and I gasped. She *did* throw the ball at her face on purpose!

For a tense moment, Natalie and Jessica stared at each other. I wondered if there would be a smackdown in the hall right then and there.

Natalie was a *beast* on the court even when Ms. Johnson was there to referee. Who knows what moves Natalie could pull in a largely unsupervised hallway?

"See you at lunch, Annie." Jessica broke first. She hoisted her backpack up higher on her shoulder and stomped off.

"I'm not *that* short." I glared at Natalie as I started to follow Jessica. But then I stopped.

Wait. Did she just say I made the basketball *team?*

"Whatever you say," Natalie responded, using the same words she did this past summer after she quoted Shakespeare in her weird way of being mean about Jessica. Only this time, her tone was playful and not annoying like back then. "Didn't you see the roster posted outside the gym?"

I hadn't! Although everyone was streaming out of the gym, I backtracked.

"Hey, watch it!" Students pushed against me. "What are you doing?"

I ignored them as I wove through them like a tiny minnow

swimming against schools of salmon.

When I finally reached the gym entrance, I saw the white sheet posted on the door. I made the team.

I made the team.

CHAPTER 19

Unlike the play, basketball practice started right away. Three nights a week to get us ready for games that would start after the holidays.

I was *thrilled* I made the team, but middle school basketball was *way* different from elementary school basketball. No more "Good job, great hustling, nice try!" Hustling and trying was expected—the bare minimum—and no one complimented us for that. But if we messed up, boy, did Coach Johnson let us know. ("You've had a week to learn these plays. You guys mess up again and it's lines till you feel like you're gonna puke!")

Jumping, squatting, running, shooting, passing, blocking, dribbling . . . my legs felt like Jell-O by the time practices were over.

And it wasn't just my body that was getting tired. It's not exactly like life gets easier for anyone right before Christmas.

For one, teachers assigned extra work. Book reports were due, tests given, projects needed to be turned in. All in a rush to cram whatever learning they could stuff in the crevices of our young brains before it would turn to mush over the holidays.

On top of that, Dad was normally very busy as the university's math department chair, but he had tons of extra work with the end of the semester approaching. That meant extra chores at home for me.

Mom was fussing about the International Food Bazaar that she and the ladies from church had been planning for months now.

With all I had going on, I couldn't believe that my mom wanted me to help out with that too.

At least it was happening after school was out for winter break. With the last day of classes on Friday the eighteenth, the bazaar itself was the next day, so there was no time for a breather before we scrambled to prepare.

Mom had volunteered to make gyoza—dumplings filled with ground pork, ginger, garlic, green onions, and cabbage, and seasoned with a little soy sauce and sesame oil. We made our own wrappers out of flour and hot water, rolled them out, and wrapped each dumpling by hand.

There were other items my mom could have made. Like kappa maki, which were relatively easy—just cucumbers and rice rolled into a sheet of nori seaweed—but the event organizers balked at that. "Seaweed? Sounds *weird*!"

But it was hard to find people who didn't like gyoza. They were pan fried so the bottoms of the wrappers crisped and browned, and then steamed so they were chewy on top. When you bit into them, the juices from the meat and vegetables hit your tongue with a splash of savory flavor. We only made them once or twice a year because they took so much time and effort. Since this was for a church fundraiser, though, my mom wanted to make something that people would be sure to buy.

The day before, my mom had made the meat and vegetable mixture and let it sit overnight in the refrigerator to let the flavors mingle. The next morning we both got up early (so much for sleeping in on my first day of break!) to make the wrappers and to assemble the gyoza. We dropped a tablespoon of the filling inside each doughy skin, pinching first in the middle, then each end, and finally tucking and gathering the extra dough to form a neat, crescent-shaped morsel. Tak helped roll out the dough since his little fingers weren't nimble enough to form the pleats.

Then we heated up some oil in our largest skillet and neatly arranged the dumplings in a circle that fanned out like a flower, each gyoza a petal. When the bottoms browned, my mom added a little broth and then covered the skillet immediately with a lid to steam the dumplings. When they were cooked, she put a plate on top and flipped the whole thing over. We added oil and repeated.

Several hours later, all the dumplings had been filled, pan fried, and steamed. Each of us had three, dipping them first in a mixture of soy sauce, chili oil, and vinegar. My stomach growled after finishing my share, but my mom wouldn't let us have any more.

"Only if there are some left over after the bazaar," she scolded.

Tak and I frowned. We knew there wouldn't be.

Then my mom and I both had to get ready. I really, *really*, really didn't want to, but we were going to the bazaar dressed in our kimonos.

I'd only worn one a few times before in my life. They were stiff and uncomfortable, and my mom yelled at me for not acting a little more "ladylike" when I had mine on.

She had me watch while she put hers on.

"There's a special way to do it," she explained as she wrapped soft towels around her midsection first. "If you don't learn how, you're going to have to pay someone to help you."

"Really? How much?" The thought of having to *pay* someone to dress you piqued my interest.

"Twenty-five? Maybe thirty dollars."

Whoa. I paid more attention because who had that kind of money?

My mom carefully adjusted the kimono around her waist. She undid it and tried again.

"Unless you get someone who knows what they're doing, it's going to look sloppy." After twenty more minutes of pleating, folding, adjusting, and cinching, Mom finally had her kimono on. It was a soft mint green adorned with pink and white blossoms that cascaded over one shoulder and pooled at the bottom hem. She wrapped a contrasting silver obi over it with an elaborate pattern woven into its fabric, and tied it in a type of knot that made it poof in the back. Finally, she tied it all together with a pink cord. She had her hair pulled back in her usual bun, but stuck in a long tortoiseshell kanzashi ornament for her hair. I had to admit that the final effect was stunning. She was beautiful.

"Now your turn."

I sighed and held up my arms so she could go through a similar but less involved process with me. I was going to wear a yukata, which was like a kimono, but not as fancy. Normally, Japanese people only wore these during the summer since they were light and made out of cotton, but "no one here will know the difference," Mom assured me. Plus, a kimono like the one my mom wore would cost hundreds of dollars, and as my mom put it, "No need to buy something so expensive that you're only going to wear a few times."

"Oof," I complained as she spun me around, tying everything tight to make sure nothing would slip during the event.

"Just pretend you're getting dressed for a play. Like the one you want to try out for next. What is it again?"

"*The King and I.*" I stopped grousing. My parents said I could try out, but I could tell my mom wasn't thrilled when her first comment was, "Only if you keep your grades up."

When my mom finished with me, she turned me to face the mirror. My yukata was pink and covered in a dragonfly pattern.

"You don't look half bad when you dress up," she assessed.

At the bazaar, the church basement was teeming with people milling about tasting all the treats, drinking coffee and hot cider from Styrofoam cups, and laughing. They wished each other "Merry Christmas!" loudly and often as a segue to moving along, especially when they had run out of things to say to each other.

"Jackie! Oh, Jackie, hiiii!" Mrs. Kelly made her way to us. She wore an off-white Irish fisherman sweater over a Christmasy red-and-green-plaid skirt. "Jackie" was what my mom let Mrs. Kelly call her since "Chiaki" was too hard for her to pronounce.

"Oh my goodness, look at you!" I stifled a cough as Jessica's mother approached and her overly floral-scented perfume enveloped us. "Did you find your table? Here, let me help you find it."

Even though my mom and I were holding several containers of gyoza, it took us what seemed like forever to reach our station because Mrs. Kelly kept stopping to show my mom off to people.

"I know, isn't this amazing? Why, she looks just like a *doll*, doesn't she?"

The hair on the back of my neck rose. I don't know if I was feeling annoyed because I didn't want to be here in the first place, or if it was the stuffiness of all the people packed in the room, or my arms hurting from not being able to set the trays of dumplings down, but something about the way Mrs. Kelly talked about my mom was bugging me *big-time*.

Every time people stopped to ooh and aah, my mom just nodded and smiled. When they asked questions about her kimono, she answered them politely, never losing patience, even when asked if it was a "real one from China."

I called this my mom's "flight attendant" mode.

Around the time my mom graduated from college in Japan, a lot of women dreamed of becoming flight attendants. She was one of several hundred the airline hired that year, out of almost twenty thousand applicants. "Very competitive," my mom told me with pride. "My English was one of the best out of all the applicants." This always confused me because she was so shy and reserved around other parents now.

Didn't flight attendants have to interact with tons of people every day? I remembered a university picnic where one of my dad's colleagues asked her, "So how 'bout you, Mrs. Inoue? Do you work?" When she responded that she used to be a flight attendant, that professor laughed and said, "Oh! So basically a sky waitress! Can you get me a tomato juice, no ice?"

I was only around five then, but the memory of seeing my mom shrink remained as clear as if it happened yesterday. She didn't *actually* shrink, but it seemed like she did, or like she deflated or *something*. Before that, she used to tell me about all the cities she had visited as a flight attendant and what she was able to squeeze in during her layovers—shopping the Magnificent Mile in Chicago, marveling at the stained glass in the Duomo (I guess that's a church?) in Milan, and visiting Anne Frank's house in Amsterdam. But after that man had made fun of her job, Mom *never* talked about it in the same way again.

Come to think of it, that's when she stopped talking about herself to other people in general. So maybe she wasn't really shy. She was *wary*.

When I told her that maybe someday I could be a flight attendant, too, she shook her head.

"No, you need to have a job that people *respect* here. You can do better than I did."

No one said anything to me about my outfit for the International Food Bazaar. Maybe because my increasingly surly mood was making me look decidedly un-doll-like? Or like the type of doll that murders people while they sleep. . . .

When we finally made it to our table, we set out paper plates, napkins, and toothpicks. We filled several plates with three dumplings each and sold each helping for a dollar.

"Now what are these?" Jessica's dad, Professor Kelly, stopped by our table.

"Gyoza," my mom responded.

"Giyo-what?"

"Gyoza," my mom repeated. "Asian dumplings."

Professor Kelly handed me a dollar and I gave him a plate. He didn't use the toothpicks we provided, but used his fingers to pop an entire one into his mouth. Although I loved the salty, vinegary dipping sauce we ate our gyoza with, we skipped bringing any. Mom said it would be too messy and that they were plenty delicious without.

As Professor Kelly smacked his lips and licked his fingers, I thought, *Mom was right. Again.*

He chewed and sucked on his teeth. His eyes grew wide. "These are *pot stickers*, not *gi-oh-za*!"

My mom and I traded looks. *Pot stickers?* We'd never heard

them called that before. In our house, they had always been *gyoza*.

My mom dialed up her flight attendant mode. "Pot stickers? Yes, thank you!"

I pulled at my collar. At this point, I was really glad that I was wearing a summer yukata and not the heavy silk kind my mom was wearing. It was getting really hot in here. Or maybe that was just my face.

I didn't like how people were talking to my mom.

I don't know why it bothered me now, all of a sudden. Maybe it was because none of my own friends were here and so it became clear that no one talked with my mom like she was a friend. It was hard for me to pinpoint *how* they were talking with her....

Until the church administrator stopped by our table. Mrs. Briggs—I liked her.

"Hey, Chiaki!" she greeted my mom warmly. "Everyone has been saying how delicious your dumplings are."

"Thank you." My mom smiled back. And in a real way, not like she was dealing with passengers on a trip across the ocean.

"Say, would you mind helping me at my table? Just for a few minutes. I see that you brought a helper with you." She turned her attention to me. "Would you mind terribly if your mom helped me while you stayed here? Just for a few minutes."

I nodded. "It's fine."

As they walked off, it occurred to me what the difference was. Mrs. Briggs just talked to us like . . . she talked with everyone else.

But the Kellys . . .

All of a sudden, it struck me. They talked *down* to her. Like she was a thing, like a doll—not a person, like she didn't even know what the name of the dish *she* made was.

I sat down, feeling hot and dizzy. *No, that can't be it*, I thought. *They've never been that way to me . . .* Or had they?

"Annie?" I heard a voice call my name. "Annie, are you all right, sweetheart?"

All of a sudden, I felt really weak and had to put my head down. Yesterday's basketball practice was brutal. Maybe that was what was hitting me now. Like a ton of bricks.

Then I smelled the lavender of Mrs. Kelly's perfume and felt her cool hand on my scorching forehead.

"Oh, Jackie!" Mrs. Kelly exclaimed to my mom. "She's burning up! I have to head home to tend to Jessica. Let me drive Annie home, too."

Next thing I knew, I was in her car on my way home with her clucking and cooing at me in her reassuring way. "Oh, dear. You must have been working so hard. I know Jessica is worn down to the bone, too. That's why I didn't make her come tonight. I sure hope a good night's sleep will do the trick for you. What a way to start your break."

I was wrong about the Kellys, I thought as I lay down on the soft car seats, the cold leather providing relief to my pounding headache. *They weren't talking down to us.* I pushed my negative thoughts about them away. It was me in my fevered state just imagining it. Mrs. Kelly was like my second mom, taking me home to where my dad was waiting for me.

My real mom finished up at the church because she had promised she would.

CHAPTER 20

Some "break" it turned out to be. After the bazaar, I stayed in bed for several days straight, getting up only to go to the bathroom. Even though my mom had strict rules about no food in the bedrooms, she brought okayu up to me so I didn't have to move any more than I needed.

Okayu is what my mom always made us when we weren't feeling well. After boiling some leftover rice in chicken stock, she flavored the porridge with a pinch of salt and bits of umeboshi pickled plum.

I felt so miserable, though, that I couldn't finish it. I ate as much as I could since Mom made it special for me, and because I knew the umeboshi were hard to come by—it was always hit or miss whether the Asian food store over thirty minutes away would have them in stock.

I was so sick I couldn't even taste the bright salty-sour plum, and the hot spoonfuls only made me feel hotter. But when I threw off my covers, I shivered and couldn't get warm again, even when my dad piled extra blankets on me.

Then the coughing began, and I couldn't sleep despite the fatigue that seeped into every pore of my body. In my feverish haze, I remembered seeing Tak stand in my doorway clutching Tiffany the Triceratops. Any other day, I'd yell at him for playing with my stuffed animals, but I couldn't muster up the energy. I heard him whispering to my mom, "Is she gonna be okay?"

By Christmas morning, I was finally able to make my way downstairs. Tak and my mom had decorated our small fake tree together with colored lights, paper chains, and popcorn strung with cranberries. A month ago, we had gathered pine cones from the neighborhood and had been planning on painting them white and sprinkling them with glitter. It looked like Tak and Mom went ahead and worked on them without me, which was fine. I was too weak to care.

We unwrapped our presents, including the ones from Santa.

"Look!" Tak shouted at his math flash cards. "Santa got me a game!"

I looked over at my dad and he seemed amazed. "Santa must have heard what a good boy you were! Annie can help you with those," he told Tak.

I smiled. *Better him than me.*

Dad opened up several new silk ties with the bright patterns he was so fond of. "I couldn't wear these in Japan." He grinned. "They're great!"

That's another aspect of life in America he loved. The freedom to wear flashy ties.

As was our Christmas tradition, Tak and I both received one new stuffed animal each. His was a roly-poly bunny with floppy ears and mine was a large grinning cat. Even though I knew I was getting a little old for stuffed animals, I still gasped when I unwrapped it.

"It's like the Cheshire Cat!" I exclaimed.

"Sorette nani? What's that?" asked my mom. "I thought it would be nice to have a cat in your room again. Even though it's for decoration—not for snuggling. Like Dr. Wang said, okay?"

So, the *Alice in Wonderland* reference wasn't on purpose . . . but I loved it anyway.

Also in line with Inoue Christmas tradition, Tak and I each received a new outfit. He immediately tossed his off to the side in favor of the Man-At-Arms Masters of the Universe action figure I bought him. I held my new pastel-striped sweater close, though. I loved the shiny silver threads woven through it. With each day that passed in middle school, I couldn't help but care about clothes more and more. The new jeans from Santa weren't the trendy acid-washed ones that a lot of other kids wore, but they were lighter-colored than the dark denim ones that my mom had insisted on buying me last year.

Mom's present was small, but tied with a fancy red-and-green bow. She carefully unwrapped it to reveal a pair of turquoise-and-coral earrings. The bright colors contrasted with each other, but also worked well together.

"Kirei, they're so pretty!" My mom held them up to her ears.

"Put them on, put them on!" Tak jumped up and down on the sofa.

"Hey, calm down!" Dad scolded him. Tak didn't stop.

"Not right now. For church." Mom set them down.

That made Tak stop.

In past years, church on Christmas Day signaled an end to the magic of Christmas morning. We understood that attending the service to celebrate the birth of Jesus should be the *real* focus of the day, but . . .

I coughed, and I *swear* I wasn't acting when I did.

Mom and Dad traded looks.

"Do you think we should go?" Dad asked my mom hesitantly.

Tak and I sucked in a breath and didn't dare say a word.

"Hmm . . ." My mom thought for a moment. "Aoi definitely should stay home. I'm feeling fine, but . . ."

"We've all been exposed. We wouldn't want to get anyone else sick." Dad nodded solemnly.

"And Annie would be all alone if we went and she didn't. On Christmas!" Tak played his part.

A soft snow began to fall outside our window.

We never knew if we were going to have a white Christmas or a cold and dreary gray Christmas here in Topeka. It looked like this year it would be a white one.

"The roads might get tricky," Mom mused. "Will any crews even be working to clear them today?"

"I guess we could miss church this year," my dad said slowly.

Years ago, Dad told us he didn't know how to "do Christmas" when he came to the US. Neither his family nor my mom's celebrated it in Japan when they were kids, so he had no idea what the fuss was all about. But a kind professor invited him to his house one winter break when my father was still a student. "Felt sorry for me to be alone, I think," Dad explained, and there he experienced his first American Christmas.

"It was nothing like I had ever imagined," he had told us. "I remembered every bit of it, so my children could also have a real American Christmas one day."

Since that professor had attended Christmas services with his family, Dad had always insisted we go, too.

The church we went to looked so pretty during the holiday season, with a tall, *real* tree, covered in so many decorations that the limbs looked tired trying to hold them all up. Red-and-green poinsettias livened up the entryway and the steps that led to the pulpit. For the Christmas services, the best singers always led the hymns. But when we heard that we might not go this year . . .

I could tell Tak wanted to jump up and down on the sofa. I did, too, but I held on to him tight. We didn't want to seem too excited! Although there was no denying that the Christmas service *was* beautiful, not going meant I'd get to stay in my pj's with a purring Chibi at my feet.

"You know, Mrs. Briggs stopped by and dropped off some grapefruit and to check on you while you were sick," my mom began. "Maybe we could have that? Are you hungry?"

So, rather than going to church this Christmas morning, my mom peeled wedges of that ruby-red fruit the kind church administrator had brought us instead. We piled it into crystal bowls my parents had received as a wedding gift, and Tak helped drizzle the slices with golden honey.

Dad was home from work, Mom was relaxed, Tak was happy, and we were all surrounded by presents and the warm glow of the fireplace, where wood crackled and sparked. When we bit into the bright tartness of that grapefruit that contrasted with the sweet honey that lingered on our tongues, it was like waking up to the sunshine. In that moment, it was like *all* our dreams—ones that we didn't even know we had—had come true.

CHAPTER 21

A few days after Christmas, reality settled in again. I felt *much* better even though my cough lingered. I started to feel antsy. Auditions for *The King and I* were coming up and I hadn't prepared at all!

Jessica's family was skiing in Aspen with her aunt, uncle, and their cousins. I wished she were around, so I could ask her opinion about what song I should use in my audition. For *Annie*, Sam didn't specify what songs we should sing. But for *The King and I*, she was *very* clear about how we each should choose a song that was *not* part of the actual musical. I guess hearing "Tomorrow" sung a gajillion times did her in.

In some ways, it was great because there was so much flexibility and we could choose the song that best suited our voice and range. In other ways, though, it was daunting because there were so many songs that *weren't* in *The King and I* that it made my head swim!

One evening, my dad brought a copy of the musical home from the local video rental store so that we could watch it as a family.

"It has explosions," Tak told my dad. "But you have to watch closely, or we'll miss them." I couldn't tell if Tak was playing the same joke I played on him, or if he still believed that he missed the "explosions" from the time we watched together. When he looked my way and grinned, I had my answer. I grinned back.

We squeezed onto the sofa and Tak and I laughed at the stubborn and haughty king's antics. We listened in rapt attention at Anna Leonowens's wise advice and beautiful singing.

At least I *tried* to. My parents talked throughout the whole show! First my mom commented, "Is this actor Thai? I don't think he's Thai. I don't think the young woman who plays his new wife is, either."

"I don't know," Dad responded. "I don't know any people from Thailand."

"I visited once when I worked for the airline and they didn't look like *that*." My mom crossed her arms while she watched.

"Well, this *is* set in the past—" Dad responded thoughtfully.

At this point, I gave my parents the stink eye. I got in trouble when *I* talked while they were watching the news—but here they were with their running commentary! All I wanted was to lose myself in the love story between the young Tuptim and her boyfriend, Lun Tha. It was pretty hard to, though, when my mom piped up, "I'm pretty sure the person who wrote this wasn't Thai, either."

At the end, my dad stopped the tape and pushed the rewind button on our VCR. "Omoshirokatta ne!" He exclaimed how fun the movie was to watch.

My mom didn't say anything.

"But I didn't catch any explosions. Did they happen when I went to the bathroom?" Dad asked.

"*Tons* of explosions while you were in the bathroom!" Tak and his potty sense of humor were delighted. *Sigh.*

"So, your school is really going to do the same musical?" My mom seemed skeptical.

After watching the video, it was pretty clear to me that the high schoolers would be cast in the major roles. A middle school student would most likely play Anna's son, and *maybe* (and that was a *big* maybe) Tuptim could be played by a middle schooler, too. But that was it. At the most, the rest of the middle schoolers who made the cut would have bit parts like one of the royal children.

"It's with the high school. And the director from this summer," I explained. "There are a lot of good singers at the high school." I thought of Jennifer, the girl who ended up playing

Pepper in *Annie*. She'd told us she did summer theater to keep her acting chops sharp—because competition for parts at the high school was brutal.

"Hmm. I'm not worried about lack of talent . . ." My mom frowned.

Well then, what *was* she so concerned about? Sometimes my mom could voice her disapproval without saying much at all. Now I began to wonder what exactly she had against *The King and I*.

"Maybe Topeka is more sophisticated than people give it credit for," mused my dad.

"Hmm," Mom said again.

On the last Friday of break, I was in my room warming up my voice with arpeggios and sirens.

"OoooooOOoooooOOOoooo," I made my voice rise and fall.

Through the walls, I heard Tak mimic me. "OoooooOOoooOOoo."

I slapped the wall. "Stop it!"

"OoooooOOoooOOoo."

I kicked the wall this time. "Stop it, or I'll come in there and *make* you stop." I coughed. My cold was hanging on, but I knew I must be getting better because my little brother was acting like a turd again.

A knock on my bedroom door, and then my mom entered my room before I could even say, "Come in."

Uh-oh. No more okayu and pampering for me. I knew I was in trouble.

"Aoi, I've scheduled a doctor's appointment for you. Come on."

"What?" I kind of wished she was here to punish me for threatening my little brother, not to take me to another doctor's appointment.

"I told you about this yesterday."

"No, you didn't. And what for? I feel a ton better."

"I didn't? Well, I meant to. Now, *hurry up!*"

Back in the exam room again, Dr. Wang listened to my heart and lungs.

"Well, the good news is that it's not pneumonia. I've been seeing a lot of patients with similar issues. It's been a bad flu season."

I sighed with relief. *So I had the flu. What's the big deal? I'm better now.*

"But the coughing?" my mom asked. "Still bad at night, even before she got sick."

"Hmm." Dr. Wang studied me thoughtfully. "No more stuffed animals?"

"Not on the bed, no."

"No cat in the bedroom?"

I shook my head.

Dr. Wang checked my chart. "You know, eczema, allergies, and asthma often come together. Your lungs sound fine, though, so I think I'd like to check for allergies. Would that be okay with you?"

I gulped.

"All right then. Would you mind waiting a minute?" Dr. Wang left the office.

All of a sudden, I felt sicker than I had for days, but a different kind of sick. *What if I was allergic to Chibi?*

Dr. Wang's nurse knocked softly on the door before appearing with a tray of vials.

"We're going to do a skin prick test for dust mites, mold, cats . . . to see if any of those things are what's bothering you. For kids, we usually do this on the back; for adults, we do this on the forearms. Do you have any preference?"

"Back," Mom answered.

"Arms," I answered at the same time.

The nurse looked back and forth between us and laughed nervously.

My mom looked my way and nodded. "What she wants."

"Arms," I whispered weakly. I cleared my throat. "Arms," I repeated in a voice I hoped sounded strong and fearless.

As the nurse swabbed my skin with alcohol and pricked me,

I looked away. They weren't needles and it didn't hurt much at all—just little pinches—but I half wished I had agreed to have them on my back because I couldn't help but wince when the nurse pushed the allergens into my skin.

"There, all done!" The nurse wrote some notes on the clipboard she carried with her. "Now, I know you know this, but don't touch them, even if they itch. In fifteen minutes, we should know."

Even though I hated this, this office, these tests . . . I couldn't help but be fascinated by what was going on.

Two areas on my arm began to grow red and *very* itchy.

Two welts formed. One continued to grow . . . and grow.

Halfway through the process, the nurse came in and checked my arms. She scribbled again on her clipboard. "If you feel faint or dizzy or *anything*, you just holler, okay?"

While I didn't feel faint *or* dizzy, I did feel a sense of dread at the welt that was taking over my forearm.

After the fifteen-minute timer sounded, Dr. Wang and her nurse both appeared again in the room. The nurse took a small ruler and measured the size of the "weal," which is what they called it. The first weal was just a histamine, a type of control to see that the test was working. But the second weal . . .

After more scribbling in my chart, Dr. Wang sat down and began.

"Aoi, you are *definitely* allergic to cats."

My eyes began to water, and not from allergies.

My mom let out a sigh.

"Does this . . ." I tried my hardest to keep my voice from cracking. "Does this mean we have to . . . Do we have to . . ." I couldn't even say the words.

"Shoganai," my mom said to me gently. "What can we do? I know someone who loves cats. I'm sure she would be happy to take care of—"

Dr. Wang interrupted her. "Now, this doesn't necessarily mean you have to give up your cat."

That caught both my mom's and my attention.

"Allergy shots have proven to be very effective." Dr. Wang handed us some sheets of information. "They're time consuming and you'd be seeing a lot of me, but once you're finished with them, they would help. A lot."

Shots. I shuddered at the thought of needles.

"Time consuming?" My mother frowned. "So, she will miss a lot of school?"

"Well," Dr. Wang began. "She would need to have a shot once a week and this would last for several months . . ."

A shot a week? I was old enough now that I wouldn't bolt down the hall to avoid one, but needles still gave me the heebie-jeebies something awful. I could deal with my vaccinations that came along with my annual checkups, but *once a week*?

"I know that sounds like a lot, but we can work with Aoi's

169

schedule to ensure she misses as little school as possible. After each injection, we'll keep her around for a bit, too, to make sure she's tolerating the allergen without any issues. The good news is that once she's done, she won't be allergic anymore. Your cat, what was her name?"

"Chibi," I answered.

"Chibi. That's a cute name! Well, Chibi will most likely be able to snuggle with you again. How does that sound?"

Mom turned to me. "Dou suru, Aoi?"

I took a deep breath and nodded. "I'll do it."

CHAPTER 22

By the time school started in January, I had completely recovered from my cold. But even though all of us were on break, I still felt behind when classes resumed. My legs were weak from not exercising while I was sick and my voice was still a little hoarse.

Auditions for the musical were happening in three days and I still hadn't chosen a song. Based on what I had observed during *Annie*, serious actors would have their song memorized. How was I going to do that if I hadn't even chosen one yet?

Add to that my basketball team resuming its three-nights-per-week practice schedule *and* the fact we just had our first game this Saturday. All I'll say about it is, we have our work cut out for us. My last doctor's appointment showed that I only had three more inches to go before Muggsy Bogues and I were the same height. My last game showed that I needed *a lot* more than height to help me play better.

And even though I might not have felt all that rested from winter break, it was clear my teachers were raring to go. Like the snow that was plowed into drifts on the side of the road, we all were assigned an avalanche of homework our first week back.

Mrs. Olds was like the abominable snowman with all the assignments she piled on us.

"Can you talk with her, please?" I joked with Ben during lunch one day. "Since she obviously *loves* you."

Ben laughed. "But don't you see? This is the sick and twisted way she shows her affection."

"You mean, instead of candy—?"

"Fractions." Ben's face was dead serious.

"And instead of smiles—?"

"Word problems involving volume and surface area, that's right!" He broke into a silly grin.

We both *had* to make the musical. We just *had* to.

"What did you decide on?" I asked Jessica during one of our hour-long phone conversations. I held the phone up to my ear while I did sit-ups. For basketball, I had to get my strength back and *fast*!

"'I Could Have Danced All Night' from *My Fair Lady*."

"Oooh, smart choice," I said. Ms. Tracy had said actors sometimes use songs from other musicals that were similar to ones in the production they were auditioning for. "I Could

Have Danced All Night" was sung by a woman who was fall-ing in love. By selecting that, I could tell Jessica wanted the role of Tuptim.

"How 'bout you?" asked Jessica.

"I don't knoooow!" I whined as I splayed out flat on the floor, my abs burning from the punishment I had just inflicted on them. *I* wanted to play Tuptim, too, but then I caught a glimpse of myself in the mirror. I hardly resembled any sort of princess, and the ratty sweats I was wearing didn't help any, either. I learned my lesson from *Annie* not to aim too high.

"The only songs I know the words by heart to were the ones in *Annie* and 'Physical,'" I finally answered.

"'Physical'? You mean the one by Olivia Newton-John?" Jessica burst out laughing. "You can't sing that."

"You're telling me! The lyrics are . . . I mean, not exactly audition-appropriate. Ugh." Even though I was stressed, the thought of doing that made me giggle, too. "Unless, you know, if I was trying out for Tuptim. Since it's more of a 'grown-up' song."

"Yeah . . ." Jessica responded. But then she was quiet long enough that I thought the line had gone dead. I wished I could take back what I said about auditioning for the role I knew *she* wanted.

"But I won't because everyone says I look like I'm ten," I added.

"You *do* look young!" Jessica finally spoke up again. "But

you'd definitely get their attention with that song choice!"

"You mean, I'd definitely get detention?"

"Annie's been on the phone forever!" Tak shouted downstairs.

That little rat, I thought. He'd probably been eavesdropping on our whole conversation as well. Ever since I'd been feeling better, it was like he was trying to make up for lost time.

"But seriously," Jessica said, calming down. "What are you going to sing?"

"I don't know how quickly I can memorize a new song," I grumbled. "And I bet Sam is still on *Annie* overload. It would be a bad idea to use a song from this summer—"

"I got it!" Jessica shrieked so loudly that I had to hold the phone receiver away from my ear. "'Red River Valley'!"

"Red River Valley"? That was from third-grade music class. In fact, it was practically the only tune our music teacher had us sing for *months*. Over and over until it was time for our unit on recorders. We didn't love those screechy, plastic ear-torture devices, but boy were we happy to have a break from that song!

"Don't tell me you've forgotten the lyrics." Jessica sounded exasperated.

"No, but . . ."

"Red River Valley" was hardly the type of song that would blow anyone away.

"I know *you're* probably still sick of it, but I doubt Sam is."

Jessica made a good point. Brushing up on the lyrics of an old song would be way easier than learning a whole new one.

"Red River Valley" it was!

In addition to audition stress, my allergy shot treatments also began that week. Even though Dr. Wang said her office would try its best to get me appointments outside of school hours, my first one fell squarely during first *and* second period. We took it, though, because Mom wanted to get me on the schedule as soon as possible. As much as it pained her for me to miss school, this was the first appointment that was open.

The shot itself, while awful, didn't take much time. It was the waiting afterward that did.

"Just to make sure you don't have a bad reaction," Dr. Wang explained.

I opened my copy of *Alice's Adventures in Wonderland* and pulled out a folded sheet of the lyrics for "Red River Valley." I was pretty sure I still knew it by heart, but with auditions tomorrow, I didn't want to take any chances!

To my horror, my mom also had reading material: the *TIME* magazine with "Those Asian-American Whiz Kids" that I *thought* I had hidden, and hidden well.

I looked back and forth between my lyrics and my mom placidly studying the articles. It was unusual to see her reading in English. She read the newspaper that was tossed onto our front porch every morning, but it took time, and they would pile up on our kitchen table. Normally, she preferred the Japanese publications her sister shipped to her every so often from Japan.

"Mama, nani yonderu no?" I asked in Japanese, as sweetly as I could muster. *What are you reading?*

"Oh, just about all these *amazing* kids!" Mom flipped a page.

"Oh yeah? How so?" I didn't really want to hear her answer, but maybe my talking to her would stop her from reading that closely.

"Just that so many go to good schools. Harvard, MIT . . . By working hard, you know. Wouldn't you like to go to one of those schools someday?" My mom eyed my sheet of lyrics. "Because I think you need to work harder if you do."

College? I couldn't believe my mom wanted to talk about college.

"Mom, I'm *twelve*."

"But you will be in eighth grade next year, just one year until high school. How will you stand out? Are you making the best use of your time now? Don't you have any homework from the classes you're missing?"

Fact is, I *did* have homework. Math homework. But her pointing that out to me made me not want to do it at all.

"I made the basketball team, *and* I'm doing theater!" I almost shouted. "I'm working on memorizing my song here. I think that's a good use of my time."

"How *is* basketball?"

Ugh! Those three words might have seemed like a simple, innocent question to anyone listening, but *I* knew what my mom was getting at. So what if all my shots were blocked during my first game? It just meant that I was really going for it, and in my defense, some of those calls were big-time iffy. And it's normal to be a little rusty at the beginning of the season, especially since I had been sick. She was trying to hint that maybe I *shouldn't* be focusing on basketball. That maybe there was no future in it. That maybe . . .

While I was getting myself all worked up, Mom had returned to that *darn* magazine and read some more.

I fixed my eyes on my sheet of lyrics. I saw the words, but wasn't able to focus on them at all.

My mom finally broke the silence. "You know, here it says that there's less discrimination in math and science fields. That you will be judged more objectively . . . if you go down that path."

I wasn't having a reaction to my shot, but I was having a reaction to this! My stomach clenched at the same time I broke out into a cold sweat.

I hated that magazine. I didn't see myself in those pages at all. Those kids didn't sound like me *at all*. But my mom was reading it like it was a how-to manual on what to do with me. That darn magazine . . . no, that *damn* magazine!

CHAPTER 23

Although I had waited forever for this time to come, when the three-day audition window for *The King and I* rolled around, I found myself regretting that I didn't have at least another week to prepare.

As I hung out backstage that evening, I wished Jessica were with me to offer encouragement. But both she and Ben auditioned yesterday when I had basketball practice. It was bad enough that neither of them were here, but what was even worse was that I didn't feel ready. During my vocal warm-ups, my voice shook.

"Nerves are completely normal." Ms. Tracy's words of advice from this summer came back to me. "Nerves just mean you care. So, acknowledge that you have them, that they are normal, and move on."

I am nervous because I care about this audition, I told myself.

Hello, nerves, I acknowledged them. *You are normal.* I repeated these words in my head as I waited for Sam to call my name. *You are normal. Nerves are normal. I am normal.*

And then—in a way that was so beyond normal—I *totally bombed* my audition.

It's hard to know exactly what went wrong—I think my mind blocked the worst of it out because it was so horrendously embarrassing. But what I do remember went something like this:

When I stepped out onto our middle school stage, it was way less intimidating than the university concert hall where the *Annie* auditions took place. It was just our gymnasium, where we had all our morning assemblies, only this time I was looking down from the stage rather than up toward it. Sam was no longer a stranger to me and I'd heard our choir director was nice. I saw her in the halls all the time. I took a deep breath. *See? This is all familiar territory. Nothing to be scared of.*

Only this time, there was no kindhearted piano player to give me a reassuring wink and a nod . . . and I would be singing something I had only chosen three days ago.

"Oh, hey, Annie!" Sam greeted me. Even though she was gruff and scary at first, once I got to know her, she was still gruff and scary, just not as much.

"Hi, I'm Annie Enoway." I cleared my throat. "But I mean, I

guess you know that, um . . ." I laughed nervously.

"Yep, sure do." Sam checked her watch. "Whatcha gonna sing for us today?"

"'Red River Valley.'" I looked over toward the nice grandpa-like piano player . . . who was *not* there. *It's okay*, I told myself again. *Get ahold of yourself, Annie! Geez.*

I began.

"From this valley, they say you are goin' . . .
I will miss your sweet eyes and bright smile . . ."

Whoa, wait, did I just mix those two up?

*"For they say you are takin' the sunshine
That has brightened our pathway the while."*

I took a deep breath at the end of the first verse and watched Sam and the choir director for their reaction. They didn't seem to realize that it should have been "bright eyes and sweet smile," not the other way around. I kept going.

*"Do you think of the valley you're leavin'
Oh, how lonely and dreacly it will be."*

"Dreacly"? What the heck is "dreacly"?

"Do you think of the hond fart you're breakin'."

Oh no. There's no way they missed that one.

"And how sad it will be to cast me."

I know that's what I was thinking, but did I actually sing that?

Even though it was cold in the gym, I actually began to feel warm, *very* warm, like I was going to ignite. But I was determined to finish the song, determined to redeem myself. I didn't know how, but I would.

Sam held up her hand. "Thanks, Annie." But even worse than her stopping me in the middle of the song was what she did next. I heard a crinkle of a wrapper and then watched as Sam poured herself a handful of peanut M&M's.

I scurried off that stage and out of the gym as fast as I could.

Hond fart?

If there were a rabbit hole I could have fallen down at that moment, I would have leapt into it, and gladly.

I wish that was all there was to the audition, but there was also an optional choreography portion. I hadn't even focused on it up until now because I was sure my singing would be a slam dunk after all my experience this summer. Now I knew I had to at least try to dance, or else I'd have no shot at all.

After eight of us had sung, we were ushered into a classroom where Ben's aunt, Midge Prescott, taught us all a short dance.

On a scale of one to ten, I was a seven in terms of how confident I felt about my singing.

In terms of my dancing ability, I was a negative seven. I'd never had any dance training. I assumed lessons were expensive, so I never asked for them, and my mom never offered. A lot of girls in my grade had been learning since they were toddlers, though.

"I looked into Thai dances, and from what I can tell, there is a lot of this type of posture—" Midge stopped and posed with bent knees and flexed feet and then hopped on one foot across the stage. She swept her arms in a wide circle and assumed a different pose, this time with her wrists flexed and bent at an angle perpendicular to her arms.

"Okay, girls, space yourselves apart and follow along."

Over the next thirty minutes, Midge taught us a quick dance that involved a lot of similar postures and a lot of hopping on one foot. In the *King and I* video I watched over break, there's a part in it where Tuptim puts on a play based on *Uncle Tom's Cabin* for the king. Its main character, Eliza, was a dancer whose moves involved a lot of hopping across the stage in her effort to escape the evil men pursuing her.

The hopping wasn't all that hard—my basketball legs were more than prepared for that—but remembering the moves . . .

I just didn't understand how all these other girls picked them up so easily.

When Midge added the music to our dance, I thought it would make it easier, but it actually made it harder. Just one more thing I had to pay attention to, on top of my hands and legs and head and right and left.

Jennifer, the girl who played Pepper in *Annie*, saw that I was near tears. "Hey, just follow me, okay? We'll probably form two rows on the stage and I'll make sure I'm in front of you. How does that sound?"

I nodded and looked down. When she went out in the hall to drink from the fountain, I wiped my eyes. Jennifer was in high school, so I just assumed she would ignore me. She reminded me of Mrs. Briggs from church. How she just talked to me like she would with any other person, not caring at all that I was just a lowly seventh grader. Unlike a couple of the other high school girls who had ignored me the whole time.

When the eight of us were onstage, Midge stood off to the side.

Just like Jennifer suggested, I stood in the second row behind her.

"Ready, everyone?" Midge pressed the play button on the stereo next to her.

At first, everything seemed to go fine. With all my attention on the kind high schooler in front of me, I managed to go right when I was supposed to go right, and hop left when I was supposed to hop left. I might have been a split second off coming out of a pose or two, but all things considered—surprise, surprise—the dancing was actually going much better than my singing had!

With the final pose only seconds away, the eight of us prepared to spin, turn, and then high-kick to the side with our right legs.

Spin, turn, high-kick, THUMP.

THUMP was . . . *not* part of the dance. I kicked as high as I could with my right leg, perhaps a little harder than I should have, maybe with a bit more energy than was called for. *Why?* Maybe it was because I was so excited to make it through the dancing part of the audition alive that I forgot I hadn't actually made it through yet.

THUMP. When I kicked my right leg as high as I could, I guess I put so much force behind it that I forgot to keep my left leg strong and rooted to the floor.

THUMP. I fell hard and *loud* on the stage. The remaining seven dancers completed their last three moves—arm swoops, hop to the back (right past me), and pose.

I didn't know what else to do, so I hopped up as quickly as I could, double-timed my arm swoops, hopped to the back, and posed with the rest of the dancers like nothing had happened, like I had not just performed the most colossal wipeout ever seen in the history of Kansas theater.

The music ended, and with it, so did any hope that I would make the play.

CHAPTER 24

At least I had basketball. Well, sort of anyway.

I was far from the star of the team. That honor was Natalie's, and pretty much Natalie's alone. She was to our seventh-grade team what Danny Manning was to KU's college team. I was more like Scooter Barry. Never heard of him? Yeah, well, it was because he was a hard worker who didn't score much. Not the stuff of headlines. Like Scooter, I didn't make a ton of baskets either, but that wasn't my job. My job was to get the ball to Danny Manning, aka Natalie "Skyscraper" Moreno.

Even though she and I weren't friends, we were teammates, so we *had to* work together. I needed to put my negative feelings toward her aside when we were on the court.

The day after my disastrous audition, we had our second

game. It was perfect timing because I needed something to keep my mind from replaying "hond fart" and *thump!* over and over again. Our opponent was another middle school in Topeka. Auburn Hills Middle School students lived way out past the mall, past the stretch of road where there were five different churches in a row. These kids' houses sprawled across at least an acre of land. My mom used to drive out there and admire the huge homes, especially ones near the lake.

"That one has its own tennis court!" she liked to point out. "I went to an open house for that one. It has a pool . . . *indoors.*"

Knowing these kids lived in a place my mom only dreamed of living made me want to crush them even more. Like bugs instead of the "Eagles" they claimed to be.

Tweet! At the start of the game, Natalie jumped higher than the Auburn Hills center and tipped the ball to me—on purpose, not an accident like in our first scrimmage. Like we had gone over in practice, Natalie ran to the basket as hard as she could and posted up. We made eye contact and I hurled the ball to her. With her long arms up and ready, there was no way her defender, who was a good half foot shorter than her, could get it. Natalie's team nickname wasn't "Skyscraper" for nothin.' Layup. Two easy points.

Auburn Hills' ball. Even though their point guard was at least a couple of inches taller than me, she didn't have pent-up frustrations about making a total fool of herself onstage yesterday. I stuck to her like glue. Where she went, there I was. I stole the ball from her three times in the first half.

Back and forth the teams traded leads throughout the first three quarters.

Near the end of the game I stole the ball from the opposing guard a fourth time. As I turned to run back down the court, the other team's guard was finally as frustrated and fed up as I was. At least I'm assuming she was because she pushed me hard from behind, sending me sprawling across the court.

Truthfully, she didn't push me *that* hard, but I careened forward out of control like she did. I slid, rolled, and left a sweaty smear across the gym floor. For extra effect, I just lay there until two teammates came to help me up.

Tweet! Foul called and two free-throw shots for me. I hadn't scored anything the entire game. Natalie had scored over twenty points, and I'd had a number of assists (meaning I'd passed the ball to Natalie), but points? In that arena, I had *nothing*.

My team was down 33–34 with only two seconds left in the game. If I made these two shots, we would pretty much be guaranteed the win. Sure, there *were* teams that had launched desperate shots with only that much time left and won. But those types of miracles usually only happened with pro or college teams, not ones in seventh grade at the beginning of their season.

The referee handed me the ball after the girls lined up on either side of the key.

Like I practiced at home with the hoop across the street, I bounced the ball twice and locked my eyes on the basket. I made sure to use my legs as I unwound and released the ball. I flicked my wrist, followed through with my hand, and left it up pointing toward the basket. As I released the ball, it sailed through the air . . . *clunk, clonk* . . . it bounced around the rim a couple of times . . . but then dropped in the hoop!

Tie game! Not to mention this basket was my first official point of the season! A cheer sounded from the—I wouldn't exactly call it a crowd—more like the small gathering of reluctant parents who probably didn't really want to be here. My dad's voice was mixed in there, too. He wasn't very loud, but I heard him anyway. At the very least, we would head into overtime.

That is, unless I made this next shot. In which case, we would . . .

I blocked out any thought of winning for the moment. Everyone disappeared—the spectators on the bleachers, my dad's hopeful gaze, my teammates on the bench locking arms. I concentrated only on the task at hand, which was to make this last free throw. Following the exact same routine as before,

I released the ball and it hit the backboard hard—*clonk!*—and then fell into the net. It sure wasn't a pretty one, but a basket's a basket.

We won! Wait, not yet—there were still a few seconds left on the clock. The ref blew her whistle and handed the other team the ball. I bounced up and down and waved my arms in the opposing player's sweaty red face. The end-of-game buzzer sounded, and our win was official. We won. We won!

My team surrounded me, patted me on my back, and gave me high fives.

"Good job, Annie!"

"Dang, girl! You have ice running through your veins. That's what we should call you—'Ice'!"

"Way to pull through, Annie!"

Even Natalie, who I hadn't really liked at all this past summer, congratulated me.

"Nice flop, Shorty!"

"What flop?" I feigned innocence. "And it's 'Ice' now, thank you very much."

"You're the best actor I know." Natalie grinned. "Not a half bad ballplayer, either. Way to win it for the team."

Natalie had made twenty-five points that game. "I made two points," I pointed out. "If anyone won the game for us, it was you."

Coach Johnson came up and gave us both fives. "Kirsten was a beast on defense, and Angie's offense was on fire. And never discount the importance of making the clutch play, Annie! The *team* won the game," she pointed out.

I have to admit, it felt pretty good. *Team.* To be part of something bigger than just myself.

Then my dad wandered toward me with the tallest man I'd ever seen in my life. He lumbered over toward Natalie with a slight limp, and had dark hair streaked with gray. He was holding a pink jacket, though it looked more like a handkerchief in his enormous hands. Pretty clear now where Natalie got *her* height! "Vámonos, Natalia." He spoke to her in Spanish.

"'Kay, Dad," Natalie responded in English, just like I did when my dad said something to me in Japanese. She put her jacket on halfway.

"See ya later, Shorty." Natalie gave me a high five. "Sorry, I mean 'Ice.'"

I never realized that Natalie was actually "Natalia," too, just like I was actually Aoi.

As Natalie and her father walked away, I heard him scold her for not putting her jacket on completely and letting one sleeve trail behind her. I knew this must have been what he was saying because Natalie groaned, stopped, and put the rest of her jacket on quite deliberately. Up until now, I had only considered Natalie as a teammate at best. But as I watched this interaction, for some reason it made me feel like maybe someday we could be friends, too.

On the drive home, my dad was even more excited for me than I was.

"Wow, Aoi, that was like the game last week against Missouri!" As KU Jayhawks fans, we hated the Mizzou Tigers with a passion. I hated the Puke Poo Devils more, but Mizzou was a pretty close second. Last week, KU had won a nail-biter against Mizzou 78–74. At home. The crowd went *wild*.

Our middle school game took place on a sleepy Saturday morning where only the parents attended. And not *all* the parents, either. Just the parents who lost the coin toss or drew the short straw or whatever and had to wake up early on the weekend even though that was the only time they could sleep in. If our game was as exciting as he seemed to think it was, then the other parents wouldn't be looking as grouchy as they were. "Dad, our game wasn't anything like that."

We had watched a recording of the KU-Mizzou game together the day after it took place since Dad had to work when the game was actually on. You'd think that since the semester ended he would have a bit of a break, but now there were "semester-beginning" duties that the department chair had to handle, too. We were able to keep from hearing about the results of the game, though, so it was just as exciting as watching it in real time. No way that my game this morning was anywhere near as exciting as the KU-Mizzou one, even the *recording* of the game.

"You ran the point like Scooter Barry!" Dad exclaimed. "And those last two free throws won the game! It's not easy to shoot like that under pressure."

"Maybe . . ." I gazed out the window as we drove home, white snow drifts covering the dull gray trees against the chilly bleak sky. I tried to keep my mind off the colorful costumes and cheerful music from *The King and I*, but my mind kept going back. Although the cast hadn't been announced yet, I assumed I wouldn't be part of it. I sighed. It would have been nice to have something like that to work on during these cold, drab months.

"You know," Dad mused. "Scooter Barry's father was a free-throw pro. One of the best ever! But he shot underhanded."

While Scooter Barry wasn't all that well-known, his dad, Rick Barry, played for the NBA. He was *very* famous, especially for his super-reliable underhanded free-throw shooting technique.

I knew what my dad was getting at. "Ugh, Dad. No way am I shooting granny-style."

My dad laughed. "Sou ne. Kakko warui ne."

"Yeah, Dad. Not stylish. *At* all."

Maybe basketball would be my thing. This morning's game sure felt awesome. But I didn't know why afterward, I felt the need to push away my dad's shooting suggestions. Maybe it was because I knew what my mom would think about basketball as my new dream, and maybe I noticed how Dad didn't compare me to the short but powerful NBA sensation Muggsy Bogues like he had in the past, but instead to the dependable workhorse Scooter Barry.

Or maybe it was because my teammate's comment that made me happiest was Natalie's . . .

"You're the best actor I know."

CHAPTER 25

On Monday, I doodled a basketball in the margins of the handout Mrs. Olds had Ben (of course!) distribute. As Mrs. Olds droned on, my cartoon took shape. I could almost hear the roar of the crowd as my mind wandered to the court where I was on the same team as Muggsy Bogues. He had just stolen the ball, but instead of running it up the court himself, he motioned for me to cut to the basket. With lightning speed, I outran the other team *and* the clock as it counted down—five, four, three . . . And just as the buzzer was about to sound, I jumped as high as I could. Muggsy lobbed the ball at me—*alley-oop!* I caught it in midair, right over the basket, and then . . . *SLAM DUNK!* The crowd roared. Ben (who just happened to be in the audience) rose to his feet and cheered—

"Miss Enoway!"

When I heard my teacher announce my name from a

distance that felt dangerously close, I slid my arm quickly over the sketch.

"Yes, Mrs. Olds?" I looked up.

She held a pink slip in her claws—I mean, *hands*.

"Seems they need you in the office." She raised an eyebrow at me in a way that made me think she didn't know what this was about, either.

"Um . . . okay." There were only ten minutes left in class, but ten minutes in this class felt like an hour.

"Better take your stuff with you." Mrs. Olds's hard, washed-out eyes glittered as she narrowed them at me, like this little blip of disturbance to her class regimen was *my* fault.

I packed up everything as quickly as I could and glanced back at Ben as I left the class. He grinned at me and I grinned back. Prison break! We were always happy when any student was spared from the agony that was "Math with the Monster." I had no idea why I was called out of class, but whatever the reason, it would be better than having to spend more time in that Dungeon of Dull.

When I opened the door to the front office, I was greeted with a sneaker to my rear end. "Hey!" I yelped as I spun around.

It was Jessica. God, I wished she'd stop with the butt-kicking! Whatever happened to a good old-fashioned "Hello"?

"What are you doing here?" I wondered why *she* wasn't in class, either.

"Waiting for you, silly!" Jessica jumped up, tucked a few papers and a couple folders under her arm, and waved to the office assistant in the back. "Thanks, Mrs. C!"

"Of course, sweetie!" Mrs. Cunningham waved back.

Jessica grabbed my arm and pulled me through the door and back out into the hallway.

"Don't I have to check in?" I showed Jessica my pink slip, still not sure exactly what was going on.

"I just did that for you." She grinned. "*I* got you out of class."

"You did? Why? And *how*?"

My friend pushed me down the hallway in front of her toward who knows where. "Mrs. C and my mom went to school together," Jessica explained. "So, when Mom dropped me off today—I overslept, in case you were wondering why I wasn't on the bus this morning—I asked her if she wouldn't mind pretty-please-with-sugar-on-top calling you out of class to help me."

"Help you? With what?" With every question Jessica answered, it only led to more from me.

Sometimes Jessica's life felt so different from mine that it was hard understanding what was going on. First, I wouldn't be in such a good mood if I overslept to the point of missing the bus *and* my first two classes. *My* mom would have dropped me off, sure, but she would have chewed me out first. And my mom certainly didn't have friends here who were so close that they'd call their daughter's best friend out of math to wander the halls.

Jessica knocked on the door to one of the eighth-grade classrooms. A teacher I didn't know well opened the door and Jessica handed him a folder. "From the office," she told him.

He took the folder and closed the door behind him. Since Jessica continued walking down the hall, I assumed that meant I should follow.

"This doesn't seem like a two-person job." While I was happy to get out of Mrs. Olds's class, Jessica clearly was onto something I had no clue about. I didn't like feeling like she was keeping something from me (and was having fun while doing it!).

Jessica stopped in front of Mr. Malder's classroom. Even though this was another class in the eighth-grade hallway, I knew this one. Mr. Malder was the most popular teacher in the school. His English class wasn't about papers and grammar. It was skits and reenactments, speeches and movies that parents had to give permission to watch. Every eighth grader *prayed* they'd get this English class and not the other one with Mrs. Lloyd. She was nice enough, but she loved Charles Dickens and pretty much only Charles Dickens and she looked just about as old. Maybe they were childhood friends (ha!).

"Fine, *you* do this one, then." Jessica handed me a folder.

When I knocked on the door, the teacher opened it a crack. "From the office," I said.

But Mr. Malder didn't just take the folder. He opened it and looked inside. "Oh, great. Can you come in for a minute?"

Jessica and I traded looks. We were being invited into magical Mr. Malder's kingdom! We tiptoed our way behind him. A student was at the front of the classroom presenting.

"Let's see, I know it was here somewhere." Mr. Malder looked through the stacks of paper on his messy desk. His pencils were topped with cute trolls with wild green hair.

As Jessica and I waited, my attention turned to RJ Butterfield, the boy giving his speech at the front of the room.

"I think it was great that we nuked the Japs," he said. Clear as day and with the same ease someone might say, "Nice morning, isn't it?"

All the blood felt like it was draining from my body and my hands turned ice cold. *What did he just say?*

I looked around, but there was barely a reaction. A girl checking her hair for split ends. A boy picking his nose. But the rest of the students were facing forward. Like they were listening. They *had* to have heard.

"'Cause they bombed us first, you know? Pearl Harbor. They wanted to take over America, make us speak Japanese, ching chong . . . ching chong." Mr. Malder looked up briefly, but then continued signing the forms in the folder I handed him. *He heard too but . . . why wasn't he doing anything? Saying anything?* I turned to Jessica. She was playing with one of the troll-topped pencils on the teacher's desk. At this point RJ looked at me, like he *just* realized I was there. I glared, daring him to continue.

"No offense." Clearly, he didn't see me as a threat at all. And then to drive home this point, he laughed. *Heh heh . . . heh.*

All those eighth graders turned to see who RJ was addressing his comments to. *Me.* The class was *silent.* The teacher was *silent.* I didn't know it was possible for silence to be loud, but it was. It was *deafening.*

All the blood that had rushed out of my body rushed back in. And it was boiling.

Mr. Malder put down his pen and handed me back the folder. "Can you take this back to the office and save me a trip? Thanks!"

I staggered out of the room as fast as I could manage. Before I said anything or did anything I would regret.

This time, it was my turn to speed down the hall.

Jessica trotted to keep up. "Isn't Mr. Malder cool? I totally want him for English next year. Hey, slow down, why are you walking so fast?"

I needed to get as far away from RJ, Mr. Malder, *everyone*—and that included Jessica—in that class as I could.

Jessica ran to catch up with me. I was so mad I was shaking.

"Hey, what's wrong?" My friend's easy-breezy attitude disappeared when she saw my face.

"What's *wrong*? RJ is what's wrong. Didn't you hear what he said?"

Jessica frowned. "RJ? You mean in Mr. Malder's class?"

"And don't get me started on Mr. Malder—" *And you*, I thought. *You didn't say anything, either.*

"What *did* he say? I wasn't listening. . . ."

I stopped and looked into my best friend's eyes. Jessica seemed genuinely confused. "Did he say something bad?"

"Yeah, he did!" I responded. I recounted what I'd heard of his speech word for word.

"Oh my God!" Jessica looked aghast. "I wasn't listening, I swear! Besides, RJ's a butthead. Everyone knows that."

Maybe she really didn't hear, I thought. I *hoped.*

Jessica shifted back and forth on her feet. I could tell she was uncomfortable. People who looked like her generally were when presented with situations like this.

"I bet Mr. Malder wasn't paying attention," Jessica said. "He *was* signing a bunch of stuff."

That's another thing that happens. They make excuses for people they like and refuse to *see* that maybe they aren't as great as everyone thinks they are. I replayed what happened in that room. The kids turning to stare at me. Mr. Malder looking up. *He* heard. I know he did. But Jessica . . . Jessica was playing with the troll's-head pencil.

I took a deep breath and chose to believe that at least Jessica didn't hear what RJ said in that room. Because not believing my best friend was just something I couldn't bear.

Jessica seemed to sense my decision. "Come on! I have just the thing to make you forget all about jerky ol' RJ."

Jessica speed-walked down the hall and turned the corner. I followed her, trying to be excited to know what was up—*finally*.

"Here we are!" We stopped in front of a bulletin board outside the music room.

"Here we are, *what*?" My nerves were already worn thin, and my impatience was about to bubble over.

Jessica unzipped her Christmas present—a fancy oversized purse covered in the designer's logo—and pulled out a couple of sheets of folded paper.

She held one up to the bulletin board and pushed a tack through one corner. She put the other one up too and did the same. "Hey, can you tell me if this is straight?" She lifted the unpinned corner and lifted it up to the right.

"Really? *This* is what you needed help with?" I crossed my arms. The trauma from RJ's speech had just started to wear off and all I felt was tired now. I even kind of wished I was back in math class and this adventure with Jessica never happened.

"Is it straight or not?" Jessica laughed.

"It's straight!" I blurted out with exasperation. "No, wait, bring it down a little. . . . You didn't *really* think you needed two people to do this, did you?"

Jessica ignored me as she did the same thing with the other sheet. "It totally does! Now, can you read it from where you're standing?"

"Read it? No . . ." I was so busy wondering what Jessica was up to that I didn't even think to ask what these papers were about. "Are those . . . ?"

I was barely five feet away, but I dashed to the bulletin board anyway, and nearly ran into the wall in the process.

Omigod, omigod, omigod. These were the cast announcements for *The King and I*! Jessica wouldn't have made such a grand production of it if I weren't part of it, right? Because that would have been cruel, and best friends aren't like that!

I scanned the list. Of course, the main parts of the king and Anna went to high school students whose names I didn't recognize, but holy moly—

"Jessica, you're *Tuptim*?" I thought for sure that Jennifer would get that part since we all knew she was talented *and* a high school student, but . . .

"Keep on reading," Jessica urged.

I scanned down the list. "Ben made it, too?" He was going to be Louis. As far as middle school roles go, it was a pretty good one!

"Come on, Annie, don't make me have to point it out for you." Jessica was getting flustered.

It was then that I saw my name. MY NAME.

ELIZA: Annie Inoue

It took me a second to process this news. I fell down *hard* in the choreography part of the audition. I never in a million years imagined I'd be cast as a lead dancer.

Overall, my part in the musical was small, but Eliza was the main character of the short dance that the servants put on for the king.

I'll take it.

After convincing myself that I wouldn't be part of the production at all, this was good news—no, this was GREAT news!

"We're gonna be in the play?" I asked, not quite believing this stroke of good luck, especially after the morning I'd just had.

"We're gonna be in the play!" Jessica shrieked back.

We grabbed each other's hands and jumped up and down. With each jump, I stomped down RJ's words. Down, down, down where they wouldn't bother me anymore.

"Girls? Why aren't you in class?" The school nurse stood in the hallway with her hands on her hips.

"Mrs. C asked us to post these," Jessica replied without an ounce of guilt or missing a beat. "Just finished!"

Then Jessica grabbed my sleeve and pulled me after her as we walked as quickly as we could from the scene.

I could feel the nurse's eyes on us as we passed her, but then the bell rang, and we disappeared among the students who poured out of the classrooms.

Eliza. I am Eliza. I floated instead of walked to my locker and then to my next class, I focused on this thought instead of RJ's ugly words. *I am Eliza*, I repeated to myself as I ignored other questions that tickled and scratched at the edge of my mind like a tag on my sweater—such as *how* had I managed to get so lucky after such a disastrous audition? *Why* did Jessica have the casting sheets before anyone else? And did she *really* not hear what RJ said?

CHAPTER 26

School, basketball, theater rehearsals, doctor's office. My schedule was jam-packed. Sometimes I wished I had a potion like the ones Alice had in Wonderland to get everything done.

I thought coffee might be that potion. One morning, I casually grabbed the instant Folgers Crystals to make myself a cup when my mom stopped me.

"What are you doing?"

"Umm . . . I thought I'd have some coffee like you guys."

"We have coffee because we're adults. You're twelve. Twelve-year-olds don't drink coffee."

Why not? I thought but didn't ask. Dad let me have Sanka sometimes. How different could Folgers be?

Because my mom could read my mind, though, she answered. "It has caffeine and caffeine is a . . . drug."

What? I almost burst out laughing. I countered with, "So, Dad and you do drugs?"

As soon as I blurted out this smart-alecky question, I wished I could take it back.

Tak almost spat out his milk and his eyes grew wide. "You do?" He looked back and forth between our parents.

My mom's eyes flashed. *How dare you disrespect me?*

"Stimulant. Mom meant it's a 'stimulant,'" Dad jumped in. "And it stunts your growth. You want to grow taller, don't you?"

I sighed and put the coffee back.

Mom wasn't done with me yet. "If you're so tired, maybe we should rethink your basketball and theater commit—"

"I'm fine!" I interrupted. "Daijoubu da yo."

I'm fine.

And really I was. *The King and I* and basketball were helping me get through the cold winter months that usually got me down. When the wind cut like knives through my overcoat and chilled me to the bone, running around in the gym and scrimmaging with my teammates warmed my body up in no time.

But musical rehearsals warmed my *soul*. With the high school students as part of the production, rehearsals held an entirely different vibe from this summer. The adults in *Annie* were nice and everything, but it wasn't like any of us orphans *wanted* to hang out with ol' Daddy Warbucks and thirtysomething Miss Hannigan when we weren't rehearsing.

The high schoolers, though, were *cool*. Kevin, the senior who was cast as the king, was over six feet tall. He played football during the fall, and now he was on the swim team too. Technically, he was blond, but he buzzed off all his hair for the first rehearsal, just so he could look as much the part as possible.

"I have to shave the rest of my body when I race, anyway," he casually remarked when all our jaws dropped. "This way, I don't have to spend money on swim caps this season."

Michelle, who played the schoolmistress Anna Leonowens, had dark messy hair, and wore all black clothes and clunky boots that she laced up only halfway. Her eyes looked sunken from all her black eyeliner. She smelled like a fireplace, but on the first day of rehearsal when Sam said, "No smoke breaks, either, okay? No matter *how much* you might feel like you need one," and looked right at her, Michelle shrugged and explained that her friends smoked, not her.

"Yeah, okay." Sam was clearly not convinced at all.

Michelle just looked away. She clearly couldn't care less.

But when she took the stage, she changed *completely*. She became a bright and assertive do-gooder. She was maternal, earnest, and openhearted—all the things that Michelle clearly was *not*. Or maybe she was, but she just hid it really well.

In any case, she was *awesome*.

But perhaps the most intriguing high schooler was Kent Wright, who played Tuptim's boyfriend and forbidden love, Lun Tha. He was fifteen years old and not quite as tall as Kevin, but he was thin and muscular and—I'm not saying this because I liked him or anything, but because objectively speaking it was just the truth—*so* good-looking it was almost distracting. With a wavy mop of dark brown hair and piercing black eyes, he was the closest person to a movie star any of us had ever seen.

Jessica was the middle schooler with the biggest part. She was Tuptim, the youngest and reluctant new wife of the king (he had more than a few). Jessica was a little older for our grade—she turned thirteen in September, so technically Kent was only a couple of years older than her.

The high schoolers were pretty nice to the middle schoolers. I guess it didn't hurt that we idolized them. All of us except for Ben. He thought they were full of themselves and in return they treated him like a pesky little fly.

I still liked Ben, though.

While Jessica rehearsed her romantic scenes with Kent, Ben, offstage, substituted his own song lyrics for the real ones, kind of like he did when he made up his own dialogue during summer rehearsals for *Annie*. When Tuptim and Lun Tha secretly meet and lament about how they have to kiss in the shadows,

Ben whisper-sang to me, "We sing very loudly, so we get caught right away. We knew this was wrong, but . . . just had to burst into song."

He also drew funny pictures in the margins of our script, like a scene from math class with Mrs. Olds as the devil, complete with horns and a pitchfork. The rest of us were clearly in hell, judging by the flames he drew around all of us.

I laughed and laughed when Ben showed me. But then I remembered what Ms. Tracy had told us about our copies of the scripts. "Wait, are we allowed to draw on these?"

Ben's eyes widened and he grabbed an eraser. "Oops!"

It felt so good to laugh with Ben again like we did last summer. Even though we had two classes together, we barely interacted during first-period science since neither of us were morning people. When he wasn't letting out monstrous yawns, he had his head down on his desk, always turned to his left. I was still sleepy in science, too, which made it easy to slip into my daydreams. Like imagining I was seated to the left of Ben and that's why he always tilted his head that way. In math, Mrs. Olds had seated us next to each other before winter break, but she separated us when she caught me smiling once. Ben had murmured something to *me*, but of course it was *my* grin that got us in trouble. Because Mrs. Olds felt the need to squash any sign of happiness when she was around.

"Tsk, tsk, Annie. Flirting with the boys again, are we? Girls can be such one-celled amoeba brains, can't they, class?" It was so embarrassing to be called out like that I wanted to shrink as small as a mouse and skitter away, never to be seen again. Or at least not in math class.

To their credit, *none* of the girls in the class laughed. For one, what she said didn't make any sense—Natalie was the best student in the class by far! We all detested Mrs. Olds. She said things like that to us *all* the time. A couple of meathead boys let out prehistoric-sounding snorts like Bigfoot might make, but otherwise the class was silent. Mrs. Olds simpered and smiled to herself like she was the funniest person in the world. When she turned to scratch her white chalk across the dusty board in front of the class, Ben mouthed "Sorry" to me.

After that, neither of us talked to each other in that class.

Even though we sat together at lunch, Jessica sat with us too. I don't know why, but I had been feeling a little distant from Jessica for the past couple of months. At the beginning of the school year, I figured it was because we were just at a new school, and it would take us a little time to find our groove, especially since we didn't have recesses to hang out during anymore, and we only had PE and lunch together. But that feeling grew after I made the basketball team and I had three practices a week plus weekend game commitments. We didn't see each other at all over the holidays since I was sick, either. She called a few times, but it wasn't the same as elementary school when she would come over and make believe we were space shuttle pilots in my sycamore tree, or when I'd go over to her place and we'd play with her dolls and stuffed animals. When we sat together at lunch, I made sure to talk with her as much as I did with Ben.

But, since Jessica had a bigger part than either Ben or I did, I figured it was fine for me to spend more time with him, especially when she was devoting all her attention to her castmate Kent. Jessica's acting had really matured since we first auditioned for *Annie*. I mean, she *really* seemed to be in love with Kent . . . I mean, "Lun Tha."

Since I had basketball practices on the nights that there weren't theater rehearsals, I often found myself doing homework backstage with Ben when we weren't working on the parts that we were in (which was pretty often).

"Wow, how'd you figure out that answer?" Ben asked during one rehearsal, looking over at the math handout I had just completed. It might have just been me being paranoid, but it seemed like Mrs. Olds was deliberately assigning us even *more* homework once rehearsals began. But this was Mrs. Olds we're talking about, so I'm sure I wasn't imagining it.

"This question?" I asked him. He nodded.

The question Ben was stuck on wasn't that hard. But I knew not to say that, and just showed him the steps I took instead.

"I'm not sure this is the best way to solve it, but I did it this way."

"Oooh, okay!" Ben smacked his head. "Of course!" Then he copied down my answer.

I frowned. "Won't Mrs. Grumpy-Face take points off if you don't show your work?"

Ben shrugged. "I dunno. She usually takes it easy on me."

Of course—teacher's pet.

But then I remembered something Jessica told me last week after rehearsal after I told her how I helped Ben with his homework. "Guys don't like it when you act smarter than them."

"What if you *are* smarter than them?" I responded.

Jessica sighed. She was getting impatient with me. "Then *act* like you're not. Guys don't like *brains*."

I don't know why all of a sudden Jessica talked to me like she had so much more experience with boys. Or that she had insight into how I could get Ben to feel the same way I felt about him. But I listened to her because I *so* needed him to like me.

So, today I played it different. I peeked over at Ben's worksheet. There was a problem there that was a *little* more involved than the other ones. When Ben wasn't looking, I *erased* the answer to it on my own handout.

"How'd you figure that out, Ben?" I asked.

He seemed surprised. "You couldn't do it?"

I shrugged. That wasn't exactly lying.

He sat up straighter and went through his steps. "Well, first I did this . . . and then this . . ." He erased a miscalculation and then penciled in the correct one. "And then got this!"

"Oooh." I tried to sound surprised and amazed. "I get it now!"

Ben beamed. I could have gone on forever pretending like this for that smile! There was another set of problems that was also due tomorrow, but he had already finished them. Even though I hadn't started those, I put away my homework at the same time he did.

I had felt a little weird about playing dumb like Jessica had advised, but when Ben smiled at me, I knew Jessica was right.

Even though things were different in middle school, she was still my best friend.

CHAPTER 27

Jessica's singing had really improved since the summer, too. Not that she was bad before, but now she was even better! Even though Jessica's "vocal coach" (I had no idea that there was such a thing before Jessica told me she had one) said she was technically a "mezzo-soprano," Tuptim's high notes didn't seem to worry her as much as they did when she was Annie.

When Sam stopped the music during one of her songs and wanted to practice a certain phrase over again, instead of looking nervous like she did this summer, Jessica tossed her hair back and said, "My singing coach and I will work on that."

Jessica's mom had given her these singing lessons for her birthday. I could totally tell they helped!

Asking for singing lessons for Christmas briefly crossed my mind, but everything was so hectic, I felt bad about adding to that. My birthday wasn't until May, so I decided to put them out of my mind until then. What I really needed were dancing lessons because Midge sure wasn't holding back on the choreography!

If the moves we learned for the audition seemed hard, the actual dance she wanted us to learn for the musical was a hundred times more elaborate.

The first day she showed us what it would look like, she danced all the parts, but like she was on fast forward. "So, you're Eliza and this dance is showing how you try and escape from the evil Simon Legree. Your part is going to look like this. You gals start out here, and then you come through here. Then you go through here and pose. Then hop, hop, hop—"

My eyes widened when she kept on going . . . and going. The cat-eyed glasses perched on her nose bounced along with her bleached-blond curls that spilled from her high ponytail like a bubbling fountain.

"When the narrator talks about climbing a mountain, there are gonna be three guys here on their hands and knees and you're gonna walk over their backs—"

Wait, what?

"And then when the narrator talks about the river, oh my! You'll crouch down here, and these girls will wave sheets of 'water,' know what I mean? No? Well, you just wait until the angel shows up and the sheets of water turn to ice so you can cross the river—"

Was I supposed to take notes? None of the other dancers

were. They were just nodding their heads like these directions made all the sense in the world.

"And then the grand finale! Swoop, swoop here with your arms, and swoop, swoop there, now bow, kick—and don't forget to keep your supporting leg stable—"

Midge paused at this moment to give me a sly wink.

"Oh, and I had almost forgotten. You're escaping to find your lover, George, and you're going to be carrying a dolly—also named George—throughout this dance. And that's it! Whaddaya think, Eliza?"

I gulped. "Cool . . . ?"

"Great!" Midge clapped her hands, once and loud. "Your turn!"

My what?

Before I could have a heart attack and die right there on the stage, Midge slapped me on the back and cackled.

"Kidding, darling! I'm just kidding!"

I let out my breath while managing a weak smile.

Midge wheezed; she was still laughing. "Oh, sweetie, the look on your face. No, no, don't worry, I'll get you through it. Midgey always does! But you gotta practice at home, too. You got some mirrors there?"

The only mirrors in my house that were large enough for me to practice in front of were the mirrored sliding doors to my parents' closet in their bedroom. Mom raised an eyebrow when I asked if I could practice in there, but she said I could as long as I didn't make a mess and left as soon as she needed the room back.

One nice aspect about the dance is that Tuptim narrates it as it happens, so it's almost as if I had directions while dancing it. Midge provided me with a cassette tape of the music to work with, too. Sundays seemed like the only quiet day of the week anymore, so that's when I decided to work on it at home.

At first, it was dreadful. Those full-length mirrors really highlighted how far I had to go before I could dance the way Midge showed us (she made it look so easy!). But they were also really helpful. When I was finally able to look at myself and my dancing without cringing, I could figure out how to correct some of my mistakes.

For instance, I thought I was holding my back, non-hopping leg up high, but I really wasn't. When I hoisted it up higher, it looked way better in the reflection, even though it was a much harder position to hold. But I could do it—my legs were still strong from basketball, even though I could hardly move over winter break. I needed to arch my back more, too, and lengthen my neck. When I shook my hands and fingers, I needed to exaggerate the movements more, especially if I wanted everyone in the audience to see—

"Again?"

My mother called out sharply from the kitchen.

"What do you mean, 'again'?" My father sounded tired and tense.

"You know how much money we have, but you still send *that much* home?"

"We can afford it."

I stopped working on my pose and cracked the door open an inch, so I could better hear what my parents were talking about. They were speaking in Japanese and my mom was talking especially fast, so I had to concentrate to understand.

"I'm the one who handles the finances, you know that, and I'm telling you *we can't*."

"But I'm the oldest. It was my responsibility to take care of them—"

"I'm not saying that you *shouldn't* help, but why do you feel you have to give to the point it hurts *this* family? Aoi should have lessons, tutoring—"

"She's doing fine!"

"But she could be doing *better*. My sister's kids have lessons and tutoring after school. They're going to get into the best schools. Aoi needs to start thinking about that, too."

"She's *twelve*!" Dad responded with what *I* was thinking. "And *I'm* the only one providing for this family!" My father hardly ever raised his voice, but when he did it was scary.

"And *I* do everything here because you work all the time!"

I felt a pang of guilt at my mom's words. With school,

basketball, and now the musical, I had less time to help with chores. I didn't have much time to play with Tak, either, so my mom absorbed the bulk of his shenanigans.

"I'm department chair." My dad was starting to sound beaten down. "I have to get this grant in on time, or . . . It'll get better once I've sent it in."

"I just find it *very* interesting what parts of America you find so easy to adopt, but what parts of Japanese life you just can't seem to leave behind—"

Tak's door creaked open and he appeared, clutching his Man-At-Arms action figure I had given him for Christmas.

"What are they fighting about?" he whispered. Since he barely spoke Japanese at all, he had to ask me to translate a lot of the time. At this moment, I kind of wished I didn't understand what they were saying, either.

"Dad said something about the way the steak tasted tonight," I lied. "Mom's telling him if he doesn't like her cooking, he should try making dinner himself sometime."

"Dad said *that*? He should know better." Tak looked relieved. "But it *was* kind of tough. I had to chew *a lot*."

I nodded. "Me too."

"Maybe I could make dinner sometimes," Tak responded with a thoughtful look on his face. "I'm pretty good with a knife now."

"You are!" I agreed as I hustled him back into his room.

"But I think we should just let them work it out. Hey, think of something we could do, and I'll play with you later, okay?"

"When?"

"Thirty minutes? But you have to be good for that whole time. Do you think you can do that?"

"Of course I can!" Tak scoffed, like asking him to be quiet and well behaved for half an hour was no challenge at all . . . even though all of us had yet to see it happen.

I went back into my parents' bedroom, pressed play on our cassette player, and turned the volume up until my parents' voices were muffled.

Hop, hop, hop, hop . . . I would definitely not be asking my mom for any dance lessons anytime soon . . . if ever.

Run, Eliza, run. Hop, hop, hop, hop. As Eliza ran away from the evil Simon Legree, I imagined her running (or hopping, I guess in her case) toward a better future.

I'll make you proud, I thought as I pretended the pillows I piled on the floor were the mountain I needed to climb.

I'll make my dreams come true, I thought as I imagined the river turning to ice, so I could cross it.

I just hope I can do both, I thought as I crouched down into one of my final poses and waited for the angel to come down and rescue me.

CHAPTER 28

"So, what do you think the deal is?" Ben asked while we were watching rehearsal a couple of weeks later. We were both sitting backstage since neither of us were in the scene Sam was directing at the moment.

"What deal?" I asked. "You mean, what's going on between those two?" The two leads—Kevin, the giant, bald jock-turned-theater-nerd, and Michelle, who we dubbed "Moody Michelle"—were clearly having issues. It was unsettling how quickly Michelle could change from sunny to dark and glum, just like the weather in Kansas. Kevin was a star football player and swimmer. More than a few of us wondered why he decided to try his hand at theater his senior year.

"No, Sam. *Her* deal. Why do you think she's bothering with dinky little theater productions in Topeka if she was a big-shot Hollywood director before?"

"Well, she's from here," I answered slowly. "And she's staying with her mother, right? Maybe she wanted some more time with her." I guess *I* had been so impressed with the caliber of our productions and that so many people wanted to be a part of them that it never occurred to me that Sam might think they were beneath her.

"I don't know . . ." Ben sounded dubious.

The scene wasn't going so well. I could tell not because I had been paying much attention at all, but because Sam pulled out a box of Raisinets this time and threw a couple down her throat. She gulped them without chewing, like they were aspirin and could cure the headache that was happening before her eyes. They were trying to block the scene, so in addition to her usual dark and angry way of dressing, Michelle wore a wide hoop skirt (one that she would be wearing for the actual performances) over her ripped jeans. It was pretty clear Kevin and Michelle *hated* each other from the way they stood—arms crossed and facing opposite directions. When they were forced to look at each other, it was like they were shooting daggers out of their eyes.

"I was doing it that way because Michelle said—" Kevin was explaining something to Sam when Michelle interrupted.

"Oh, don't you blame your 'acting' choices on me." She drove the point home with air quotes around the word *acting*. I always found that annoying. I'm pretty sure Michelle did, too, but she did it *specifically* to get under Kevin's skin.

Kevin flung up his hands and yelled in frustration at Sam. "See? Do you *see* what I have to deal with?"

"*You?*" Michelle scoffed. "*I've* had to deal with some punk *jock*, saying, 'Gee! What if I try out for the school musical? Even though I've never been in a play *ever*!' Waltzing off the football court—"

"*Field!*" Kevin yelled. "It's a football *field* and *we don't waltz*!"

"Not to mention *disrespecting* the *craft* of acting!" Michelle screamed back.

"Oh, you wanna talk about *disrespect*? You coming in here with all your *knowledge*. With all your 'expertise'"—Kevin threw some "air quotes" right back at Michelle—"telling the *king* how to do this, do that, like you're some big know-it-all—"

"To be fair, Kevin," Sam said, trying to get the situation under some form of control, "*Anna Leonowens* tells the king—"

"Yeah, but would it *kill* you to give me some credit? The king ain't no dummy, and she treats him like he is. She's real smug about it, too. Like she thinks she's better than me."

Michelle crossed her arms. "Think? No, I *am* better—"

"Okay, *knock it off*, you two!" Sam hollered.

There *were* times in the play that there were tensions between the king and Anna, but this particular scene in which Anna teaches the king to dance was *not* one of them.

"I'm thinking maybe she's not as big a deal as she says," Ben continued to muse.

I couldn't believe with the drama between Kevin and Michelle that just blew up in front of our eyes, Ben was still laser-focused on Sam.

I liked Sam. But maybe I also wanted to believe that we were good enough that a Hollywood director found us worth her time.

"*She* never said she was a big deal," I countered. I didn't want to argue with Ben, but I also didn't like the way he was trying to take Sam down. I didn't see what his problem was with her. It reminded me of how Natalie was critical of Jessica over the summer. Even though we were friends now, I still didn't agree with her about that! I didn't see why people had to dig for underlying motives or weird reasons for why the world was the way it was. Couldn't people just get the part because they were good, and Sam just direct in Topeka because she felt like directing here?

Ben was quiet, and I worried for a second that I'd annoyed him by disagreeing with him. Sam wasn't exactly a friend, but I still felt like I needed to defend her.

"You're right," Ben agreed. "It was Ms. Tracy and my aunt who talked her up."

Sam popped another handful of candy in her mouth. "Are there issues with this musical? Yes. But this is what we got, and we got to make it work. Look, I don't care if you don't like each other in real life," she said to Michelle and Kevin, her voice getting louder and louder. "I don't care if you have voodoo dolls of each other that you stab with needles in real life. Because this ain't real life, and *you* signed up for this."

"Come on, think about it," urged Ben. "If you were doing well in Hollywood, would you come back *here*? Topeka's the type of place you can't wait to get out of, right? Or that you come back to—maybe—if you have kids. And I don't see Sam as the 'mom' type, do you?"

A good place to grow potatoes. That's what the name "Topeka" actually means. My dad said when he heard that, he knew this was the place for him. "Because . . . I *love* potatoes!" Whenever he told this story, he would smile real big, but my mom would smile in that small, tense way that made me think she didn't love potatoes nearly as much.

"So, time to suck it up, pull up your big-kid pants, separate fact from fiction, and *act*, for cryin' out loud." Sam was red-faced and shouting at Michelle and Kevin by this time.

The more I thought about what Ben said, and the more I watched Sam, the more I wondered if he was right. Directing plays and making these stories come to life so that people were transported to another place and time seemed like a great way to live one's life. But if being here was Sam's dream, it sure didn't look like she was enjoying it right now.

At that moment, Jessica plopped herself beside Ben and me. "What's going on?"

"Where've you been?" I asked. She was breathless and her face was flushed. I'd hoped Jessica and I would be able to hang out more since we were doing another theater production together, but our parts didn't overlap much. She was always rehearsing with "Lun Tha."

Kent arrived a couple of seconds after and he crouched down next to Jessica.

"Oh, nowhere," Jessica responded to me, but she was looking at Kent.

"Yeah, we were just . . . rehearsing." Kent looked straight ahead. Jessica smiled at him before she looked down and then away.

I went back to observing the drama between Kevin, Michelle, and Sam unfolding onstage. But out of the corner of my eye, I noticed Ben was watching my best friend and her costar, like there was an even bigger story happening right next to us.

CHAPTER 29

The weeks sped by and before we knew it, it was time for our show. The beginning of March was usually at the tail end of practically three months of cold, gray, and miserable weather in Topeka, but for the musical, we dressed like we were in warm and balmy Thailand.

Michelle and Ben dressed in proper 1800s British clothing, which meant a long-sleeved dress complete with a hoop skirt and *lots* of fabric for her, and beige, knee-length knickers and long socks pulled up high for Ben. In addition, he wore a brown vest over a prim collared shirt with a floppy bow-tie-like ribbon completing the boyish look.

I couldn't help grinning when I saw him.

"What?" Ben scowled. I had heard the high schoolers making fun of "Louis, oh little Louis!" earlier.

"Oh, nothing," I replied. But my face contorted in an effort to keep from laughing.

Ben played with the little tie around his neck. "Does *this* amuse you?"

"No, no." I shook my head and looked away to keep from cracking up.

"Or is it my fashionable *socks*?" Ben lifted his leg up so I could get a closer look. As if I needed one.

I blinked. They were so ridiculous.

"Then it must be my *knickers*, eh?" Ben hiked up his poofy knee-length pants and I could hold it in no longer. I burst out laughing.

"I can't believe you're making fun of me!" Ben acted all wounded.

"I'm not, I'm . . ." I was laughing so hard I was almost crying.

"Yeah, yeah." Ben broke into a lopsided smile. "No fair that I have to wear *this*, and you get to wear . . ." Ben waved his hand vaguely at my costume. "You look nice, by the way."

My heart skipped and fluttered.

Then he bounded away before I could respond.

Those of us who played Thai characters wore looser-fitting costumes than Anna and Louis Leonowens. I wore a short-sleeved silver lamé crop top and billowing, high-waisted maroon-colored pants with slits in the sides. Parent volunteers made all our costumes and one of them made sure to sew a smattering of glittering sequins over my pants, too. I pulled my shoulder-length hair back into a tight, high bun. A mom who was helping with everyone's hair and makeup had bobby-pinned any stray hairs to my head.

"Cover your eyes," she commanded, before she coated my hair in a fine mist of hairspray. When it dried, my hair felt like plastic.

Then I traced my eyes in black eyeliner. It was stage makeup and my mom never allowed me to wear any, so it felt *really* over the top. But when I thought about it, it was still less than what Michelle used every day, so I decided it was probably okay. The next step was to paint my lips a dark cranberry color, and that was it. I was stage-ready.

My castmates' process was a little more involved.

For every Thai character other than Kent, who had dark brown hair—and Kevin, who was bald—they had to drape a towel over their shoulders and have a parent volunteer help spray their hair black.

It felt strange to have so many of my castmates all have black hair now, like me. But it felt even weirder when they coated themselves in bronzer, their pale arms and legs now tan like mine, or even darker.

But my stomach downright flip-flopped when they applied their eyeliner, too, and when they did, they made sure to angle the lines up, mimicking the slant of my own eyes. Suddenly, memories of kids slanting their eyes at me on the playground flooded my brain. It was only a couple of kids, and only once. We were playing tag, and I made sure to shove them *hard* when I was "It." When they fell to the ground and cried, I said, "Oops," but not "sorry." I didn't tell my parents because talking about these types of things only makes them more real. So I sucked it up, pushed it down, and forgot about it. Only I guess I hadn't. Even though this incident happened more than five years ago and lasted less than five minutes, I remembered. My face grew hot as I watched my castmates apply their makeup. I liked this cast. They wouldn't be like those kids all those years ago. But I still bristled, like I was on alert.

"Whaddaya think?" Jessica bounded over. "Do I look like you?" Her transformation into Princess Tuptim was complete. I barely recognized her—gone was her pale complexion and freckles that were perfect for her role as Annie. In its place was a deeply bronzed face, thinner and more grown up than during our last production.

"Like me?" I was confused. "Why would you want to look like me?"

"Well, *you know*." Jessica sounded exasperated.

"I'm not *Thai*." I mimicked her tone right back to her. I regretted it right away, though, when Jessica looked hurt.

"Well, same difference, right?" She pouted.

It *wasn't* the same. But I didn't know why I felt so on edge tonight. *Must be nerves*, I thought. And then I felt bad for taking my jitters out on Jessica.

"Hey, you look great." I changed my tone. She still looked kind of mad.

"I'm just worried about the mountain-climbing part of my dance," I explained.

Jessica's expression softened. She nodded. "Oh yeah, it's tricky, isn't it?"

It was. Midge made it look so easy, but stepping on the boys' backs was actually really hard. They were on their hands and knees, and they had to stay completely still as I stepped on them. I had to balance and pose at the top, which was annoyingly difficult because it turns out cloth over skin is *slippery*. In practice, I fell off their backs at least half the time. I would be so mortified if that happened during a show.

Kent walked by and Jessica's eyes followed him.

"Break a leg, okay?" She squeezed my hand.

"Thanks. You too." I barely got my words out before Jessica turned and ran off after Kent.

Mom was skeptical when she heard the middle and high schools were going to put on a joint production of *The King and I*, but you know what? We pulled it off. *We pulled it off!* Even watching in bits and snippets from backstage, as soon as the curtains parted, I could tell we were going to knock everyone's socks off. The orchestra played together and in tune. Michelle and Kevin transformed into Anna Leonowens and the King of Siam onstage. Whatever bad feelings existed between them disappeared, or they actually fed their performances. I guess it's called "chemistry." Whatever it was, together they were *fantastic*.

Sparks flew between Jessica and Kent, too. At least I could sense how much Jessica's character, Tuptim, longed for her boyfriend, Lun Tha. Kent had a beautiful and powerful singing voice, almost to the point it overpowered Jessica's. Still, they sounded great together and I applauded for them as loudly as I could backstage. Since my dance wasn't until Act II, I was thoroughly enjoying the first one.

At intermission, though, I felt the nerves coming on. My hands grew cold. I paced back and forth in an effort to calm myself and to warm up my body.

"Hey, Annie," Sam called out to me.

I stopped.

"Relax. You'll be fine."

I nodded, not feeling fine. "Okay."

"Want some Raisinets?" Sam fished a yellow box with red lettering out from her jacket pocket.

"Um . . . sure." I held out my hand.

Sam sprinkled some into it. They were a little warm and

about to melt, so I popped them all in my mouth at once. She poured herself some directly from the box into her mouth.

"Look, kid." Sam chewed as she talked. "I've been doing this a long time and sometimes you just get a feeling about a show. This one's going well and it's only opening night. Don't wanna jinx it, but I think it's . . . special. You're gonna knock 'em dead. Okay?"

I knew Sam well enough to know that she was not an optimist and was of the mind-set that if something could go wrong, it would. So to hear her say these hopeful words put me at ease.

I nodded again, this time like I meant it. "Okay!"

I don't know if it was the little rush of sugar from the Raisinets or the pep talk, but by the time Act II started and it was time for my dance, I was ready.

A *gong* announced the beginning of the dance number, "The Small House of Uncle Thomas." Jessica began to narrate and the flutes began to play. Then she announced my name— Eliza. That was my cue.

Once onstage, I took a deep breath and concentrated on the music and my movements. I dove into the story of Eliza, the enslaved girl running away from the evil King Simon Legree.

The spotlight followed me as I hopped across the stage. It stayed on me when I posed and did my deep knee bends. It shone on me as I climbed the mountain (without falling!) and hit my pose on top. This was nothing like when I played one of the orphans in *Annie*. Except for the one time Jessica invited me to join her for a bow at the end, the spotlight was *never* on me. The rest of the dancers were in sync and the singers were all in tune.

When it was time for Eliza to cross the raging river that the angel turned to ice, Jennifer Miller—like she saved me during the audition—saved Eliza. Jennifer played the angel who showed Eliza how to skate on the ice. Following her lead— step, pose . . . step, pose—the angel guided Eliza to the other side of the river. Then she gave me a wink and a small smile that seemed to say, *You've got this, you're almost done!*

With that, the rest of the dance sped by. When it was over, the entire dancing cast turned toward the king and Anna onstage, who clapped politely for us. Then we bowed to the audience out there in the darkness of the high school auditorium. Their applause rose up and surrounded us like a golden thunder.

CHAPTER 30

After the performance, the cast gathered in the auditorium lobby to chat with family and friends before we packed up and headed home.

Not surprisingly, a crowd surrounded Michelle and Kevin. Her parents were unexpectedly normal. I don't know who I thought they'd be, but it certainly wasn't a mild-mannered man in a crumpled suit and a mom in a pastel cable-knit sweater who looked like she used to be a cheerleader. Michelle looked happy, but by the way her jaw clenched at her parents' "Could you believe that was our baby girl?" comments, I didn't expect her cheerful mood to last long.

"Shorty's got hops!" Natalie bumped me in the shoulder from behind. "But seriously, I didn't know you could dance! You were awesome!"

I smiled. "Thanks, Natalie!"

"Hey, I have to get going, but see you at Saturday's game?"

"Yeah, see you then!"

Natalie waved at me as she hustled through the crowd and out the school doors. It was nice of her to come to opening night even though she was busy, *and* we'd perform for the whole school later this week. But there was a reason Natalie was the best basketball player on our team—she practiced even when we didn't have to.

I surveyed the crowd for my parents but couldn't find them. I spotted Professor and Mrs. Kelly instead. They were with Jessica, who was surrounded by a throng of admirers. I hadn't seen her parents much since that time at the International Food Bazaar. A twinge of guilt hit me when I remembered how I felt about them that night. But I wasn't feeling well then and tonight I felt *great*.

"Yes, Jessica was the lead in *Annie*, but since she's still only in middle school, Anna Leonowens's part went to a senior. And rightly so!" Mrs. Kelly was sparkling tonight, in both her mood and her getup. Her rhinestone earrings were so large, I wondered if her ears would start to protest.

"I couldn't believe it was our girl up there tonight!" Professor Kelly boomed. "All in love with some *boy*!"

"Dad!" Jessica smiled and playfully smacked him on the shoulder. "It's called *acting*."

"Your singing was lovely, dear," a nice matronly woman with

silver hair and thick glasses complimented her. I recognized her as their neighbor Mrs. Wade. "You've improved so much since this summer!"

Mrs. Kelly's smile didn't waver as she jumped in before Jessica could answer. "Well, that *was* her first real show. She has a *vocal coach* now, Mrs. Wade." She paused, waiting for a response. When the neighbor only nodded and didn't express any sort of amazement, Mrs. Kelly turned her attention to me. She hugged me so close I could barely breathe.

"Annie. Annieeeee!!! You were so wonderful up there!"

I let out a sigh of relief when she let me go.

"Oh! You were the dancer, weren't you?" Mrs. Wade turned toward me and placed her hand on my shoulder, her touch as light as a feather.

"Annie's never had formal training," Mrs. Kelly mentioned.

Mrs. Wade's eyes grew wide. "No lessons?"

I shook my head.

"Ever?"

"No, ma'am." I looked down. Even though the spotlight felt like home, I felt bashful about the attention I was getting out here.

"Well, isn't that something? You were like a professional, dear. And I'm not just saying that. I might not look it, but I used to dance, too—"

"Now, where are your parents?" Mrs. Kelly interrupted. "I'm

sure they must be so proud."

I scanned the crowd, wondering the same thing. They'd said they'd be here tonight.

When I spotted them, I excused myself. I was grateful how Mrs. Kelly rescued me from any more of Mrs. Wade's compliments.

I waved to my parents and my little brother.

"Annie!" Tak hopped up and down on one foot like he was Eliza. Once he reached me, he grabbed on to my hand.

"Wow, this is hard." Tak continued to hop. "How'd you do it for so long?"

"Basketball," I answered as I led him back to our parents.

"Well, what did you think?" I asked my parents once I reached them.

"It was fun!" my dad responded. He looked like he meant it.

"It was good," my mom answered. She looked relieved. Then she gave me a once-over. I was still in my silver top and slit pants. "Aren't you cold?"

I laughed. My parents were never lavish with the compliments, but I was in a cheerful mood because *I* knew we did well. *I* did well! And Jessica's neighbor—a total stranger—seemed impressed, too.

Then, a woman I had never met before, an *Asian* woman, approached my parents. She was with Kent, the high school boy who played Lun Tha.

In a quiet voice, she asked, "Sumimasen, Nihon no kata desu ka?"

My mom turned toward her in surprise.

Kent mumbled to us, "My mom wanted to say hi."

But my mom and his mom were already saying more than hi. They talked a mile a minute, smiling and going on about where in Japan they were from, how long they'd been here, how come they hadn't met before (Kent just moved here last year), would you like to have tea sometime, etc., etc.

Kent and I just stood there for a few seconds without saying anything. I hardly ever talked with him during rehearsal since our scenes never really overlapped and because he was a high school boy.

"The show went pretty well, huh?" he blurted out.

"Yep." I nodded. "You were good."

He nodded back. "So were you."

"I didn't know your mom was Japanese."

"Yeah. She saw your last name on the program and figured you might be, too."

He looked around some more and so did I. Where was Ben? I spotted his family with Jessica's. At the same time, Jessica turned in my direction. I gave her a little wave but I'm not sure she saw it. She looked our way, but when she did, it was like she was seeing right through me and Kent. Her head swiveled abruptly back toward her parents and Ben. My stomach flip-flopped—that seemed weird.

"You and Jessica are friends, right?"

"Yep."

"Cool."

I could tell Kent was as uncomfortable with this conversation as I was. But I wasn't exactly pleased with how I was saved from it.

"Well, well, Miss Enoway. Now I see how you've been spending all your time instead of on your homework."

Mrs. Olds had crept up on us without me realizing it. Although Kent's mother mentioned how they had only moved to Topeka last year, I could tell she gave him the heebie-jeebies as well.

"Oh, hey, I have to say hi to Kevin. Could you, uh—" Kent fidgeted as Mrs. Olds's eyes came to rest on him.

"I'll let your mom know." I finished his request for him.

Then he left as quickly as he could.

My dad—I'm guessing he was tired of Kent's mom and my mom's chatter—showed up next to me. He held out his hand to Mrs. Olds.

"Hello! I'm Annie's father, Hiroshi Enoway."

Mrs. Olds took his hand and shook it . . . like a fish would.

"Nice to meet you. Mr. Enoway. Or is that Professor Enoway? I heard that you teach at the university?"

"Mrs. Olds is my math teacher." I signaled to my dad with

my eyes: *Yes, THAT math teacher.* I hadn't turned in my homework that week because I hadn't finished it yet, so I began to sweat. Maybe there were a couple of assignments from last week, too—I didn't remember exactly since my focus had been on the musical. I hoped she wasn't here to rat me out.

His eyes widened as he shook Mrs. Olds's hand more vigorously. "Oh, *Mrs. Olds*! Annie talks about you all the time—"

I tried to telegraph to my dad that he was overdoing it without my teacher seeing.

"All good things!" he continued, making it worse. No *way* Mrs. Olds would believe that!

"Is that so?" Mrs. Olds turned her pale eyes on me, her gaze almost clammy in its coolness. "I was thinking it would be nice to talk with you more sometime. A meeting, perhaps? I'd love to discuss Annie's . . . progress."

"Of course!" My dad released my teacher's hand.

"Well, then." Mrs. Olds left without saying anything to my mom, who was just finishing up her conversation.

Onstage, I was a dancer in a warm country halfway across the world and in a time more than a hundred years ago. Offstage, I was in a high school lobby suddenly feeling very cold in my flimsy costume and worried about what developments the "real" world had in store for me.

CHAPTER 31

We had four more performances of *The King and I*—one for the middle school and one for the high school, and then two more over the weekend. Each one was better than the next, except for the Sunday matinee. It wasn't *bad*, but it was a little low energy since it was our last one. We were all just so sad that it was coming to an end! Like Sam mentioned, this production was *special*. In fact, Tak loved it so much he begged my parents to bring him to both weekend shows. My mom came with him once (and sat with Kent's mom in the audience), and my dad brought him for the final one.

During each show, I was transported like a dream into a different place and time. I bathed in the spotlight for the ten minutes that it was on me.

After each show, I basked in the compliments that I finally started to feel comfortable with. A little, anyway.

Ben's aunt Midge hosted the wrap party that followed our last performance.

"I don't know about you being out late on a Sunday night," my mom frowned as she pulled up in front of Midge's house.

"Tomorrow's a teacher in-service." I froze in the back seat, worried that my mom would change her mind about letting me attend the party. "And a lot of adults will be there." She was always suspicious about gatherings at night, and especially so for this one since high school students were also invited.

"Oh, that's right." My mom put the car in park. "And you did work very hard on this. Have fun!"

I almost fell out of the car. My mom wasn't telling me that I needed to work harder *and* she told me to have fun!

"Just don't do anything stupid."

I laughed. *That* sounded more like her.

I tried to enjoy myself at the party since this was the final time the cast would all be together. I was intimidated by the high school students before auditions, but now they were like big brothers or sisters. Part of me couldn't wait to go to high school like them, even though the seniors wouldn't be there anymore by the time Jessica, Ben, and I got there.

Sam was walking around talking to everyone and letting them know what a good job they did.

"You gonna do theater in college?" she asked Michelle.

"Maybe, I dunno."

"Well, you should. You're super talented."

That type of encouragement from Sam made even Moody Michelle smile.

I remembered Ben's comments about how maybe Sam wasn't that big of a deal, and why would she be in a place like Topeka if she were. I liked Ben and everything, but he was wrong. Our school production for *The King and I* was pretty dang good, and Sam was pleased as heck with us. I could tell from the way she laughed and joked with everyone.

Or maybe she was just happy it was over. The thought made me put down the chocolate cake doughnut I was about to eat, suddenly not hungry for it anymore.

"Okay, everyone, gather round!" Sam yelled at the top of her voice so even the kids who were downstairs came stomping up. Jessica, Ben, and Kent burst through the door in the kitchen that led to the basement. I had wondered where they were but when I arrived, I pretty much immediately parked myself at the table where all the potluck items were. My mom was an excellent cook, but there was so much food here that I normally don't have at home that I couldn't help but stuff my face. I practically dove into the chili con queso dip.

In between crunches, I waved at them. Kent gave me a nod, but Jessica and Ben were talking with each other so they didn't see me. At least I don't think they did because they didn't wave back. Still, that dip was *good*, and I couldn't bring myself to leave it just yet.

Sam looked around to make sure we were all there. "So, look, guys. You did good. No, you did *great*. I've been involved with theater, TV, film, you know, all that, for a while and not everything goes well all the time. In fact, most of the time it's pretty mediocre. But every once in a while, everything comes together and when that happens, well . . . it's totally awesome."

We all cheered at that moment, as much for Sam as for us. She could be tough, but honestly, she really knew how to make us better.

"I'm gonna miss you all. I'm gonna miss *this*. But I *am* happy to let you know that we have something really cool planned for the summer, too."

I looked toward Jessica. She seemed just as surprised as I was. She turned to Ben, who shrugged. He didn't know what this was about either.

"It's gonna be an under-eighteen all-kids production. So, not with Topeka Repertory, but with Ms. Tracy's theater school."

"Aww!" Jessica groaned loudly. Something in Sam's glance our way made her stop, though.

"I know it might seem like a step down from last summer with *Annie*, but what's exciting is that *you're* going to be more involved. We're gonna be doing the play *Alice in Wonderland*, which, okay, yeah, I know it's not as mature-sounding as *The*

King and I, but if you ask me, it's *way* more age-appropriate *and* we're gonna do something different with it."

Sam reached into the bag next to her and pulled out a stack of photocopied scripts.

"During the next few months, if you're so inclined, I want those of you who are interested to rewrite these with *your* take on the story."

Alice in Wonderland? ALICE IN WONDERLAND? This story was only my go-to, my comfort read, my favorite tale of all time. I knew it backward and forward and upside down.

"Who's interested?" Sam looked nervous all of a sudden, like maybe none of us would think this was as neat of an idea as she thought it was.

My hand shot up in the air. Jessica's did too, but maybe not as enthusiastically, but I didn't care. So did Ben's.

"For those of you who want to take a stab at it, turn in your written scripts at your school's front office by noon on the last day before summer vacation. I'll swing around and pick them up then." Sam began to distribute copies to all of us who had our hands up. She stopped in front of Kent. "No?"

"I don't know if I can yet." Kent's arms were crossed.

"Well, how 'bout you take one while you figure it out?" Sam shoved a copy into his arms.

As I flipped through the script, everyone and everything else dropped away. The play was a little different from the book, but my ideas for it came fast and from everywhere, like the silver balls pinging back and forth inside a pinball machine.

I was sad that *The King and I* was ending, sure. But I was so happy that I'd have *this* to look forward to this summer.

It's curious how dreams work. I dreamed of being Annie, but then I was cast as only one of her orphan friends. Dad had encouraged me to take the experience in, though—to learn. And I did. I dreamed of being in *The King and I* and even though I botched my audition, by some miracle I was able to get a bigger part than I did in *Annie*. It wasn't the lead, but I had a taste of the spotlight. Now, I realized that patience was finally going to pay off, because it was leading up to this—the biggest dream of all.

I've paid my dues, I thought. *It's* my *turn*.

I was going to be Alice and the summer show was going to be my Wonderland.

ACT III
ALICE IN WONDERLAND

CHAPTER 32

It's funny how no matter how much you want to hang on to your dreams, they slip through your fingers. Like when you're having the best dream—the type you want to linger in just a moment longer—but with the first rays of sunlight, it's gone and you can't remember it at all. Just a whisper of the feeling you had while in it.

That's kind of how the weeks after *The King and I* went. Harsh like the sound of a morning alarm clock, reality pounded away at my dreams.

First, there was the basketball to the face. Not literally, but what happened during practice this week sure felt like it.

I was super thankful to have something to do after *The King and I* finished. As the KU Jayhawks advanced in their search for an NCAA basketball championship, everyone on my team was filled with basketball fever. Coach was especially fired up, with her being a mega Jayhawks fan and all.

Before our last game with our crosstown rivals, the Shawnee Mustangs, Coach had us work on our jumping.

Tweet! She blew her whistle and we jumped as high as we could.

Tweet! Jump!

Tweet! Jump!

Tweet! Jump!

Over and over again until we were sweating buckets. When our legs felt wobbly like Jell-O and we were all about to pass out, she stopped us with one loud, extra-long whistle.

"Annie, get up here!" she barked.

Was I in trouble? I was trying as hard as I could . . .

"I want you all to watch this." Coach tweeted again.

I just looked at her, unsure of what she wanted me to do.

"Jump!"

So, only I went through the drill again and again in front of everyone else.

Why was she torturing me?

Coach finally stopped, and I put my arms on top of my head. I breathed in and out as deeply as I could so I wouldn't collapse.

"Did you see that? *Did you see that?*" Coach walked down the line, yelling in everyone's faces. "Did you see how high she was jumping? Did you see her let up? No!"

I smiled in relief. So I wasn't in trouble! I was happy that Coach saw how hard I was pushing myself.

She stopped right in front of Natalie. "Now, Annie's so short that no matter how high she jumps, it's not going to make that much of a difference. But *you*—if *you* tried that hard, do you know what a difference you'd make?"

My smile turned into a gasp. All the air left me and I felt myself deflate like a punctured basketball. What Coach said was so unfair in so many ways.

Natalie made a *huge* difference in all our games. She was our best player and almost always our highest scorer. She left it all out on the court *every single time*.

So did I . . . but this was the first time I'd ever heard that I didn't make much of a difference! True, I didn't score much. I was lucky to make two baskets, if that, but that wasn't my role. Still . . .

At the end of practice, Natalie found me right away. "Hey, are you okay? I don't think Coach meant it that way."

I was hoping maybe I had misheard, but Natalie's words confirmed that I hadn't. Just like Jessica made excuses for Mr. Malder, Natalie was making excuses for Coach. "It's fine." I smiled weakly.

"No, it's not. That was *not* cool of her. You want me to say something? I'm gonna say something."

This reaction was a little different from Jessica's. I studied

Natalie's expression. *Would you really do that for me?* I wondered.

"Natalia, can you come here?" Her dad waved her over before I could answer.

"Sorry, just a second." Natalie jogged over to Mr. Moreno, who was talking with Coach.

"Do you really think she has that kind of potential?"

Coach looked at Natalie. "She's the most gifted player on the team by a mile. A lot of these girls aren't going to play beyond middle school. But Natalie's good enough she could make the high school team *now* if that were an option. She might be college material if she dedicates herself."

"College?" Mr. Moreno's eyes looked distant. "I was scouted, too. Senior year. But then . . ." He lifted his right leg and slapped it before he brought it back down with a *thump.* "Damn knee blew out."

"How are your grades?" Coach asked.

"Straight As," Natalie's dad said as he puffed out his chest.

Natalie looked back and forth between her dad and Coach.

"We're talking real *possibilities* here. If she keeps her grades up through high school, maybe even a scholarship to a school like Stanford."

"Stanford?" Natalie's dad looked thoughtful. "Isn't that like Ivy League?"

"No." Coach smiled. "It's *better.* I think she could go

there . . . if she puts in the work."

"What do you think, mija?" Mr. Moreno gazed down at Natalie. "You think you can put in the work?"

Natalie squeezed the basketball she was holding between her mighty hands.

She looked at me and then back at Coach. I wasn't sure what was meant by that glance, if anything.

If someone had said that about me and my basketball abilities, I wouldn't have waited even a millisecond before responding with the loudest "Heck, yeah!"

But Natalie responded with a serious "I can . . ." and she trailed off.

It was raining when my dad drove back home. He chattered. "Big game against Oklahoma State this weekend. Would you like to watch it with me?"

"Sure." I didn't feel like talking much.

I followed the raindrops as they made their paths down the window. They went in one direction until bumping into another. Then they would change their course and flow another way. I came to terms with the fact that I was no Muggsy Bogues. I wasn't even a Scooter Barry. I was "not bad for middle school." Even though it hurt to hear, in my heart I knew it was true. No NBA or college ball for me, probably not even the high school team. I was happy for Natalie, though.

She lived and breathed basketball.

Can a person have too many dreams? I didn't know the answer to that question, but maybe dreams needed room to grow, like plants. They take time, and if you have too many of them, do they crowd each other out so none of them get enough sun?

When I got home, I stashed my basketball inside my closet and opened up my *Alice in Wonderland* script.

Natalie wasn't the only one who was going to make her dreams come true.

CHAPTER 33

Every afternoon when I came home from school, I opened up my copy of the script Sam had given us, scribbled down ideas, and wrote until it was time for dinner. Alice and her adventures in Wonderland reminded me of all the new and often uncomfortable situations I encountered at WMS. Maybe I'd put a middle school spin on the story? But if I were Alice, would I cast Ben as the Rabbit with me chasing after him?

"Aoi, come here. Right now." Even though my mom was down in the kitchen, her voice was loud enough that it seemed like she was right behind me.

I dropped my pencil, startled. Mom had been in a pretty good mood ever since meeting Kent's mom. They had tea together a few times and Kent even came over once. He made it clear it wasn't his choice, though—that he had to help run errands afterward.

"Have you decided whether you're going to do the summer play?" I asked him after my mom insisted that I emerge from my room.

"I don't think so." He shrugged. "I have to visit my relatives in Japan."

I nodded. "I had to spend a summer there a few years ago when my grandpa died and Mom needed to go back."

"Yeah, mine's not doing too well." With his toe, he nudged one of Tak's toy cars out of the way.

I'd overheard my mom and Mrs. Wright talking about her dad the other day. Even though Kent's mom was going through a tough time, helping her seemed to help my mom. I'd never thought of her as someone who needed to socialize since she didn't seem to like big gatherings, but she seemed so much happier on the days she saw Mrs. Wright. The guard she put up, that *wariness* she wore like armor when we went out, was gone with Mrs. Wright. It was such a contrast with how she normally had been when she didn't have a friend like Kent's mom.

But the way she said my name just now did not sound happy. *At* all.

I got up and ran down the stairs. Even though it was dinnertime, the way Mom said *right now* made me think that wasn't why she called for me. Each step filled me with dread.

"Yes, Mom?" When I reached her, she was holding a piece of paper in her shaking hand. On the table was an envelope—its return address: Westridge Middle School.

Uh-oh.

"Do you know what this is?" My mom's voice was ice cold.

"Uh . . ." was all I could get out. If it was my report card, I was in as much trouble as Alice was when she nearly drowned in her own tears.

"Tadaima!" My dad's cheerful voice rang through the house as he opened the front door. "I'm home!"

"Hi, Daddy!" I couldn't have been happier to see him at that moment. I was about to run and greet him, but a look from my mom stopped me like a steel door slamming shut in front of me.

My dad set down his briefcase and loosened his tie. "Finally, some good weather! Annie, do you want to shoot some bask—"

"No," my mom interrupted. "Aoi won't be doing anything for a very long time."

Dad took in the scene that was unfolding before him. "What's going on?"

"This." Mom extended the paper toward him.

Dad's normally cheerful face twisted and contorted until it was as scary as Mom's.

"A C-minus, Aoi? And in *math*?"

I'd never been in trouble at school before, let alone in a meeting that my parents demanded I attend. Not to mention the fact that my parents had actually hired a babysitter to watch Tak, as opposed to bringing him along with us, which is what they usually did. We waited in Mrs. Olds's room after school the Friday before spring break. Normally, this would have been an awesome day. The first day of a whole week off from school! But my stomach had been in knots since this morning and I could barely eat lunch, even though it was just Ben and me (Jessica had been missing a lot of lunches lately). I couldn't focus on anything all day.

My parents and I didn't talk as we sat in the front row of cramped student desks. There was nothing left to say—for the past few days, I'd tried to explain that I'd make up the work, that my C-minus was because of missed classes due to my allergy shot appointments so I'd work extra hard to catch up on all the concepts that I'd put off studying, that it was only a quarterly progress report (not my actual grade for the semester), and that middle school grades didn't matter anyway.

The last comment didn't go over so well.

I never thought I'd be happy to see Mrs. Olds, but I breathed a sigh of relief when she finally entered the classroom. *Let's get this over with*, I thought.

"Hello, Mr. Enoway, Mrs. Enoway." Mrs. Olds sat behind her large imposing desk instead of pulling up a student seat next to us. "I'm glad you called to arrange this meeting. I must admit, I was as surprised as you were with Annie's mid-semester grade."

My father shifted slightly in his seat. "Oh? Did you mention to Annie that her grades were dropping—?"

"Well, now. I didn't complete a lot of the grading until just before report cards were due. In *my* class, I expect the *students* to take responsibility for their own learning."

"Of course," my dad agreed. "Annie maybe took on too much this past quarter."

I gulped. *That wasn't why!* "Is there . . . anything I could do to bring my grade up?" I asked. I didn't want my parents to make me give up the activities I truly loved.

"Well . . ." Mrs. Olds regarded me with a glimmer of a smile behind her thin, wrinkled lips. Since she was usually not a smiley sort of lady, her expression made me especially nervous.

"If Annie turns in all her missed work the day after spring break, I can give her up to fifty percent credit for it."

Fifty percent? That was still failing. It would bring up my average a bit, but—

"I wish I could offer more, but that wouldn't exactly be fair to everyone who was able to finish their work on time now, would it?" Mrs. Olds responded before I could object. She pulled a stack of worksheets from her desk drawer and slid it across the table toward us.

"Thank you for . . . for allowing her that opportunity." My mom spoke softly as she took the papers and set them in her lap. "We are very disappointed in our daughter."

Mrs. Olds turned to her in surprise. Like she didn't expect that my mom could talk. She sniffed. "Yes, well, don't be too hard on her. I realize many of your people are gifted mathematically, but she *is* a girl."

There were so many things wrong with what Mrs. Olds said that the three of us just sat there for a moment, stunned.

"'A girl'?" My mom finally broke the silence.

"'Our people'?" Dad blurted out at the same time.

My teacher was not fazed. "It's no secret that Asians tend to be especially adept at math and science. Did you happen to read that recent *TIME* magazine article?"

It took all my willpower not to bang my head against my desk.

"Yes," my mom responded, in full flight attendant mode. "I've seen it."

"Maybe the fact that Annie is a girl is working against that. Girls tend to do well in elementary school academically, but the boys tend to overtake them by high school, especially in math and the sciences. A pity."

"A pity, *indeed*." Dad stared straight through Mrs. Olds like he was trying his best to control himself. I'd never seen him that mad, but she didn't seem to notice.

"If that's all, then . . ." Mrs. Olds stood up and held out her limp-fish hand to my father first and then to my mother. They shook it as quickly as they could without being rude.

"Have a nice break, Annie," my teacher called out to me in her singsongy way as the door closed behind us.

"Tondemonai sensei da ne!" *What a ridiculous teacher!* As soon as we reached the parking lot, my mom let loose.

"You had said she was bad, but I had no idea *how* bad. My best students are girls!" My dad stomped to the car.

I couldn't believe this turn of events. I thought I'd be in *huge* trouble, but now we were actually united in our opinion of my awful teacher. Maybe this meeting would result in everything working out in my favor!

"*I told you* it wasn't me!" I joined in. "You understand now, right? She's *impossible*."

My mother stopped in her tracks and addressed me in rapid-fire Japanese.

"No. You are in this mess because of *you*. And while your teacher is awful, *you* are going to prove her wrong. Don't think for one minute that you're not in trouble anymore, do you understand me?"

I shrunk from my mother's anger. "Yes, but . . ."

"You are not to go *anywhere* this break. You will sit at home, and work on all this and only this. Get in the car."

"But—"

"Right *now*." My mom swung open the door to the back seat for me. I climbed in and flinched when she slammed it shut behind me.

"It was the musical." My mom sat in the front seat and faced forward as she continued to yell. "You spent too much time on it, that's why this happened. Aoi, you need to get your head out of the clouds. This acting, these plays—" She waved her hand around like she was batting an annoying fly from her face. "These are fine as a *hobby*—but they are *not* going to help you in real life."

I lowered my head and picked at a loose thread on my pants. I didn't say anything back during my mom's talking-to of a lifetime, though. I'm not *stupid*. But . . . she was *wrong*.

Dad started the car. "I agree that Annie needs to make up the work, but she was very good in—"

"I know there are many opportunities here, maybe some Aoi wouldn't have had back in Japan. But she's not going to *play basketball* or *act* for a living." She spat out those words like they were poison.

"I know I'm not going to play basketball for a living!" I shouted. I wanted to show my mom I *was* practical. I was.

"So, do you think you're going to act, then? Aoi, have you watched TV lately? Haven't you noticed that *there's no one who looks like us*? What movie have you seen that makes you think that's an avenue that's open to *you*?"

"What about *The King and I*?" I sassed back. *We just watched that over winter break. How could she forget?* Clearly, Mom was only seeing what *she* wanted to see.

"Aoi, those actors *weren't like you and me*. They were more like your castmates."

I'm pretty sure my mom was wrong about the actors in the musical we'd watched over Christmas break, even if she was right about the actors in the school version. I pulled at the thread on my pants to avoid fighting any more with my mom. It broke, so now there was a hole in my pants, too.

"There's that fellow on *Star Trek* . . . ," my dad began.

My mom snorted dismissively and looked out her window.

Dad knew better than to say anything else. This conversation was over.

When we arrived home, my mom shoved the stack of math assignments into my arms. I stomped up the stairs as Mom and Dad stayed downstairs to pay the babysitter.

As soon as I reached my room, I slammed the math papers down on my desk. I sat down and picked up a pencil. I stared at my first worksheet. Problem after problem. How was *this* stack of busywork going to help me in real life? If anything, it would kill me with boredom before I had a chance to finish seventh grade.

My parents came upstairs, but then headed straight into

their own bedroom without saying good night to me. *Fine by me.* When their door clicked shut and I heard their bath running, I opened my desk drawer and pulled out my version of the *Alice in Wonderland* script I had been working on. Just to be safe, I taped a math worksheet on top to camouflage it.

I pulled out a notebook that I'd had for years. It was blue and covered in clouds with silver linings—it was so pretty I couldn't bring myself to write in it. Until now.

I pulled the cap off my favorite pen. It was one my aunt sent me from Japan and had cute rabbits—like the White Rabbit in Wonderland—and it made thin, perfect lines in a midnight-blue ink.

My pen hovered above the first page as this scene filled my mind:

A roar erupts from the crowd as I lift the hem of my glittering gown and make my way up the steps and onto the largest stage I've ever been on. A man in a tuxedo hands me a golden statuette. It's heavier than I imagined it would be. I set it on the podium and—hands shaking—unfold a piece of scratch paper. "Thank you so much for this honor," I begin once the crowd has finally quieted down. "First I'd like to thank the Academy—"

A gust of wind from outside blew away this particular dream. The *tap-tap-tapping* of tree branches on my window reminded me to get to the task at hand.

Instead of writing my Academy Award acceptance speech, I began with—

Alice sits outside Westridgeport Middle School waiting
for her ride to arrive. She opens a book as a WHITE
RABBIT hops across the school lawn.
WHITE RABBIT
(Checking its neon-colored Swatch)
Oh man! I'm gonna be late.
The White Rabbit bounds into the school. Alice looks both
ways and decides to follow.

I'll prove you wrong, I thought as I wrote line after line of my script. *Just you wait.*

CHAPTER 34

For the rest of spring break, I pretty much stayed in my room and only came downstairs to eat, if that. I didn't mind, though, because it gave me more time to work on my middle school take on *Alice in Wonderland*. Jessica's family was in Hawaii for the week, and basketball season had ended with a disappointing second place in the seventh-grade district-wide end-of-season tournament. Despite Coach's earlier comments, I played my hardest anyway. I even fouled out, which is pretty unusual for a point guard. Time after time, I planted myself in front of an opponent charging her way to the basket. The goal was to get knocked over to draw the charging foul. Only the ref said I wasn't set for a full second, so *I* got called with blocking fouls instead. I was red with frustration, but at the end of the game, Coach approached me.

"Hey, Annie?"

"Yeah, Coach?" As a team, we had already listened to her "You're still all winners in my book!" speech, so I wasn't sure what else she needed to tell me.

"I just wanted to say . . . to tell you sorry about the comments I made, you know, when I was trying to get Natalie to jump higher."

At first I acted like I didn't know what she was talking about. In fact, I was kind of stunned she was apologizing in the first place. Adults are always telling us kids we need to, but I'd never had anyone like Coach admit to being wrong to someone like me.

"You *are* short, but you can . . ." Coach paused, like she was rethinking what she was going to say next.

Be anything you want to be? I thought. Before I could stop myself, I blurted out, "Dunk like Muggsy Bogues and play in the NBA?"

Coach threw her head back and laughed. I guess I had my answer.

"Oh no, please don't be mad, Annie. I've just never had a girl ask me that before." Coach's face grew thoughtful. She crossed her arms as she contemplated her answer. "Truthfully, there hasn't been a woman yet who has dunked the ball, and there's not a women's NBA league. A woman was drafted into the NBA once, but she never ended up playing. I'm not saying it's impossible, but these are the odds you're looking at."

I nodded. Although this wasn't the answer I hoped for, Coach was telling me the truth. "Thanks, Coach."

"So." Coach held out her hand. "We good?"

I took it and shook. In my mind I had already put basketball aside. But with her apology, I was able to put some of the hurt away too.

As I bounced my basketball, I wondered how Coach realized she had hurt my feelings. All of a sudden, it struck me. *Natalie must have said something.* Instead of being annoyed, though, I thought back to RJ and his stupid speech and how no one said anything and how that was much, *much* worse.

I ran down the hall feeling lighter than I had in a while.

I guess you could say doing math worksheets and not having my best friend around was a lonely way to spend time off from school, but I tried to think of it more as not having any distractions. I divided up all the math assignments I missed (which were—I admit—*a lot*) and made myself do a few every day.

It was harder to concentrate today, though, and it wasn't just because I had to shove my cat off my desk three times already. My cough had practically disappeared with my allergy shot treatments and so Chibi was allowed back in my room.

When I had to pick her up and move her *again*, I briefly wished she weren't. I contemplated just kicking her out, but then I knew she'd just mewl and scratch at the door until I let her back in. Tyrant!

Around lunchtime, my dad knocked on my door.

"It would be fun to watch a movie tonight, don't you think? Want to come to the video store with me?"

I hadn't started on my math for today yet since I had spent all morning on my writing . . . but a movie sounded great and I didn't want to sit through anything that Tak chose.

"Mom's out running errands with your little brother." Dad always knew what was on my mind. "You've been working hard, and I think you deserve a break!"

An idea popped into my head that made me hop out of my chair so quickly it almost toppled over.

"Yeah, sure!"

At the Blockbuster video store, my dad looked through the new rentals while I scanned through as many videos as I could.

There are *actors who look like me*, I told myself. *What does Mom know?*

I searched and searched. Sure enough, people who looked more like Jessica and Ben were on most of the movie posters and video jacket covers I found. Occasionally, there was someone who was Black, but not often. In the family movie section, there were a lot of cute cartoon animals. But nobody who looked like me.

I wandered into the aisle with the musicals and spotted the video for *The King and I*. I picked it up and read the back, hoping to find the actors' names. Maybe then I could find more movies that they were in, too.

Yul Brynner played the king. Hmm, that didn't *sound* like an Asian name. But I wasn't *sure*.

An actor by the name of Rita Moreno played Tuptim. *Moreno*? That was Natalie's last name. Definitely not Asian!

"Excuse me." I located a store employee. He wore a blue polo shirt and looked like he was about the same age as my high school castmates from the play. "Can you recommend more movies with Yul Brynner in them?"

The teenager—"Chad," his name tag read—took the video from me and scanned the back. "Yul Brynner?" he confirmed. "Sure! He was in a classic called *The Ten Commandments*...."

I followed Chad to the section with a bunch of old movies. He searched through them for a few seconds before spotting the video. He took it off the shelf and handed it to me.

"Aaaand . . . let's see. He was in *The Magnificent Seven*, too. You like Westerns?"

I shrugged. "Maybe."

Chad searched the aisle and handed a copy of that to me as well. "How's that for starters?"

I was busy studying the back of both video jackets. "Good, I think. Thanks."

"Anytime. Let me know if you need anything else."

My heart sank as I came closer to the conclusion that Yul Brynner was *not* Asian. I wasn't sure *what* he was, though. He played an Egyptian in *The Ten Commandments* and an American cowboy in *The Magnificent Seven*.

"Hey!" I hollered louder than I meant to at Chad. I interrupted him helping another customer so I was doubly embarrassed.

But he hustled back over like he was used to customers yelling at him.

"What *is* Yul Brynner, anyway?" I asked, not really knowing a better way to put the question.

"What *is* he?" Chad looked blank for a moment.

"I mean, like, is he Asian? Is he Egyptian? Is he—"

"Ah! He is *Russian*." Chad seemed supremely pleased to be able to provide me with this bit of knowledge.

"Russian?" I was confused. "Why didn't they cast an Asian actor, or an—"

"It's all about the big bucks, that's why they call it show *business*," Chad explained.

"Huh?" I still didn't get it.

"Yul Brynner was a big name. People pay money to watch movies with big-name stars in them."

"But how do you get to be a big name if you're never cast?" I stared at the videos Chad had handed to me.

He shrugged. "*That* . . . I don't know."

"Hey!" another customer shouted at Chad.

I returned the movies to their shelves and wandered through the aisles again.

As a family, we all watched *Shogun*, an American TV miniseries about Japan in the 1600s, but the Japanese actors in that were actually Japanese. Not Japanese American like me. There was a guy who played an Asian exchange student in the movie *Sixteen Candles*. Jessica *loved* it, pretty much because the male lead was what she called a "hunk." He *was* really good-looking, but I didn't like the story as much as she did. The way the Asian exchange student was the butt of a lot of the jokes and always introduced with a gong sound made me squirm when we watched it together. Jessica laughed and didn't understand why I didn't think it was funny, too.

"Didn't want either of those?" Chad motioned to my empty hands when I bumped into him again.

"They weren't what I felt like tonight." I shrugged.

He frowned. "No one, and I mean *no one*, leaves Blockbuster empty-handed. Not on my watch. Come with me." I followed as he strode away.

We stopped in the section for movies that had been released within the last year or two.

"*Princess Bride?*"

"I've already seen it."

"Are you a 007 fan?"

I shook my head. "Not really."

"I am!" My dad found me. He hadn't selected anything yet, either.

Chad shook his head. "I'll find something you *both* like," he assured me. "*Dirty Dancing?*" he suggested next.

Ugh. Jessica had mentioned it was good, but no *way* was I going to watch a movie called *Dirty Dancing* with my dad.

"*Karate Kid?*"

"Seen it."

"How about the second one?" Chad sure wasn't giving up.

The second one? We saw the first one on video a while ago. Tak was only two, but he drop-kicked his stuffed animals and then threw them around the house after watching it, so I actually think he got the gist of it. He might like this one, too.

I traded looks with my dad. Although the second *Karate Kid* came out in the theaters a couple of years ago, we had missed it—like we did a lot of movies.

"We'll catch it on video," he always promised, and here was our chance. Dad nodded.

"Enjoy!" Chad looked triumphant as he handed a copy of *The Karate Kid Part II* to me.

Back at home, we sat mesmerized as Daniel LaRusso traveled to Okinawa with his teacher, Mr. Miyagi. The plot itself didn't interest me much, and my mom and dad actually laughed at some of the Japanese (even *my* Japanese was better than that!). There were intimate scenes in which Mr. Miyagi reconnected with his long-lost love. But they spoke in English to each other . . . wouldn't they speak in Japanese?

"People are lazy," my mom explained, with some of her first words to me since our meeting with Mrs. Olds. "If the actors spoke in Japanese, then the audience would have to read subtitles."

"Which a lot of people don't want to do," my dad added. "Movies are for relaxing!"

But Daniel's girlfriend was *Japanese*. In fact, she looked a little bit like my mom!

I checked the video jacket. *Tamlyn Tomita*. "Tomita" was a Japanese last name, for sure, but "Tamlyn" was definitely not a Japanese first name.

She was a Japanese American actor.

Japanese *and* American.

Like me.

CHAPTER 35

Ha! My mom was *wrong*. There *were* other actors who looked like me out there. Maybe a long time ago, like when they filmed *The King and I*, there weren't enough, so Hollywood filmmakers had to find actors who weren't Asian to play Asian characters, but not anymore! Hopefully, there would be more and more of us in the theater, TV, and *maybe* even blockbuster movies, too.

Us. There were so few Asian Americans around me that "us" had usually meant just me and my family. The thought of "us" as a bigger group was both exciting and a little scary as well. "Us" as a group of people who weren't just math and science "whiz kids" but actors, and maybe artists, and singers, and athletes as well. Maybe *anything we wanted to be.*

I powered through the rest of my script rewrite for *Alice in Wonderland*. I wrote Alice with me in mind. Why not? I bet I could play Alice as well as anyone else. Instead of falling down a rabbit hole in the beginning, I imagined Alice following the White Rabbit into the middle school, where there was a long, dark hallway. So long that she couldn't see the end of it, but she was so curious about where it led, she followed the rabbit anyway. When I wrote about the Queen of Hearts screaming, "Off with her head!" I thought of Mrs. Olds. It almost made my awful experience in her class worth it, if only for the material. *Almost.*

Writing about scary women screaming about decapitation reminded me to complete the rest of my missed assignments. Just in time, since they needed to be turned in tomorrow!

On the first day back from spring break, I was filled with all the promise of the new season. Pinkish-purple redbud trees bloomed along the streets, and a sweet wind with a hint of sunshine propelled me into the school.

During math class, I turned in my stack of missed assignments to Mrs. Olds.

"Very good, Miss Enoway. I'm delighted you've finished these. Though . . . it would have been better to have done them the first time around. Wouldn't you agree?"

"It won't happen again!" I smiled, determined not to let my least favorite teacher and her backhanded compliments get to me.

I searched for Ben as I walked back to my seat. Usually in this type of situation he would wink, or flash me a conspiratorial smile. But when we made eye contact today, he just looked away. . . .

Right, I thought. *No reason to give Mrs. Olds any more ammunition.* That was fine—I'd just talk to him at lunch!

In the cafeteria, Jessica hadn't arrived by the time I'd gone through the lunch line. Ben was sitting at our usual table. But even though we were barely five minutes into our lunch break, he had already finished all of his hamburger and fries!

"You might want to chew," I joked as I plopped down next to him. "How was your break?"

Ben shoved three fries in his mouth and didn't look up. "Fine," he mumbled.

His normally pale face was red and peeling. Like Jessica's during the summer when we spent too much time swimming at the club her parents belonged to.

"Did you go someplace fun? Looks like you got some sun."

"Hawaii. And thanks for pointing that out." Ben motioned to his face.

Hawaii? That's where Jessica and her family went. *Did they travel together?* The Kellys and Prescotts were friends, but she would have mentioned if they went to the same place. I knew some families traveled with each other, but not mine.

There were a lot of people we were friendly *with*, but not any who were close enough that they'd say, "Hey, whaddaya think about hanging out in Hawaii together?"

Ben was acting really weird—usually he was all jokes and funny stories, but not today. *Should I ask why?* But his sunburn looked really painful and I guess I'd be annoyed if someone pointed that out, too. Plus, it was clear he was hungry, so I was probably making a big deal out of nothing.

"Hey, have you seen *Karate Kid Part II*?"

Ben shrugged. Was that a no or a yes?

I kept going. "We watched it over break! Daniel LaRusso's girlfriend . . . Kumiko? Was that her name?" I don't know why I acted like I wasn't sure what her name was. But Ben's silence was making me increasingly uncomfortable and I didn't know what else to do other than keep on blathering.

"Yeah, Kumiko. I thought she looked a lot like my mom, but my little brother thought she looked more like me."

Ben finally stopped stuffing fries in his mouth and looked right at me. I breathed a sigh of relief. It was the first time today that he'd made any eye contact at all.

"What do *you* think?"

"I think . . ." Ben studied my face. "I think she's not quite as ugly as you are."

What?

The bite of hamburger in my mouth just sat there. He was

joking, right? If he was, I found it very hard to laugh. Still . . .

"Ha ha, very funny." I chewed and swallowed even though the food had suddenly turned to cardboard. I didn't know what else to do or say. For a moment, I wondered if I were actually here, or if this was an absurd version of the Mad Hatter's tea party. I had been working on my script so much that maybe it had seeped into my dreams. Or nightmare, in this case. I willed myself to wake up.

"No, I'm serious." Ben's green eyes that used to twinkle when we talked darkened, hard, instead. "Jessica's family and mine *were* in Hawaii together. And you know what? I told her I liked her."

Ben liked Jessica? I wished I hadn't swallowed that bite of hamburger because it was all I could manage to keep from throwing it right back up.

"But she told me she couldn't like me back because *you* liked me."

Now it was my turn to avoid making eye contact with Ben. Cymbals crashed and trumpets blared inside my brain. It was like an entire pit orchestra tried to drown out the sound of Ben's voice.

But I still heard. *Ben liked Jessica. Jessica told Ben I liked him.*

"I thought to myself, that's too bad, because you're simply too ugly for me."

I stood up then, so quickly that I almost knocked my milk

281

into his lap. I looked around, for the exit, the path for the quickest getaway I could find. Before the tears that were building up behind my eyes could fall.

It was then that I saw Natalie. She was sitting three tables away with the rest of our basketball team. She looked up. "Annie?"

Like a robot, I turned in her direction. She motioned me over and I felt my legs carry my body over toward her and my team. She scooted over so there was space for me, and I was barely able to put my tray down before the tears started flowing.

"What's wrong?"

"What happened?"

"Annie, are you okay?"

The well-meaning questions that rained down on me only made me cry harder.

Natalie didn't say a word. She only patted my back and handed me the coarse brown cafeteria napkins.

My team huddled around me and protected me from curious stares and whispers. When the tears finally stopped, I was able to blurt out, "He likes Jessica, not me." The tears started again. "And . . . he . . ." I took deep breaths to try and get the awful words out. "He said . . . I was ugly!" I covered my face with all the napkins I could find, not caring if they were already soaked with my tears.

"He said *what*?" Natalie's eyes narrowed as she stood and swiveled toward Ben. Her fists clenched.

"No, don't!" Part of me wanted Natalie to beat Ben up, but part of me didn't want that. No matter how much he had hurt me.

"You're not ugly." Natalie sat when our teammate Angie pulled her back down.

Of course, she *had to* say that. But I remembered how two neighbor kids used to call me "Flat Face" during soccer matches on our street. I kicked their shins instead of the ball to make them stop.

"Flat Face" isn't something you call someone who's pretty. I thought I had pushed that memory down and moved on. I was supposed to forget about it, too, but I couldn't. Like what Ben said. I would remember this forever.

Mom was right. No one who looked like us played the love interest in any movie or show we had seen. That is, until *Karate Kid Part II*, and Ben had let me know what he thought about her.

Kirsten left the table and headed toward the dwindling lunch line.

By this time, I was able to control my tears and in its place was just an aching emptiness—a hollow, shattered feeling in my chest . . . I guess that's why they call it heartbreak.

"Jessica told him I liked him," I went on. "I don't know why she would do that. I thought she was my friend."

Kirsten returned with a giant chocolate chip cookie and handed it to me. "From the lunch lady."

Natalie's expression was hard. "Look, Shorty. Jessica and Ben? They're not your friends."

I bit into the cookie from Kirsten. It helped fill the emptiness, at least a little. "I know you're right about that jerkface over there, but Jessica's been my best friend since kindergarten. She shouldn't have said anything to Ben, but . . ."

Natalie traded looks with Angie and Kirsten.

And then she told me *everything*.

CHAPTER 36

I had exactly fifty-five minutes to cool down between my lunchtime conversation with Natalie and my final class of the day—PE . . . with Jessica.

Fifty-five minutes wasn't *even close* to enough time.

"She said you only got the part in *The King and I* because you're Asian," Natalie told me. Even though those were Jessica's words and not her own, it was like she was tasting something bad when she repeated them. "She's been telling everyone it's too bad that people who actually deserved the part didn't get it."

"We don't believe that at all!" Angie exclaimed.

Kirsten nodded. "You were really good!"

"She wasn't even there!" I joined in. But a little part of me broke inside when I heard this. My audition *was* disastrous. I thought I redeemed myself during the actual performances, but maybe I didn't. Maybe people were just trying to be nice when they congratulated me.

Or maybe it was a bunch of pity for ugly little ol' me.

Jessica also had been complaining that our carpool arrangements were *so unfair* and they ended up having to drive me *everywhere*. Mrs. Kelly always offered, though, and said, "It's no trouble at all!" We took it at face value. Guess it *was* trouble, after all. Then Jessica had been telling people, "I wouldn't want to ride in their gross old car anyway. It doesn't even have air conditioning!"

Finally, Natalie also told me that Jessica's mom was on the Regional Arts Council and her parents were "patrons of the theater." I didn't know exactly what that meant, but Natalie explained that since they donated lots of money, Jessica would always have a leg up in auditions.

Anger, sadness, shock, betrayal, fed-up-ness—there was a whole lot of *stuff* going on inside me by sixth period and it let itself out in the form of . . .

A swift kick to Jessica's butt.

It happened after we all changed into our gym clothes and before we lined up for stretches. Coach Johnson had just received a note from the office.

"I have to return this call. Girls, do your warm-ups until I get back, okay?"

As Jessica made her way to her spot, I ran up behind her and kicked. *Hard.*

She yelped and whipped around. "What the heck, Annie?"

"Just saying hi." I kicked again. "You do it to me, what's the big deal?"

"Yeah, but not as hard." Jessica dodged a third kick from me. "What is your *problem*?"

A couple of our classmates glanced our way. I positioned myself in the row behind my former friend and acted like everything was normal. The other girls stopped paying attention. They weren't focused on their warm-ups or stretches, either, but took Ms. Johnson's momentary absence to chat and goof off instead.

"Oh, I don't know. Maybe it's because you told Ben that I liked him and now he hates me." I spread my arms out and high-kicked across my body, not kicking Jessica this time, but really wanting to. High kicks were part of our warm-up routine. Nothing out of the ordinary here!

Jessica froze and looked as guilty as a kid caught stealing cookies red-handed. "I . . . I thought I was helping. I mean, *you* weren't going to ever say anything, so . . ."

"So you thought you'd ruin my life?" I high-kicked again, coming closer to Jessica this time.

"Would you stop that?" Jessica batted my foot away. "Well,

what about *you* and *Kent*? *You* knew I liked him, but I know you're trying to steal him from me."

I snorted so loudly that several girls stopped their own conversations and turned our way. "You *know* that's not true. Our moms are friends. That's it."

"Then why else would he not—?" Jessica began to ask a question, but she stopped.

"Oh my God, you told Kent you *liked* him?"

"*No!*"

I could tell Jessica was lying by how red her face turned, like a big red balloon, ready to pop.

"Maybe he turned you down because he's in *high school*!"

"But . . . I'm *thirteen*. He's a young tenth grader, and I'm an older seventh grader . . ."

Jessica looked so pathetic, like it was just beginning to dawn on her how unrealistic her reasoning was. I almost felt sorry for her. *Almost.*

I remembered what Natalie told me. "Plus, I know *what else* you've been saying."

Jessica's big red balloon face deflated right in front of me. Her mouth opened and closed, but no words came out. She reminded me of a fish flopping on the ground, gasping for breath.

Like our friendship.

"Okay, girls, y'all warmed up?" Ms. Johnson had returned.

She clapped her hands. "C'mon! Get in a line and number off—one, two, one, two!"

We played dodgeball that day. Normally that was a cause for celebration—way more fun than running laps, endless sit-ups, or an aerobics video. But I had to sit out a lot because I kept on hitting Jessica in the head with my ball.

"It was an accident!" I feigned innocence after the third time. "You know Jessica was my friend." But I said "was" real softly, so it sounded more like "is."

Coach sighed. "Just say sorry, okay? Jessica, you gotta move faster, too."

"Sorry, Jessica," I said sweetly as I glowered, my eyes showing I was *anything* but.

Jessica hustled out of the locker room as quickly as she could after class. She wasn't on the bus, either, but that wasn't a big surprise. Ever since winter break, she had talked about how "not cool" it was to ride the bus, even though she *knew* I usually didn't have a choice. She had sometimes offered to pick me up, but she stopped halfway through the winter. Now that I knew these weren't *real* offers and she accused me of trying to "steal" Kent from her, it made sense why.

I opened my tattered copy of *Alice's Adventures in Wonderland* on the bus. It opened to this passage I had underlined:

"I could tell you my adventures—beginning from this

morning," said Alice a little timidly: "but it's no use going back to yesterday, because I was a different person then."

I tried to remember why I had marked this passage, but I couldn't. Like Alice, I wasn't the same girl today that I was yesterday.

Then the words swam and swirled like the events of the day in my brain.

Thwap! A wadded-up paper ball bounced off my head and into the seat behind me. I looked up to catch a little twerp sneering at me from five seats ahead.

I looked down at my worn and well-loved copy of my favorite childhood story. Slowly, I ripped out the title page and table of contents. I crumpled them up and threw a paper ball back.

I missed.

Of course I did.

CHAPTER 37

The thing about anger is that it can really feel like it's burning you up, like having a spotlight as hot as the sun aimed *right at you*. But once it's gone, there's . . . nothing. It's like being on a completely empty stage. No set, no costumes, no orchestra. No feelings.

Nothing.

Mom said that continuing down this path was going to lead to disappointment and hurt. She was right. Would I ever get the lead because I had the best audition? Or would I always be the orphan with the fewest lines? And when there was a play or TV show or movie with parts for people like me, would everyone say I was only cast because I'm Asian and not because of talent or hard work, or anything like that?

It was a no-win situation.

Best friends aren't forever.

The frog was not a prince in disguise. He was just a frog.

And Wonderland was just some silly words on a page, written about someone who didn't look like me for girls who looked a lot more like Jessica.

This was *reality*. And nothing crushes dreams more than that.

During spring break, all I could think about was finding time to write my version of *Alice in Wonderland*. When I wasn't writing, I daydreamed how this version—*my version*—would play out in front of an audience. Bowing at the end to a standing ovation and bouquets of flowers handed to me. All that seemed so silly now. Being in theater seemed so silly. *Acting* was silly.

The days were getting a little longer, though, so Dad sometimes was able to get out of work before dark.

On those days, he'd set down his briefcase, loosen his tie, and call upstairs like he always did. "Tadaima! Hey, Aoi, do you want to shoot some baskets?"

Only now, I answered, "I can't today. But I bet Tak would!"

Sometimes I looked out the window and watched them play. Tak could hit the rim when he shot now, but it was still really high for him. It was high for *me*.

What in the world made me think I could dunk? I thought.

Silly, silly, silly old me.

There were no plays this spring, no more basketball games.

For us middle schoolers, anyway. The one highlight was the NCAA college basketball tournament. The KU Jayhawks were still in it, and they were peaking at just the right time.

In the first round, they beat Xavier. No big surprise there. I mean, who'd ever heard of Xavier? Then Murray State and Vanderbilt.

The good news: Kansas was one of the top eight teams left in the tournament. The bad news: next up we'd play against our biggest rival—Kansas State.

Since my dad graduated from KU, we all hated K-State. Especially since they handed our team a loss at the end of January and broke the Jayhawks' fifty-five-game home winning streak. Even though Jessica didn't care about basketball, she liked K-State more than KU because "their colors are prettier." After what had passed between us, I wanted nothing more than to see red-and-blue KU mop the floor with a bunch of dejected purple-and-white Wildcats.

I got my wish.

Hardworking, not-so-flashy Scooter Barry scored more points than he ever had in that game. KU was going to the Final Four!

Even though Dad now had to work hard on managing the departmental budget, he still had time for basketball, even if it meant recording the games and avoiding any news about them (which was really hard in basketball-obsessed Kansas) until he could watch them when he had time.

Next up, the Puke Poo Devils. They called themselves the Duke Blue Devils, but we all knew their *real* name. Mom told me it wasn't "ladylike" when I called them the "Poo Devils," but Dad didn't care. He called them that, too, when Mom wasn't around. They were another team we Jayhawks fans loved to hate. Two years ago, we lost to them in the Final Four. Not this time, though.

Not this time, Puke.

For the final championship game against Oklahoma, Natalie came over with her dad to watch. Inside our small house, Mr. Moreno and Natalie seemed especially huge. I would say like Alice was when she took a bite of the cake that had the note "Eat me" on it, but I won't since I'm over that story.

They took off their shoes without us having to ask. That was one of the things I'd liked about Jessica. But when Natalie and her dad did it, too, I realized that maybe it wasn't that big of a deal when people respected the rules of our house. Like maybe *of course they should* as opposed to us being so grateful that they didn't make a big fuss about it.

Even though my mom didn't care about basketball one bit ("Now why is tonight's game any different?"), she set out bowls of freshly popped popcorn, and sliced cantaloupe for us to snack on during the game. Natalie had made chocolate chip oatmeal cookies that my mom complimented her on.

"Regular chocolate chip cookies are too sweet, but I like these. They're healthy!"

My little brother made his "Tak's Crunchy Surprise," which was basically a chaotic version of Rice Krispie treats with lots of questionable substitutions. For instance, we didn't have any Rice Krispies cereal, so he mixed Cheerios in with the marshmallows that he had blown up in the microwave. There weren't enough Cheerios, either, so he added in crushed pretzel bits.

He made a face when he tested them. "Too salty!" So then he added M&M's from yesterday's Easter candy haul. "Ugh, now it's too chocolaty!" Tak threw in a couple of handfuls of popcorn before Mom stopped him from experimenting anymore.

And you know what? It was actually pretty yummy!

That game against Oklahoma was one none of us would ever forget. The Sooners had beaten us twice before and they were seeded way above KU. But we really hung in there and by halftime, it was a tie game. Natalie, Mr. Moreno, my dad, and I screamed and shouted at the screen the whole time. We flinched every time a KU shot bounced off the rim, and cheered every time we snagged a rebound. Tak followed along and shouted "Yay!" in between shoving sticky handfuls of his "Crunchy Surprise" in his mouth. Danny Manning played his heart out like the star he was. When he sank two free throws with only five seconds left in the game, we knew we had won.

We won! The KU Jayhawks were national champions!

All of us watching jumped up and down so much the house shook. I felt my chest swell up with happiness as our team swarmed the court and hugged each other. The roars, even from the TV, filled my ears.

Sure, technically I realized "we" didn't win—it was the *team* that won, not *us*.

But for those of us who knew we would never have a chance to play like that ourselves, for those of us like my dad, who was bogged down every week with a mountain of administrative work because of a so-called "promotion" to department chair, for those of us like my mom, who might not speak English perfectly, for those of us who didn't have vocal coaches, or parents on the arts council, or who didn't look like people on the movie posters, well, that win gave us a little taste of what having a dream come true felt like.

And for a lot of us, that was as close as we would get.

CHAPTER 38

It was hard to believe there was less than a month of seventh grade left. The weeks after spring break had flown by even though I wasn't involved in anything exciting anymore.

At the beginning of the year, Jessica and I were so sad we only had PE and lunch together. By the end of seventh grade, I was relieved. I had lunch with my basketball team, and even though the season was over, they were as loyal in the cafeteria as they were on the court. When I scrimmaged against them, I often wished they weren't so tall. Now I was grateful. When they sat around me, I could barely see anyone else, and I doubt Jessica or Ben could see me. Not that they wanted to, I'm sure, but it was still a comfort.

In PE, Jessica moved to the back row of the gym for her warm-ups so I couldn't kick her butt anymore. I moved to the very front row to get the message across that I wanted to be as far away from her as possible, too.

One upside to Ben throwing my heart on the ground and stomping it to pieces was that I became a *way* better student. I did my homework every afternoon after school, even my boring math worksheets. No more daydreaming about him during class. No more acting like I didn't understand a math problem so he could explain it to me.

On the weekends, I sometimes shot hoops with Natalie while we gossiped about anything and everything. Turns out there was a lot more to her than just basketball! She had a new puppy, hated slugs with a passion, but loved math even more than she disliked Mrs. Olds. Plus, she was super interested in different kinds of music. When the weather was bad, we spent hours inside, during which she played me some of her favorite songs. She had a lot of books on her shelves that I recognized, but she hadn't read most of them yet.

"I have a hard time getting into them," she had explained. "But once I start one, I feel like I *have* to finish it, so . . ."

"It's hard to choose." I finished her thought for her. "I *totally* get it." I recommended the books I had read and liked so she could avoid the ones that would be a chore to get through. *Alice's Adventures in Wonderland* was there, too, but I didn't say anything about it.

At home, I also read a bunch, but not the silly stories I used to like. This past fall, my parents had bought a set of World Book Encyclopedias from a man who was selling them door to door. I wasn't really interested in them until now. Every so often when I was bored, I would look something up and just learn about it. Like hedgehogs, for instance. They curl up into a ball when they're afraid, and their prickly spines help protect their soft bellies. In Wonderland, they played croquet with flamingos as mallets and hedgehogs as the balls. After reading the encyclopedia entry about them, I realized just how ridiculous this was. The hedgehogs' spikes would have poked the flamingos' eyes out and Wonderland would've been a bloody mess!

Which led me to look up flamingos in the encyclopedia, too. Turns out they're pink because of the red-orange brine shrimp they eat. They're born gray, though. Were there any flamingos out there that weren't as lucky in the brine shrimp department? And did they never turn pink as a result? That, the article didn't say. I guess I could've called up the world-famous Topeka Zoo to ask, but I didn't care *that* much.

I had more time to help out at home now, too, so several evenings a week, I prepared dinner. I let Tak be my "sous-chef" sometimes. I had no idea what that was, but Tak insisted that was what he was.

"Why don't we ever make scallops?" he asked out of the blue one evening.

"Scallops? Where'd you ever hear about those?" Fresh

seafood was hard to come by in Topeka, and besides, it was *ex-pen-sive.*

Tak frowned. "On a cooking show."

Now that we didn't have our eyes glued to the TV for basketball, I guess Tak was watching a lot of those nowadays.

"If you overcook them, they're rubbery," Tak explained. "But when they're cooked perfectly—"

"'Scallops'-tte 'hotate' no koto ka na?" Mom arrived home in the middle of our conversation. She wanted to know what "scallops" were in Japanese. She thought they might be what was called "hotate," so we looked them up in the encyclopedia just to make sure. Turns out she was right. Mom's eyes got misty and distant when looking at the images. "They're delicious. And Tak's right. If you cook them too long, they turn tough."

Tak nodded as he ripped the lettuce into bite-sized portions for our salad. "I'll cook them for you one day."

"Oh yeah? When?" I chopped some tomatoes.

"In the fancy restaurant I'm gonna have."

This was new. I'd never heard him say *that* before. "Whatever happened to being a math professor like Dad?"

Tak shrugged. "I don't think he has fun at work anymore. Even with all the hot chocolate he can drink. Plus, he never gets to use a knife."

"Huh? Whaddaya mean—?"

"I asked him! He told me no, he never gets to use a knife as

300

a math professor. Chefs have *lots* of knives! When's your next play, Annie?"

Tak's ability to change the course of a conversation was like plot twists no one ever saw coming.

I felt Mom's eyes on me, standing by for a response. I didn't look up as I waited for Tak to add the rest of the lettuce to the bowl.

"I'm not doing those anymore."

Tak stopped mid-rip. "What? Why?"

"It was just a hobby," I said impatiently. "Now throw the rest of the lettuce in so I can toss the salad."

Tak frowned, the leaves still clenched in his hands.

Geez, how was he going to open a fancy restaurant if he couldn't even handle a salad? "What's it to you anyway? Come on!"

Tak threw the large lettuce leaves in the bowl as is. "You're *stupid.*"

"No, *you* are!" I retorted. It was immature of me to fight with him like this, but . . .

He hopped off the stool he was standing on, slapped his bottom at me, yelled, "You're a stinky butt!" and ran upstairs.

I took the leaves and finished the job for him. "What's *his* problem?"

"I think he just enjoyed seeing you onstage," my mom replied softly.

I don't know how my mom came to that conclusion from "You're stupid!" and "You're a stinky butt!" but, whatever.

When my birthday rolled around in May, I went to Dr. Wang's office one last time before the end of the school year. No more allergy shots, though, just my yearly checkup this time around.

"Annie!" Dr. Wang greeted me like we were old friends. I liked her, even though our extra time together over the past few months didn't make me enjoy visiting her office anymore. "How are you feeling? How are your allergies?"

"They're a lot better, thanks." I woke up to Chibi sleeping on my head this morning and I didn't cough at all. I figured she didn't need to know these details, though.

"Yes, thanks to you. We're so grateful. Right, Aoi?" My mom was still her overly complimentary self around Dr. Wang. Even after we had visited her a gajillion times in the last few months.

"I said thanks." I didn't mean to sound snappish, but I couldn't help it. I felt bad immediately after I said it. "I mean, I *am* really grateful," I told Dr. Wang. I was! What she did for me was amazing. She kept me healthy. Because of her, I could keep my cat. Maybe I could bring myself to want to do what she did, to be a doctor. Maybe it's the type of job that people dreamed about once they were a little older?

I watched Dr. Wang as she studied my chart. She was so professional, so put together. I looked around the walls with all her framed diplomas and board certifications. I bet when people heard she was a doctor, she got a ton of respect. Something that *I* sure didn't get a whole lot of this past year.

"Was it hard to become a doctor?" I asked without thinking. Mom shot me a look, too. I had overstepped and was being rude.

"Well, you do have to study. *A lot*. And take a lot of tests."

"But these tests." My mom leaned forward. "They are fair? Not like English tests or writing—"

Dr. Wang nodded. "I mean, there's a level of subjectivity in everything, but yes, I'd say the tests medical doctors have to take are probably more objective than something in less technical fields."

Mom looked pleased. I gave her a dirty look. I blurted out, "But did you always want to be a doctor?"

"Aoi." I could tell Mom wanted me to stop harassing Dr. Wang with all my questions.

But Dr. Wang didn't seem to mind. She laughed. "You know what? I *did*."

"Really?" It was hard for me to believe that hanging out in this sterile office and seeing sick people all day was *anyone's* dream.

"It really was. I had dolls and stuffed animals and I was always operating on them, and curing their imaginary diseases. . . . I once got in big trouble for cutting off my teddy bear's leg because I wanted to practice sewing it back on."

It was hard for me to imagine Dr. Wang, who was so polished and professional, as a crazy kid performing surgery on her poor toys.

"Medicine isn't for everyone." Dr. Wang didn't look at either of us as she tapped my knees to check my reflexes. "I tell people only to go into it if they *truly* want to be a doctor. I mean, no one wants a surgeon who doesn't want to be there, right? Could you imagine? Daydreaming about being a rock star and *oops! There goes an artery!*"

I looked over toward my mom, who *clearly* was avoiding looking at me. Dr. Wang's nurse, Patty, tapped on the door and arrived with a tray. What? Another shot?

"But your work, it's very interesting, right? Very fulfilling?" My mom wasn't letting it drop. So, I wasn't going to, either.

"If you're that interested in having a doctor in the family, why don't *you* become one?" I asked my mom sweetly.

Although I was being anything but sweet. *I* knew that, and so did my mom.

Her jaw clenched and she turned her blazing black eyes my way. I stared back coolly.

"That's a great idea!" Patty swabbed my arm, oblivious to the tension around her. "I used to be a secretary before I had kids. But then I went back to school!"

Now it was our turn for both of us to be surprised. "You

did?" we both asked together.

"Yep! Started with some evening classes, but then pursued my degree in nursing."

"Luckily for me." Dr. Wang smiled her way. "Nurse Patty saves *my* life every day."

I saw the needle and I looked away. I thought I was done with shots, but it turned out I needed a tetanus booster. I took in deep breaths to calm myself. No matter how many needles I'd had stabbed into my arms this year, there was still no way I could get used to them.

I felt my mom's eyes on me, but they were no longer angry like before. But I couldn't tell *what* they were. "What?" I asked her.

"What what?" she responded before she looked away.

CHAPTER 39

The last week of seventh grade, our teachers sent us home with bags of *stuff* we had accumulated over the year. Old papers, art projects, and of course—piles and piles of *worksheets*.

I didn't feel like sorting through and organizing any of it, so I just threw everything in my closet. I'd have all the time in the world later since I wasn't planning on doing much this summer, except maybe earning some money by babysitting. Now that I was thirteen, my parents agreed to let me watch other families' kids even though I'd already been watching my extremely difficult younger brother forever.

The second to last day of school, I came home to—

My mom.

In my room.

Reading my *Alice in Wonderland* script.

"Hey!" I yelled as I dropped my grocery bag of notebooks and other half-used school supplies. "What are you doing in here?"

"Helping you clean," my mother responded without a smidgen of guilt. *How dare she look through my things?*

I strode over and attempted to snatch my script from her hands.

"When did you write this?" Mom held it out of reach.

I tried again. "I don't know. During spring break."

Mom crossed her arms and held it close to her chest. "So, when you were supposed to be catching up on your math assignments and only that?"

"Yeah. Sorry." I looked down. "It's stupid, I know. I'll throw it in the fireplace right now and burn it, if that's what you want."

My mom was quiet for a long time. I looked up, ready to face the trouble I was in.

But she didn't look mad—at all. She seemed . . . sad, actually.

"Aoi," she said softly. "Why would you think I would want you to burn this? It's good."

The door to my heart opened a crack and I felt the warmth of the stage, her words, *my* words that I had written. But I couldn't deal with the disappointment again. The hurt that came with anything and everyone connected to the theater.

"Because I'm not interested in that stuff anymore."

Mom opened up the script and her eyes smiled. A little. "Who knew you had such an imagination?"

I lunged forward and finally was able to grab my work from her hands. "And I never said you could read it anyway!" I stuffed it into the trash can.

My mom stared at me in silence. I frowned and looked away.

"I'll clean up my stuff, okay?" I didn't add, *so get out*, but we both knew that's what I meant.

But my mom wasn't about to let me get away with my little tantrum.

"Aoi, the fact remains that you disobeyed me. You worked on this even when I said you weren't supposed to. So, you have to face the consequences."

I crossed my arms and scowled as I met my mom's glare. Turns out she was doing the exact same thing.

"You will take that script out of the trash right now."

The way her eyes were boring into me, I knew I needed to do as she said. And fast.

I stomped over to the trash can and pulled my script out.

"And you will turn it in to that director—what's her name? Mrs. Sam?"

What?

"No, it's Sam. Just Sam. Not 'Mrs.' That's her mom, but ..." I couldn't understand why my mother was making me do this.

"I will not have any child of mine wasting her time. You did the work, so don't throw it all away."

With that, my mother brushed past me, the tornado mess that was my room, *and* my feelings.

On the last day of school, I wolfed down my lunch.

"You're gonna choke." Natalie watched me shovel food into my mouth.

"You having a growth spurt or something, Shorty?" Angie asked.

I chugged the rest of my juice and wiped my mouth with the back of my hand.

"You mean, 'Ice'?" I grinned as I got up to return my tray. "Sorry, I have to go turn something in."

"Today?" Kirsten called out. "Shoot, was something due?"

"Yep, for me, anyway! See you in PE!" I hollered back as I picked up my backpack and practically ran toward the office.

As I rounded the corner, I almost collided with Sam.

"Annie! Geez, you trying to kill me?" She was carrying a stack of papers under one arm and a mug of coffee with her other hand. Some had sloshed on the ground.

"Oops, sorry." I opened up my backpack and rummaged around. I found a few old napkins shoved in there. Not too clean, but they'd be fine for mopping up some coffee. I threw them on the floor and moved them around with my foot while I located my script.

309

"Here." I handed it to Sam. "I know you said by noon today, so if it's too late and you don't want it—"

Sam took the crumpled script from me and opened it to the first page. "Are you kidding me? Of course I'll take it." She smiled as she scanned my words. "You might've just saved me from directing *Alice in Fartland*, written by I'm-not-telling-but-you-probably-know-who."

Ben. That jerk. I had finally gotten to the point that it didn't hurt to see him and hear his name anymore. The thought of him still made my blood run cold and fill me with a million stabby daggers.

"I'll make my decision by next week and then auditions will be two weeks after that. Did you get a flyer? I asked the front office to deliver them to all the classes a while ago. It has all the info, in case you missed it." Sam fumbled with her stack of papers while trying not to spill any more coffee.

Truth is, I *did* receive one, but I turned it into an airplane on the bus and let it fly.

I should have helped her, but I took a step back instead. "Oh, I'm not actually doing any theater this summer."

"What?" Sam almost dropped the flyers. More coffee splashed onto the floor.

We both looked down at the brown splatter. "I, uh . . ." I fumbled through my backpack to see if there were any more napkins. I felt Sam's hand on my arm.

"Hey, forget about the coffee for a second."

I lowered my backpack and took another step back. "I'm just, I dunno." I shifted my weight from one leg to the other. "Maybe writing's more my thing." Even as I said those words, I kind of wished my mom hadn't made me turn my script in at all. "But if I have to be in the play for my script to be considered, I can take it back. It's no big deal."

I reached to take my copy back, but Sam turned so I couldn't reach it.

"Never said that, kid!"

At that moment the bell rang, signaling the end of the lunch break.

"I should get to my next class." I hitched my backpack up onto my shoulder and started sidestepping away from Sam.

"Wait!" She chugged the rest of her coffee and strode toward me. "Listen. Now, this is just between you and me, but there's something I think you should know. I didn't cast you as Annie last summer because there were other forces at work and that's all I'm going to say about that. In terms of Eliza, I cast you because you got up right away even though you fell down *hard* during your audition. I heard you hit the stage way out where I was sitting. Never saw anyone wipe out like that, not cry, and get right back up. No other reason, you hear? You were good, and I'm just hoping . . ."

I stood there, stunned, as I waited for Sam to finish.

311

"Well, I'm just hoping that no one tried to tell you any different, that's all." Sam shoved the flyer at me and wouldn't move out of my way until I took it.

I walked like a zombie toward my next class. People bumped and shoved me out of their way as I trudged down the hall.

Do I really want to go down that path again? I thought. I read the flyer in my hands.

Summer Children's Theater, June 15–August 1.
Alice in Wonderland.

I didn't read any more of it. I couldn't.

So, I crumpled it up and threw it in the nearest trash can.

CHAPTER 40

A week after school was out, my report card came in the mail. B-minus.

My math grade was better than at the quarter, but still bad enough that my dad looked really sad when he saw it and read the comments:

In terms of points, Aoi's grade was closer to an "A-minus." However, her behavior and attitude were not what I had hoped for from someone with her background.

My mom was mad, but not so much at me. "Stupid woman," she muttered under her breath.

On the same day my report card had arrived in the mail, the phone rang after dinner.

Tak ran to get it, but my mom ran even faster. No telling *what* Tak would say. One time a heavily made-up woman showed up on our front porch after Tak had told someone on the phone that, yes, we *would* be interested in learning more about Mary Kay cosmetics.

"Hello?" my mom asked as she picked up the phone. "Yes, just a moment."

Mom held the receiver out to me. "Aoi, it's for you."

"Is it Natalie?"

Mom shook her head. "Chigau." *I don't think so.*

I had been in the middle of reading about fungi, or mushrooms. In *Alice in Wonderland*, there's a caterpillar on a magic mushroom. It could make people change sizes, depending on what side they ate. But in my version of the story, I changed the mushroom to a "Fun Guy" with shades selling potions from inside his jacket.

Get it? *Fungi . . . Fun Guy.*

It's dumb. I know.

I got up and shuffled to the phone. If it wasn't Natalie, I had no idea who could be calling me.

"Hello?"

"Oh, hey. Annie? This is Sam."

I paused. The only Sam I knew was the director and there was no reason for—

"Yeah, I'm calling because we're gonna use your play! You know, your *Alice in Wonderland* rewrite!"

I still hadn't said anything. I heard the words coming

314

through the receiver into my ear, but I wasn't sure how to process them.

"Hello? Annie? That's still okay, right?"

I finally cleared my throat. "Yeah, it's cool."

"Oh, thank goodness. It was the best by a mile. I might have thrown in the towel if you changed your mind." Sam sighed with relief. "So, you excited? I hope you've reconsidered auditioning..."

"I, uh..." I looked toward my mom, who was quietly wiping dishes and putting them away. Without Jessica's mom to help carpool, I'd have to ask my parents. Mom had decided to take some classes this summer and I had already agreed to help out by watching Tak. Even though it was summer, Dad was still really busy.

"I don't think I can," I mumbled.

Sam didn't answer.

"Hello?" Now it was my turn to wonder if *she* was still there.

"Oh, yeah, hi. I'm here. That's too bad, kid."

"Yeah."

More awkward silence. This was a really weird phone call. I was about to say "bye" and just hang up when Sam piped up again.

"Hey, would you mind helping me out with something?"

"Uh, sure."

"So, you know the part where you have Alice talking with the caterpillar?"

"Yeah?" *Where was Sam going with this?*

"Do you remember the part after the caterpillar asks, 'What size do you want to be?' But you changed it to, 'What do you want to be?'"

"Uh-huh."

"How did you imagine it would go? Would you mind reciting it back to me? That is, if you can remember what you wrote. As the director, it always helps to talk with the writer."

Even though I didn't have the script in front of me, I wrote and rewrote that section a gajillion times. Of course, I knew it by heart, but . . .

"Right now?" I looked around. Mom had left the kitchen and Tak wasn't around, either. Maybe she was getting him to bed.

"Uh . . . okay." I took a deep breath and became Alice, talking to the Caterpillar.

"You asked me who I was, and I told you I'm just me. I'm Alice. But that wasn't good enough for you and now you're asking what I want to be, and I told you I just want to be Alice but that doesn't work for you, either! 'Here, take a bite of what the Fun Guy is offering you to be better at this.' 'Here, take a sip of the potion he has in his other hand to be this other thing.' So, I did what you said and I became all stretched out this way, and then did what *he* said and became small again. Well, I'm done listening to both of you and I'm just gonna listen to myself from now on and I'm going to be exactly who I should have been all along."

"And who is that?" Sam read the Caterpillar's line.

"It's Annie! . . . I mean, Alice," I stumbled.

Sam was quiet again. I thought that maybe I heard her sigh. But maybe not.

"Okay, great! Thanks a lot, Annie," she finally responded.

"Sure . . . Is that it, then?" I asked.

"Yep! I got what I needed, kid."

I was drained when I hung up the phone. I had planned to finish reading the encyclopedia article on fungi, but all I really wanted to do was sleep and retreat into dreams that didn't hurt me to have.

Two weeks passed and the summer heat was beating down on us again. Mom agreed to drop me and Tak off at the air-conditioned library on the way to her classes at the university. It came as a big surprise to all of us when she announced she was going to study to be a nurse, just like Nurse Patty from Dr. Wang's office did after she had kids.

"This returning to school to start a new career wouldn't happen in Japan. Especially for someone as old as me," Mom mentioned. "But since your dad works there, I can take classes at a discount, so . . ."

"We could go together when I need to work too!" Dad smiled when she made the announcement. "On other days, I could bike. I biked everywhere when I was in Japan. Why not here?"

"Yes, why not?" Mom looked a little nervous, but more than that, she looked *determined*.

When Kent's mom heard that she was going back to school, she said that maybe she would, too, once she returned from Japan before the fall semester. Even though my mom was an adult, it made me think that maybe they needed the support of friends, too.

But this Monday morning, Mom turned right instead of left toward the library.

"Why are we going this way?" I asked.

"Because," Mom replied in her typical way.

Tak and I rolled our eyes at each other in the back seat. At six years old, my little brother was definitely less of a hyper demon and a little more human these days.

When we pulled into the parking lot of the summer theater camp, I frowned. "What's going on?"

The Kellys' Fifth Avenue had just pulled in, too. *No way!* "Mom!"

She didn't look at me as she got out of the car. It was already hot inside the Chevette, but with the windows rolled up I would just sit and bake in there.

Even so, it took me a moment to get out and follow Tak and my mom toward the theater.

"Annie!" Ms. Tracy waved to me from the front entrance. "So nice to see you again!" She gathered me into a big welcoming hug.

I couldn't bring myself to tell her this was the last place on earth I wanted to be.

Tak let go of my mom's hand to greet Ms. Tracy. He puffed out his chest and put his hands on his hips. "I'm Tak!"

Ms. Tracy hunkered down to meet my little brother eye to eye. "Hello there, Tak! We're so excited to have you in our new Beginning Theater Camp this year!"

I was so confused. *I* was supposed to watch Tak this summer.

She turned to me and explained. "There was enough interest that we were able to provide something for the little ones to get them started, so Sam and the more experienced actors could focus on—"

Then Sam walked past us in the hallway. "Annie! Awesome. Hey, we're all gathering on the stage. Wanna come with?"

Ms. Tracy took Tak's hand and my mom gave me a little push from behind.

"Let's go. Come on."

At this point, I was pretty sure aliens had kidnapped my real family and brought me here. Since when had my mom *ever* come inside to any of my activities and not just dropped me off? She *hated* interacting with all these people she didn't know.

I cast a glance behind me. *Definitely kidnapped by aliens.*

Onstage, Jessica, Ben, and a few new kids I didn't recognize were there. Ben and Jessica didn't look my way and I didn't look at them, either. I sat in the farthest possible chair from them, and scooted it another foot away just to make sure they knew *exactly* how I felt.

Mrs. Kelly was there, too. "Jackie! Jackie, over here!" She waved at my mom like it wasn't weird that they hadn't communicated for several months. When my mom didn't join her, Mrs. Kelly *clicked* and *clacked* her way with her high-heeled bedazzled sandals.

"I'll be by after class, all right, Aoi?" my mom called out to me.

"Okay." I still didn't exactly know what I was doing here, even though my mom seemed to.

"Did you say 'class,' Jackie?" Mrs. Kelly asked.

"Yes, I'm studying to be a nurse," Mom explained. She frowned and added, ". . . Maybe."

"You're going back to school?" Mrs. Kelly laughed. Not in a mean way exactly. But it wasn't nice, either. "Aren't we a little old for that?"

Mom's frown morphed into her flight attendant smile. "Yes. But *I* am not." She checked her watch. "Sorry, I do not want to be late."

I hadn't meant to listen in on their conversation, but it took all my concentration not to smile at the way my mom turned and left, with Mrs. Kelly wondering what just happened.

Sam hopped onto the stage and clapped her hands. She rubbed them together as she announced, "Hey, everyone! So glad to see you for our first day of our summer production of *Alice in Wonderland*. I'm excited about the script we're using. As you know, written by our own Annie Inoue—"

When Sam gestured my way, out of the corner of my eye, I saw Ben slump down. Ha! So *Alice in Fartland* was his. I sat up a little straighter.

"And based on everyone's auditions, the moment you've all been waiting for . . ."

Sam reached into her army jacket's pocket and pulled out a bunch of rolled-up papers. She slid off the rubber band that kept them together and handed each of us one.

Jessica's mom raised her hand. "I'd like one, too, please!"

Sam distributed them all to us before she handed the remainder to Ben. "Do me a favor, would ya?"

Ben hopped off the stage and handed a sheet to Mrs. Kelly.

My paper kept rolling up as I tried to read the cast list. I was curious who Sam envisioned in the roles I had written. Jessica would most likely be Alice, I had originally thought of Ben as the White Rabbit . . .

"But she doesn't even *look* like Alice!" Jessica screeched.

I was finally able to see the names.

And there was mine.

ALICE: Annie Inoue

I looked up. But I hadn't even auditioned!

"And she wasn't even here for auditions!"

I guess I wasn't the only one who was aware of that fact.

Jessica's cheeks turned bright red and her freckles seemed to jump from her face like Pop Rocks.

In contrast to the volcanic eruption that was Jessica, Sam was like an icy, still glacier as she waited for her to finish.

"Not on that particular day," Sam responded calmly. "But she *did* audition."

The phone call, I realized. That was pretty tricky of her. *Should I be mad?* I wondered.

"But Annie *wrote* it! So she gets to write it *and* be the lead? That's. NOT. FAIR!!!"

With Jessica's proclamation, I decided. *Nah. I'm not mad.* NOT ONE BIT.

Mrs. Kelly was up out of her seat and standing behind Jessica now.

"Mrs. Glick! I've really admired what you've done for our theater community in the short time you've been here, but I *have to* agree with my daughter. I mean, Annie, darling, you know I love you, but . . ."

Sam crossed her arms. So did I.

"As you might recall me saying, 'Mrs. Glick' is my mom, Mrs. Kelly," Sam responded in a clear voice. She wasn't yelling at all, but she spoke in a way that we could all hear. She turned to Jessica. "In *Alice in Wonderland*, there's a talking white bunny. Does Ben here look like a floppy-eared rodent? No, but my guess is he can play one. And yes, Annie's script is the one that was chosen. Correct me if I'm mistaken, but you didn't turn one in, right?"

"Well, that's because I want to *act*, not be a *writer*—" Jessica spat the word out like being a writer was a fate worse than death.

"While there *was* another script, after the tenth fart joke— and we were still in Act I at this point—I made the judgment that perhaps it wasn't suitable. Sorry, kid." Sam looked toward Ben.

Ben sank down in his seat. "Yeah, no. I get it."

Sam continued, "And you like the script, right? I didn't hear any complaints from you at auditions. And the Queen of Hearts is a great part for you."

"It's fine, but—" Jessica sputtered.

Sam uncrossed her arms and tapped the remaining papers, still rolled up like a baton, in the palm of her hand. "And do you *really* want to get into the conversation of what's *fair*?"

With that, Jessica fell silent, and Mrs. Kelly's face grew hard as the walls surrounding us.

"Well, Annie?" Sam asked. "Will you be our Alice?"

CHAPTER 41

On the final night of *Alice in Wonderland*, the roars of applause surrounded us and Tak's sharp whistles of appreciation pierced through the ruckus like exploding confetti. We all took a bow and Ms. Tracy surprised both Sam *and* me with bouquets of flowers.

"Ah-choo!" I sneezed into my roses and spotted Dr. Wang in the audience standing and applauding.

I took another bow and saw Natalie, her dad, and the rest of my basketball team jumping up and down, cheering, "SHORT-Y! AN-NIE! AL-ICE!" and pumping their fists.

I scanned the audience and there was Midge Prescott, too. She gave me a wink and a double thumbs-up.

The applause continued, so all of us took one more bow. When I stood up, I saw my family front and center, clapping and clapping and clapping.

The moment was everything I'd dreamed it would be.

After the show, Ben and Jessica ran up to me. We had cleared the air—as much as we could—over the course of the summer. Sam made it clear that this production was a team effort and she wouldn't have her cast at odds with each other.

Jessica had been under a lot of pressure from her mother. With the vocal coach *and* the acting lessons that I hadn't known were added onto her schedule once *The King and I* ended, she had felt like she was going to crack, she confessed . . . but she never actually told me she was *sorry*.

"Plus, you had your basketball *and* you did really well in *The King and I*," Jessica tried to explain to me in one of the first times we'd talked since our big fight. "We were driving past your house when I saw Kent walk out and . . . I might have jumped to conclusions and I couldn't deal with it."

"I don't really think you're ugly," Ben told me sheepishly at the end of the first day of summer theater. "I just liked Jessica and it hurt that she didn't like me back. So, I took it out on you. I'm sorry."

Now that the show was finished, it almost felt like old times between the three of us.

"Everyone loved it, Annie!" Ben ran up to me.

"Whatcha gonna write next?" Jessica bumped her shoulder into mine. "Something for me, maybe?"

I smiled. "You guys were both really good."

I wasn't lying, either. Ben was perfect as the flighty Rabbit who I, as Alice, chased after and he paid no attention to. I had liked him *so much*, so much that I even acted dumb so he'd like me more. Now that the crush was over, I realized how wrong that was. I hoped someday there would be a guy who liked me for me. But until there was, it wasn't worth acting like someone I wasn't to make him like me back.

Jessica was terrifying and *extremely* believable as the diva Queen of Hearts, who furiously ordered my head to be chopped off. But I still remembered how mad she was that I was both the writer *and* the lead of the play. How it wasn't *fair*. I couldn't help but wonder if she'd feel the same if our roles were reversed.

It was almost like old times, but not quite.

When my mom, dad, and Tak approached, Jessica and Ben left to find their own families.

"That was way more fun than math!" my dad exclaimed.

"When's your *next* show?" Tak grabbed my hand.

"Who was that boy?" Mom asked.

"Just Ben. Don't you remember him from the other plays?"

"What did you say his name was?"

"Ben. Ben Prescott."

My mom and dad traded looks and burst into giggles like they were little kids.

"What?" I asked.

"Oh, it's just that his name means . . ." My mom patted her forehead with a handkerchief. "Ben means 'poo' in Japanese and benpi means 'constipated.'"

"What's 'constipated'?" Tak's ears had perked up as soon as he heard the word *poo*.

"It means you're full of poo, but you're still having a hard time pooping," I told him.

Of course, this delighted Tak to no end. "Benpi! Benpi!" he shouted as he jumped up and down.

Ben turned our way and waved.

"Jessie-chan was very good as the Queen of Hearts." My dad tried to change the topic before Tak got us in trouble. "Very scary."

I nodded. "She's been stressed 'cause of things with her mom, so it actually was a good way to get some of her frustrations out."

My mom looked thoughtful, sad, and guilty all at the same time.

Today, all my dreams had come true and it was one of the best days of my life. But it was also a little sad because the person who'd helped me get here was leaving.

"I have to say goodbye to Sam," I told my parents. "Would you be able to wait a few more minutes?"

* * *

Sam was going back to LA now that the show was done. At least that was the official reason given for her departure. But there were also whisperings of her being *fired*, of certain members of the Regional Arts Council who were *very* dissatisfied with the summer play and her casting choices. When Ms. Tracy heard us talking about it, she mumbled something that it wasn't that at all, it was about scripts being written on in pen and not in pencil, unauthorized photocopies, and how "adjustments to the music and dialogue resulted in fines from the authorizing theatrical companies that had granted us rights to the show."

Whatever *that* meant.

So, Sam was being fired for writing on our copies of the script? Seemed like a made-up reason to me. But I wanted to believe that more than the other rumors.

Because that would've meant it was *my* fault she had to leave.

I found her in her office, gathering some items into a box. "Sam?"

She looked up and smiled. "Hey, kid! So, whaddaya think? Did you do awesome or what?"

I smiled, but the happiness of the day was gone.

"What's up?" Sam came around and sat on her desk. "You should be on cloud nine."

"I'm sorry," I blurted out.

"Sorry? For what?"

"That you have to go back to LA."

Sam laughed. "You and me both, kid! That place is a sh—"
She paused like she was wondering if it would be okay to use
the type of language she wanted to use, or if she should refrain
since she was still in the children's theater office.

I felt worse than ever. She didn't *want* to go back. I hung my
head.

"Hey. Hey!" Sam got up and grabbed my shoulders. "You
should be happy! You did so well!"

"Did you get fired because of me?" I looked up and asked her
point blank.

Sam let go of me and sat back on her desk. She sighed and
looked up at the ceiling for a good few seconds before she
answered.

"Can I tell you something? I wasn't a 'big Hollywood director' when I came here. To be honest, I was washed up, fed up,
and ready to throw in the towel." She turned to me. "You know
how many women directors there are in LA?"

I shook my head.

"Not many," laughed Sam. But she wasn't laughing like she
thought it was funny—at all. "Not only was it hard to get a
gig, but once I got 'em, the disrespect on set, lemme tell ya . . ."

Sam looked thoughtful as she pulled out a box of Mike and
Ike and offered me some. I shook my head. She poured the colorful candy directly into her mouth, as she always did.

"I loved the movies, ya know? As a kid I couldn't get enough of them. The candy, the popcorn. Getting lost in a story. So, I chased my dream as soon as I could and hotfooted it down to LA. And you know what? LA chewed me up and spat me out."

Sam stuck a finger in her mouth to loosen the gummy candy from her molars as she continued her story. "So, I came back here. I felt like that was it—I had given up. But a funny thing happened. You guys made me love it again. The directing. The collaboration to create something awesome. *The story.* That's why I eat all this movie theater candy. Helps me remember what got me dreamin' in the first place, ya know? But a couple months ago, a friend let me know that she'd opened a theater company. And they were looking for a director, so—"

"*That's* why you're going back?"

Sam smiled, and like she was truly happy this time. "Coming back here reminded me how much I loved the theater, too. And it's a chance to direct, and sometimes a chance is all you need."

I nodded, relieved that she was leaving because she wanted to.

"And you know what? That's something *you* taught me." Sam shook her box of Mike and Ike in my direction.

Me? I was confused.

Sam fished through her pockets and pulled out a card.

"Kid, I'm not gonna lie. I hope you find something else, nice and stable, that'll make you happy. Show business ain't easy. So what if you're naturally gifted and hardworking? Great. Does that guarantee success? Not at all. Will talentless hacks like Jes—"

Sam paused here like she was again wrestling with whether to say something or not. She took a deep breath and continued. "*So* many people dream of being a big star, and does everyone's dream come true? Course not. Will people with connections and money get the gig more times than you? Absolutely. But will they have a career? No. In order to stay at the top, you gotta have it *all*, and then some. And keep an eye out for the users, too. Once the leeches get an inkling that you might be able to do something for them, they come out of the wood-work, all sunshine and false promises. This business is more heartache than anything, but if it's *really* what you want . . ." She handed me her card. "I get it."

It read "Rebecca Vincent Theater Company."

"I'm pretty low in the pecking order, but if I can help in any way, look me up, all right?"

Sam threw an *Alice in Wonderland* program into the box she had packed. "See you around, Annie."

"Bye, Sam. And thank you."

Sam laughed. "No need to thank me. I just finally got out of your way."

As Sam was about to walk through the door and out of

my life, she turned around. "Hey, is Annie your real name? I thought I heard your mom call you something different."

Her question surprised me. No one had suspected that Annie wasn't who I was—ever since I started calling myself that, anyway.

"My real name's Aoi," I told Sam, curious as to why she wanted to know.

"A-o-i?" Sam repeated carefully. "Am I saying that right?"

I nodded.

"That's pretty. Why don't you use it?" she asked.

"Not many people get it right," I explained.

Sam nodded. I think she understood.

I followed Sam out the door only to bump into Jessica. I wondered how long she had been standing there and how much she might have heard. Sam walked right by her, though, like she wasn't even there. Jessica didn't say anything to her, either. The AC was on, but I got the feeling that wasn't the reason the air felt frigid between them.

Once Sam was out of sight, Jessica linked her arm with mine like she used to when we were up to our secret plans, usually shenanigans adults wouldn't approve of. She walked me down the hall in the opposite direction from where Sam had left.

"So . . ." she drawled. "Whaddaya say we get some frozen yogurt at the new place that opened near the Wendy's?"

It was so odd to be like this again, after everything that had gone on between us. Yes, we'd been civil to each other this summer, but I assumed it was because we *had* to be. I wondered if Jessica didn't think it was weird, either. I studied her expression as she continued to walk and chatter.

"I have a *great* idea for a play. *You* could write it, and I figured my mom could pull some strings with the middle school production. We'd be eighth graders and if we don't involve the high school, we'd *definitely* get the leads."

Aha.

"Really?" I feigned interest. "*Both* of us?"

Jessica looked up and away as she described her idea in more detail. "Well, I mean, it's technically about this *one* girl, but she has a best friend who's really funny."

It was amazing, really, how Jessica thought I would fall for this. I had forgiven her and Ben for dealing me some of the biggest blows I'd felt in my life.

But I hadn't forgotten.

I extracted my arm from hers and faced her. "I can't, Jessica."

Push it down.

Forget about it.

Move on.

This was how I used to deal with these types of situations. But I couldn't "push it down" and "forget about it" anymore....

I *could* move on.

334

So, I turned and walked away.

"You *can't* or you *won't* help?" Jessica called out after me, her tone hard.

I didn't answer as I turned the corner. Before, I might have felt like I owed her an explanation. I finally realized— I didn't . . . I didn't say sorry, either. I hadn't done anything wrong, and besides . . . *she* never apologized.

"Come on, Tak!" I yelled to my little brother as he stood at the base of the sycamore tree I had climbed. "You have to take your station if we're gonna get to Mars on time!"

Since *Alice in Wonderland* and Tak's beginning theater camp had ended, the last of my summer days had been spent playing with the little booger. After accidentally slicing his finger while trying to remove the pit from an avocado, he decided that maybe he didn't want to be a chef after all.

Now he wanted to relocate to Mars and become a Martian. But first he had to climb into the rocket ship. Instead, he stood there with his arms crossed. He had avoided this tree since the spring when a spider crawled on him and he freaked out so much he fell out of it. He was black and blue for weeks.

As I sat in its branches, I thought how last summer, I *truly* believed I could be anything I wanted to be. And how, during the past year, I also came to believe I couldn't be anything at all.

So which was it? Should I tell Tak that he most likely *wouldn't* ever be a Martian?

No.

While I wasn't going to be an NBA player, or a math professor, and the odds of being a big Hollywood star were slim . . . I was still going to chase my dreams. When Sam had given me a chance, I'd showed I could do it. Who knew what the future held for Tak? *I* knew he could do it.

This past year I found out it takes *a lot* for dreams to come true. They take hard work, like the hours my dad put in at the university and that Natalie was logging in at basketball camps this summer. Sometimes dreams need someone to show you it's possible, like Tamlyn Tomita in *The Karate Kid Part II* and Nurse Patty, who encouraged my mom, and then my mom, who encouraged Mrs. Wright to go back to school. But there are obstacles, like people who have their own opinions about what your life should be like, or who don't believe you deserve it, or people who want to bring you down because of their own issues and ideas that have nothing to do with you.

Dreams don't come true for anyone on their own. All dreams need a little help, and just like there are people who stand in your way, there are also people who'll open a door. I promised myself I would be one of the helpers. And maybe, just maybe . . . if we all helped each other, all our dreams *could* come true.

"Come on, Tak!" I held my hand out to him again. "I promise I won't let you fall."

Tak took a deep breath and grabbed my arm with both hands as I pulled him up into the tree with me.

AUTHOR'S NOTE

In recent years, I have been amazed at the diversity of stories that have come to be. On the silver screen, in books, TV. As a writer who is also a woman of color, I've found this development encouraging. However, I've also had recent conversations in which it's become clear that some people feel like an increase in diverse representation has meant their own opportunities have decreased. Comments such as "they only want ethnic-looking models now" or "I wasn't able to take advantage of [X opportunity] because they wanted someone 'diverse.'"

I must admit, I was perplexed. I didn't understand how diverse representation *couldn't* be viewed positively. Then I realized that some people don't understand why representation matters because they might not have known what it was like to grow up with little or problematic representation, and without role models to show how to make their dreams come true.

The idea for *Dream, Annie, Dream* came about from this realization. While this is a work of fiction, I did grow up in Kansas. I had a wonderful childhood there—I have lifelong friends from that time, and I had dedicated and caring adults and educators who encouraged and cheered me on. However, the '80s were also a time of anti-Japanese sentiment due to US-Japan trade friction. The racially motivated murder of Vincent Chin by disgruntled autoworkers happened in 1982. Few Asian Americans appeared on the screen and when they did, they were often caricatures to be laughed at, like the Chinese restaurant employees in the 1983 film *A Christmas Story*, or the foreign exchange student "Long Duk Dong" in the 1984 movie *Sixteen Candles*.

The year Annie's story begins, 1987, is also the year in which *TIME* magazine's article "Those Asian-American Whiz Kids" was published. This idea of the "model minority" portrayed Asian Americans as one-dimensional and perpetuated damaging stereotypes for years to come. Asian Americans then and now are not a monolith. While there are some doctors in our midst—like Dr. Wang, for instance—I wished to explore, via this story, the reasons *why* some Asian American immigrants wanted a career in medicine for their children. Through Annie's interaction with Dr. Wang, her conflicts with her parents, and her own ideas for her life, I hoped to represent the breadth of our backgrounds, cultures, and dreams. In fact,

Annie and her parents' experiences were developed through extensive interviews with my Chinese, Korean, Japanese, and Taiwanese American friends and their own parents' immigration stories.

While there's always a little bit of the author in their characters, Annie is much braver than I ever was. I dabbled in theater a bit, and *thought* about auditioning a lot, but self-selected out of most opportunities. I ended up participating in only a couple of productions, one of which was *The King and I*. And what a great experience that was! The girl who played Tuptim was a lovely person (not like Jessica at all), and the camaraderie that developed among the cast members was magical. Issues of appropriation, racism, and the stereotypes that permeate that particular musical—while apparent now—weren't given a second thought during that time. Some might be tempted to say, "Well, that doesn't happen anymore." Sadly, it does. Take, for instance, how Scarlett Johansson was cast in the role of Motoko Kusanagi in the 2017 movie *Ghost in the Shell*, and the cultural inaccuracies rampant throughout the 2020 live-action remake of *Mulan* (none of the four screenwriters were of Asian descent). These are only a couple of examples. I can assure you, there are many, many more.

Although the word *microaggressions* wasn't even in use during the time of Annie's story, it doesn't mean that they didn't exist. From personal experience, I can tell you that they existed in full force. Racism, privilege, the question of whether the "American dream" was meant for *all* Americans—I rarely brought up these topics because, like Annie, I noticed pointing out these instances often made people feel uncomfortable. This story is, in some ways, me sitting down with everyone and finally saying, "Let's talk."

Dream, Annie, Dream is definitely a window into the past. In some ways, it illustrates what strides have been made since then. However, I believe it also can show us what hasn't changed. Hopefully, by exploring these issues, we can work toward improving our present, and striving toward a future in which dreams can come true for *everyone*.

ACKNOWLEDGMENTS

Dream, Annie, Dream came together in the middle of the COVID-19 pandemic. It was a difficult period for many of us in so many ways, but I found myself fortunate to have the opportunity to write this story during that time. It would not have been possible without my editor, Alyssa Miele, and the HarperCollins/Quill Tree Books team. Alyssa's insights were always spot-on and her encouragement for my writing and the story itself kept me going. I'm forever grateful to have the support of such a kind and caring individual.

I am extremely grateful to my agent extraordinaire, Penny Moore. Hard-working and dedicated to bringing stories like Annie's to the world, I have appreciated your accessibility, expertise, and guidance tremendously. The publishing world is lucky to have you!

Many thanks to Tracy Subisak, whose cover art captured

Annie Inoue and her dreams perfectly. Additional thanks to David Curtis, who designed the book's jacket and interior, and to Nicole Moreno, Jessica White, and Dan Janeck, who handled the copyediting and proofreading of this story.

Although there were many difficult topics that were brought up through Annie's story, the research for it was a delight. It reconnected me with so many of my friends from childhood, college, and beyond:

Much gratitude to my brother-in-law Dr. Jeffrey Brown for his insights into what life as a professor at a small college is like. I'm indebted to my friends Bertina Yen, Steve Lin, Sarah Oh, Nina Shih, Brant Liu, Thomas Li, Jennifer Yu, Pei-Li Wang, and Irene Bryant for sharing their families' experiences immigrating to the United States. I'm grateful to Rafael Ulate, for checking my Spanish, and to my dear friend Tricia Lee Carpenter and her family for information about the workings of community theater.

To my writing group: Aileen Sheedy, Matt Merenda, and John Vincent—boy, did I ask you to read a lot of pages for our monthly meetings! Even though we didn't have a chance to meet in person while *Dream, Annie, Dream* was being written, I greatly appreciated your friendship, feedback, and virtual support throughout the process of writing this book.

To my parents who took the bold step to immigrate to the United States: Thank you for your sacrifices and your dreams for all of us. Much gratitude to my siblings and their support as well!

For my husband, Miles, and my children Leo, Tai, and Kogen: Thank you for always being excited about my books. Your help and encouragement to chase my own dreams means the world to me—I can't wait to see you chase yours, too.